NEXT
DESTINATION

Ositadimma **Chukwuemeka** Alozie

Order this book online at www.trafford.com
or email orders@trafford.com

Most Trafford titles are also available at major online book retailers.

Printed in the United States of America.

ISBN: 978-1-4669-8932-0 (sc)
ISBN: 978-1-4669-8931-3 (e)

Trafford rev. 04/18/2013

www.trafford.com

North America & international
toll-free: 1 888 232 4444 (USA & Canada)
phone: 250 383 6864 ♦ fax: 812 355 4082

CONTENTS

DEDICATION

This book is dedicated to the memory of all the freedom
fighters and the prisoners of consciences

FOREWORD

Central African Nations are my closest door neighbor countries to the outskirt of the east of Nigeria. In the years past, before my traveling to the United States of America (USA), I always listen to stories told by some of those that returned home from certain countries that constitutes the Central African countries. The stories about some of the people of those nations fascinated me a lot and drew my attention towards the understanding of the people of this "allow them they would get tired of it (as was regarded as) nations. As I developed interest in their ways of lives, I began to take notes of their traditional ways of lives and the impacts on their coexistences and standards of living because those areas fascinate me the most.

My interest on them eventually landed me to a story about Tita, a young man from a traditional religious family in a Central African country who later became a pastor in the Assemblies Mission, and so came the writing of this book 'Next Destination'.

I am also writing other books like, Faces of Fraud, Barren Womb, Agu the Disobedient. I had a bachelor of science in Business Administration in Financial Management (BSc.BA) from University of Colorado, Denver and I am currently doing Masters in Financial Management at University of Maryland University College, Adelphi and also Masters in Criminal Justice at American Military University, Charles Town, West Virginia all in the USA. I had my secondary and primary education at Eziudo Ezinihitte LGA in Imo State.

This book reader wishing to contact the author can use the address below;

Mail: Ositadimma Chukwuemeka Alozie
P.O. Box 298
Onicha, Ezinihitte L.G.A
Imo State—Nigeria
Email: osichukwu@gmail.com

ACKNOWLEDGEMENT

My special thanks go to all the good African Traditional Religious Worshippers, Believers and Observers in Central African Nations because it was through my encounter with few of them that made the writing of this book possible, and my knowledge of them took me memory lane and also fortified me literarily.

My appreciation also goes to those who are always eager to help dedicated minds to achieve their dreams so as to make their lives more bearable and worth living; those who do not hesitate to call a spade a spade even in the face of immense threat against them; those who are determined to ensure the betterments of the genuine common human, and those who refuse to cannibalize and feed on the flesh of the innocents; those whose words are the epitome of the truth, who cannot embrace egoism and egocentrism to enrich themselves through fraudulent activities; those who prefers peaceful negotiations as the best solutions to resolving conflicts, who understands that the use of force is only inevitable if all peaceful measures failed.

INTRODUCTION

This book 'Next Destination' is a true but fiction story about a young man named Tita (Prince) from a country in Central African nation who came from a poor family. He passed through the huddles to complete his basic primary education, and graduated from Primary School with a Distinction in his FSLCE, and afterwards there was no money to sponsor him, so, he followed one of his relatives to the township to learn a trade. And later he became a born-again Christian shortly after joining the Assemblies Mission in town. After becoming a born-again, he became so devoted and subsequently committed all his belongings to the church.

After years in the Assemblies Mission, Tita's role was recognized by the Ordination Council of the Assemblies Mission (OCAM) and he was subsequently ordained a Deacon and was later selected by the OCAM for pastoral training overseas at the Assemblies Mission Seminary. And he was delighted that his dream of been part of the real heaven of progress had eventually come true.

Tita in overseas was perplexed to be directed by his church officials etc to be deeply involved in all kinds of sexual behavior, consequently, he became downcast and regretted been part of the religious show. He complied with their request and their demands continued to get messier, Tita became numb of the Next Destination. He got educated as a pastor anyway, and loved bags of CFA Franc (money) and later became a 'Support Pastor' with the acceptance and absorption of sexual immorality as a condition of employment, and his stay was later terminated. Tita was left with no other option than to return back home to his village.

Pastor Tita was posted as an Assistant Pastor in his Assemblies Mission branch and was later promoted to the main pastor of the same branch, and while at home in his village, he violated their traditional law that resulted to him been exiled for nine (9) good years. He later returned to his village and became a maniac, a pure snag in everybody's shoes, and he continues to live on with the messy stinks.

CHAPTER ONE

Tita in Primary School

T ita was born in March 1961 and he is the first child and only son of Mr. Cazembi (Wise man) and Mrs. Dunduza (Venture to see) from a Central African nation, and he has three other sisters; Kalonji (Victorious), Nyahuma (Helper) and Jawanza (Dependable) respectively. Tita was born shortly after the independence of his country from colonial imperialism, so, he is one of those privileged at birth to make choices and decisions and as well excel without hindrances and/or interferences. Tita parents were peasant farmers and his father was also a laborer who worked for others when hired, and did jobs like bush clearing for farming, selling of firewood and other local jobs that offers daily pay so as to support the family. And his mother is a local mat weaver who made such carpets mostly for local needs because they lived in a local area far distanced from the nearest towns and cities, so his mother seldom make good fortune from her profession because of inaccessible roads that always hindered potential buyers from visiting their family for purchases. Although his parents were poor they were satisfied with their lots in lives and are traditional believers who strongly believed in the does and don'ts of their local tribal tradition.

Tita attended primary school and was given all the privileges he deserved so as to enable him excel in the primary school without hassles although sometimes there were delays in the payment of his school fees. The financial status of his parents could not enable them to afford him with any of his sisters in the primary school at the same time. So, his junior sisters had to wait until Tita finishes his primary school, consequently, two of his sisters didn't attend primary school because of his sake. His parents always made sure that there was enough food for him to eat every school day and wise, before and after school, and there was never a time he was starved of food during his primary school years. More so, Tita's assignments in the family were limited to ensure that he paid absolute attention to his studies so as to do well in school. His parents understood the importance of having the ability to read and write the foreign language which had became the language culture and generally accepted language as thought them by the colonial masters, therefore, they removed every huddles from his way to make him be able to communicate well in the new order which was imperative to mingle with the mixture of individuals in their country.

Tita passed through his primary school an intelligent child without failing any of his exams, and at a time he never paid his school fees within the stipulated time period before the start of his test. During a test when he had not paid his term school fees, he had encounters with the headmaster and teacher of the school who insisted that he must pay his term school fees otherwise he wouldn't seat for the test. During the 'row calls' of those who had not paid their school fees, the school headmaster Mr. Mwata (Sensible) and their test supervisor, Class 4B teacher; Mr. Tacuma (Alert) approached him on his seat while sitting for the test and asked him why he had not paid his school fees. Prior to his approach in the headmasters words "Attention Class, this is the row call of all those who have not paid their school fees in this class, if you hear your name, you please raise up your hand". And the row call started;

Tita. **Mr. Mwata called**

Present Sir (with his hand raised). **Tita answered**

Have you paid your school fees? **Mr.Mwata asked**

No, Sir. **Tita answered**

Why haven't you paid your school fees? **Mr. Mwata asked**

My father has no money to pay, Sir. **Tita answered**

When will you pay your school fees? **Mr. Mwata asked**

I do not know, Sir. **Tita answered**

He should be sent home, Sir. **Mr. Tacuma said**

Do you want to be sent home? **Mr. Mwata asked**

No, Sir. I will pay my school fees, Sir. **Tita answered**

He should be sent home, Sir. **Mr. Tacuma insisted**

Please Sir! Please Sir!! I will pay, Sir. **Tita implored**

He must be sent home Sir, otherwise he will not pay his school fees, Mr. Headmaster. **Mr. Tacuma warned**

Tita, I see you as an intelligent student, and that hurts! **Mr. Mwata exclaimed**

I want to take my test Sir. **Tita begged**

Sir, Headmaster, there is need for Tita to go home quick. **Mr. Tacuma cautioned**

Yes, I understand that . . . . (Headmaster was saying)

(Cuts in) Therefore tell him yourself to go home. **Class 4B teacher demanded**

Considering that he is a brilliant student, and that we need students like him. I wonder why his father has not paid his school fees. **Mr. Mwata said**

No matter his level of intelligence, he has not paid his school fees and he is the only person in that category, therefore, he must be sent home. **Mr. Tacuma frowned**

Tita is your father alive? **Mr. Mwata asked.**

Yes, Sir. **Tita answered**

What does he do for a living? **Headmaster asked**

He is a laborer, Sir. **Tita answered**

Does he live in the village? **Mr. Mwata asked**

Yes, Sir. **Tita answered**

Is your mother alive? **Mr. Mwata asked**

Yes Sir. **Tita answered**

Does she work? **Mr. Mwata asked**

Yes, Sir. She is a local mat weaver. **Tita answered**

Do you have other brothers and sisters? **Mr. Mwata asked**

Yes, Sir. I have three sisters only. **Tita answered**

Tita. Are you the only person in school? **Mr. Mwata asked**

Yes, Sir is only me. **Tita answered**

Sir, do you see that they have the money and they do not want to pay his school fees. **Mr. Tacuma said**

I have seen your predicament, Tita. **Mr. Mwata said**

Unfortunately in here, in this country, if you don't have money just forgets it, if you cannot pay your school fees, no free education. **Mr. Tacuma said**

. . . . Headmaster ponders a while . . . .

Tita. **Mr. Mwata called**

Yes, Sir. **Tita answered**

Do you see that all your fellow classmates have paid their school fees, leaving only you without payments? **Headmaster queried**

Yes, Sir. I am sorry Sir, but I will still pay. **Tita replied**

Tita is a complete cheater and liar, he will not pay. **Mr. Tacuma shouted**

I see to your reason Mr. Tacuma. **Headmaster acknowledged**

Indeed, he will never pay . . . . **Mr. Tacuma insisted**

Tita, will you be happy to be sent home while the others are taken their test? **Mr. Mwata asked**

No, Sir. I will not be happy. **Tita answered**

Therefore you pay your school fees period. **Class 4B teacher said**

Tita I feel for you and I am not left with any other options . . . . (Headmaster was saying)

(Cuts in), he must go home Sir and the earlier the better . . . . **Mr. Tacuma said**

Such a brilliant student! **Mr. Mwata exclaimed**

Tita does not lead all the students in his class Sir, there are others like him too. **Mr. Tacuma said**

. . . . silence observed for few minutes while scanning through his records . . . .

During this moments the teacher was busy flashing wicked eyes at Tita trying to intimidate him and make him quit voluntarily.

Tita I have gone through your past records and this seem to be the only school term you have not paid your school fees up to this time, barely two weeks before the start of your exams. And you are in your fourth grade, your parents should have understood the importance of paying your school fees on time, especially this time you are in your third term prior to entering elementary five. **Mr. Mwata said**

Headmaster Sir. This boy Tita and his parents do not know where they are. Do they think that their son would come to this school and gets all his education without their paying his school fees through to his final year if they ever want him to graduate with certificate? **Mr. Tacuma inquired**

I can pay it Sir. I can pay Sir. **Tita pleaded**

Will you shot up! How do you intend to pay that? **Mr. Tacuma shouted**

I know Sir, I can pay. **Tita continued to plead**

I said shot up. **Mr. Tacuma insisted**

Tita at this time you paying your school fees seem to be somehow beyond your capacity. **Mr. Mwata said**

Yes, Sir, but I can . . . . **Tita replied**

(Cuts in) Shot your mouth up! **Class 4B teacher stammered**

There is no need wasting time so that other pupils could continue with their text. **Headmaster said**

That is . . . . the point . . . . **Mr. Tacuma concurred**

Tita, although this is your first time of not paying as at when necessary, I will deny you the opportunity of continuing with this text today . . . (as headmaster was saying).

(Cuts in) That is it . . . . **Class 4B teacher said**

. . . . (as headmaster continued) . . . until you pay your school fees. Remember that third term exam is around the corner . . . . (as headmaster was saying).

(Cuts in) That time he will know where he is . . . . **Mr. Tacuma said**

. . . . (as headmaster continued) . . . And that only those who have paid their school fees will be allowed to take the exams with no exceptions. Therefore, when your reach home today tell your parents . . . . (as headmaster was saying).

(Cuts in) They supposed to have thought of that. **Mr. Tacuma said**

. . . . (Headmaster continued) . . . that you were ordered home in the middle of a test for none payment of your school fees for this school term, and that the exams are barely two weeks away from today, therefore, they have to act fast. **Mr. Mwata adviced**

Tita today is the last time I will see you and ever tolerate you trying to take any test or exam supervised by me without paying your school fees. Just get yourself out of this classroom with immediate effect. **Class 4b teacher warned**

Please do allow him to take his time and collect his books. **Mr. Mwata appealed**

Did you just heard what he said, that you should leave quickly, no test for you today. Did you hear that? **Mr. Tacuma said in loud voice**

Tita became confused and gradually without wasting time put his books inside his bag and left. And when he was about to leave;

Tita come and see me in my office on Monday morning before the start of lessons. **Mr. Mwata said**

Yes, Sir. I will. **Tita calmly replied**

Now, leave the classroom. **Class 4B teacher ordered**

Tita slowly worked towards the exit door.

Make sure that you do not disturb those pupils meditating for their test. **Mr. Tacuma warned**

I know Sir. **Tita said and left.**

As Tita left the classroom Mr. Tacuma walked out the door with cane and looked around to make sure that Tita had left.

Tita outside the classroom does not know what next to do, whether to go back and plead with their headmaster to allow him take the test for that day only after which he deserved no more mercy during such times. Tita soliloquized that their headmaster understood his predicament and was ready to assist him by allowing him to take the test after which his parents endeavor to pay his term school fees. Had the headmaster taken the decision alone without unnecessary interferences from that Class 4B teacher, the situation couldn't have resulted to the point of sending him home, especially when they were about to start an important test which could count towards his final grade. Tita reasoned that the involved Class 4B teacher, never helped ameliorates the situation for him because although the teacher sometimes noticed him in class when they had combined lessons, he never believed that, that teacher had grudges against him perhaps because he had been passing all his exams with excellent grades. And unfortunately, his Class 4A teacher, Mr. Kinembera (Disappearing slowly), who understood his positions and could always allow him to stay during such times was not in school, because according reliable sources; he had an emergency which he attended to and therefore could not be in school. Tita was worried because the 'promotional exams' were around the corner, if nothing happened on his payment of the Third Term School Fees, he could end up been asked to go home on the exam days. Besides, his chances of been retained without the payment of his school fees has been narrowed by the Mr. Tacuma, who had already vowed tooth and nail that he does not want to see Tita in either tests or exams venues without the payment of his school fees from 'This Day" henceforth. And unfortunately, his Class 4A teacher was not the person who supervises them on the test and exam days respectively, whereas on the test days they were supervised by the Class 4B teacher: wicked Tacuma, etc, on the exam days, they would be in other classrooms like classrooms 1-6 excluding classroom 4 respectively.

He looked at both sides of the coin to determine the possibilities of having an exam supervisor that would understand his predicament during the exam days should his parents failed to pay his school fees 'for the first time'. He landed on the probability of a one (1) and zero (0), and zero (0) and one (1) respectively. These probability outcomes implied that the chances of been supervised by a teacher who could allow him to stay and take the promotional exams was one (1) and the chances of having a supervisor who was head bent on sending him home and chasing away from the exam hall was zero (0) respectively. Looking at the other side of the coin revealed that the chances of been supervised by a teacher like 'Mr. Go Home' was one (1) and the chances of been supervised by a 'Stay, take your exams and pay later' kind of teacher was zero (0) respectively. So, putting the outcomes side by side he concluded that the best option would be to pay his school fees and be on the better side, but he was not sure if his parents could afford to pay that within the limited time frame available before the start of the promotional exams. But if his parent failed to come up with the school fees before the said date, he also stood fifty percent chances of getting lucky but there was no assurance yet.

Tita waved the idea of going back to dare the devil in his face because as he continued to ask for forgiveness, Mr. Tacuma got more angry, so, should he insist and continued to plead with the headmaster, the Class 4B teacher could eventually lose control of himself and give him unforgettable lashes on his buttocks. Thus, to be on a safer side and avoid setting the stage which its outcome could leave bitter stigmas on him, he decided to strolled home and explain everything to his father in particular. On his way home he remembered the rest of his classmates who were busy taken their test and he was forced out of the test room by the merciless Mr. Tacuma who never understood when there was a hardship in the family and never knew that 'no place is a bed of roses, and that there is no land naturally covered with mats". He reasoned deeply and began to cry as he walked his way towards home, and as he retrospect tears filled his eyes and at a considerable distance away from the school premises, he sat somewhere by the corner of the road where prying eyes could not easily spot him. In his slumber, he shaded more inward tears than those of the outside could reveal and the thought of his future occupied his mind. He was deeply touched that Mr. Tacuma never gave him the chances that he deserved and without minding forced the headmaster to a conviction that compelled the headmaster to ask him to go for good. He wondered why and when the ordinary Class 4B teacher became the headmaster of the school, Mr. Mwata himself, 'even when the headmaster showed concern for my predicament, Mr. Tacuma insisted that I must leave the exam room quick. In so many occasions when the headmaster wanted to let me alone to take my test, and pay later, Mr. Tacuma took control of the whole school and continued to push the headmaster to the point of reluctantly telling me to pack home and forgo the test. What a wicked and monstrous Class 4B teacher? a man with no heart of a human being in him, an evil incarnate".

He Tita continued to use his hands to whip his eyes clear of tears. He lamented why a whole school teacher should act so feeble minded and allow Mr. Tacuma to take decisions for him. He realized that the headmaster told him to come to his office on the next school day which was Monday morning, and suspected what could be the reason for such a summon by the head of the school. Tita reasoned that "I still don't understand the main reason for your invitation of me in your office Mr. Mwata, Sir. I hope it is for good, and never to throw me away again like a piece of trash as you did in the presence of Mr. Tacuma whom you ought to have controlled. I am afraid because everybody fears our headmaster; I fear that your call is not to punish me for my "I can do it statement". I am sorry if I did offend you in anyway but I still have to take my test. I will be in your office come Monday as you ordered me to, but "please Sir, I just want to be in school! I don't want to go home!! I can't go home!!! I ask you to let the Class 4B teacher off my back. Please Sir, let the Class 4B teacher off my good back. Off my back . . . . !

When he calmed down he picked up his bag and headed home. On reaching home, he met the presence of his mother and sisters. His mother was surprised to see him come back home during school hours, especially after telling them the previous night that they would have a test in school that day. So, like all other reasonable mothers do, she inquired to ascertain why he was not in school.

Tita, my son, is your school closed for the day? **Mrs. Dunduza asked**

No, Mama. **Tita answered**

Then, why are you at home at this time? **Mrs. Dunduza asked**

I was sent home Mama. **Tita answered**

Who sent you home? **Mrs. Dunduza asked**

The headmaster sent me home. **Tita answered**

Why did he send you home? **Mrs. Dunduza asked**

It was because of my school fees. **Tita answered**

Did you take the test? **Mrs. Dunduza asked**

No, Mama. **Tita answered**

Why? **Mrs. Dunduza asked**

I was sent home before the test. **Tita answered**

Did you tell him why your school fees have not been paid? **Mrs. Dunduza asked**

Yes, Mama, I did explain everything to him but . . . . **Tita answered**

You did explained and what? **Mrs. Dunduza asked**

He wanted to allow me after my explanation and our Class 4B teacher told him to send me home. **Tita answered**

A common Class 4B teacher masterminded for the headmaster? **Mrs. Dunduza asked**

Yes, Mama. **Tita answered**

Are you sure of what you are saying? **Mrs. Dunduza asked**

Yes, Mama, I am very much sure. **Tita answered**

Did you have previous conflicts with the said teacher? **Mrs. Dunduza asked**

No, Mama, I have had no conflicts with him and I always respect him as my teacher also. **Tita answered**

What is his name? **Mrs. Dunduza asked**

His name is Mr. Tacuma. **Tita answered**

Were you the only person that was sent home? **Mrs. Dunduza asked**

Yes, Mama. **Tita answered**

We will wait until your father comes back. **Mrs. Dunduza said**

Yes, Mama. **Tital agreed**

Mama **Tita called**

Yes, my son. **Mrs. Dunduza replied**

Our headmaster told me to come and see him in his office on Monday morning. **Tita said**

Do you know why he asked you to? **Mrs. Dunduza asked**

No, Mama. **Tita answered**

When did he tell you that? **Mrs. Dunduza asked**

It was shortly after he told me to go home. **Tita answered**

Did you molest him after he asked you to go home? **Mrs. Dunduza asked**

No, Mama, I never did. **Tita answered**

It is alright, we will discuss that with your father too, okay. **Mrs. Dunduza said**

Yes, Mama. **Tita agreed**

His mother concentrated on what she was doing and Tita went to their bedroom to keep his school bag.

In the night of that day after dinner Tita's mother told her husband that their son was home early from school that day unlike before on a test day. She explained to her husband that Tita was ordered home at the time they pupils were in the classroom ready to take the test and that according to what he told her that the headmaster of the school was the one who asked him to go home. Her mother told her husband that Tita was the best person to explain everything by himself. Mrs. Dunduza asked Tita who was sitting by next to one of his sisters to tell his father what happened, and asked him to tell his father exactly what he told her.

Papa, I was not allowed to take the test today. **Tita said**

Why? **Mr. Cazembi asked**

It was because I have not paid my Third Term school fees, Papa. **Tita answered**

Who sent you home? **Mr. Cazembi asked**

Papa, I was sent home by the headmaster himself. **Tita answered**

So, the headmaster could not allow you to take your test today? **Mr. Cazembi asked**

Yes, Papa, he said that I must pay my school fees for that to happen henceforth. **Tita answered**

My son, you are aware that I do not waste time in paying your school fees in the past. **Mr. Cazembi said**

Yes, Papa, I am surprised. **Tita replied**

This delay paying your school fees is because things are no longer as they were use to be. Things are getting a little bit harder these days because of the current government policies in this country. **Mr. Cazembi said**

This is my first time of paying late, Papa. I do understand that. **Tita humbly said**

The federal government is busy placing embargos and restrictions on both exports and imports in fear of being overthrown by insurgents put in place by the former colonial government, consequently, my customers are no longer as willing to bring out money for expenses, and that seriously affect my earning power as well as your mother's, and this is why I have not yet paid your school fees. **Mr. Cazembi said**

Papa, it is a pity. Why should the government of our country be afraid of itself? **Tita questioned**

That's what the educated ones said. The federal government sometimes contradicts itself, they government officials may have other intentions more than what are being expressed. **Mr. Cazembi said**

Papa, now that we are masters of our own desires and aspirations as a country. Why should we worry? **Tita inquired**

My so, I am far from the corridors of power, but I suspect that the former colonial masters having handed over the mantle of leadership of this country to the assumed true owners may have hidden agendas. The former colonials may handover to pacify troubled waters and did as if they have left the country in its entirety whereas they never did, and may have the intention of staging a bloody coup d'état so as to reclaim their lost power. So to facilitate their easy come back to power, the colonials could put in place their surrogate as either a President or Prime Minister of this country. So, to be on safer side and ensure that the killer never penetrates in again, there is need for adequate security measures so as to keep those that had already been infatuated with stolen authority and/or leadership at arm's length. **Mr. Cazembi said**

But Papa, I heard that the colonial masters left this country few years ago before my birth, and it was bout fifteen (15) years ago. So, I believe that the colonials must have come and gone. In that case there must be another problem with the government. **Tita replied**

What this government is doing today, it did a couple of times in the 1960's and when the seventy's came, we thought that we had schemed the colonial out of our body polity, everybody was pleased that they could now enjoy in their own home land without unnecessary and undue interferences. I hope this federal government is telling country people the truth. How can a government that has stayed on its own for such number of years still is afraid of a former colonial come back? And this government is in control of arms and ammunitions, and absolutely nobody cares to overthrow the government within. Perhaps there must be something wrong somewhere. **Mr. Cazembi said**

Papa, I overheard our Class 4A teacher the other day discussing that a militia group was trying to oust the incumbent president and his prime minister, and that after that, the prime minister could be sworn in as president because he has better plans for this country. **Tita quietly replied**

My son, I never saw it that way, but that could be the course. Does it mean that they have been lying to me all this while? In fact, the incident of the 1960's made me to believe so also. **Mr. Cazembi said**

Papa, I believe that has to do with the military and not the former colonials because the military had a hand in the formation of the militia group, and they also accused the current president of incompetency. **Tita replied**

I am with you, my son. Where will military take us to? **Mr. Cazembi worriedly said**

Papa, have this country had military leadership before? **Tita asked**

No, my son, this would be the first of its kind by the indigenes of the country if they ever succeed in plotting a takeover. **Mr. Cazembi said**

Does military rule kill a lot of people, Papa? **Tita asked**

Military rule . . . . forget about it and let us see how your school fees will be paid. **Mr. Cazembi said**

It is alright, Papa. **Tita replied**

When will you take your promotional exams? **Mr. Cazembi asked**

In about two weeks from today, Papa. **Tita answered**

Two weeks . . . . ! **Mr. Cazembi exclaimed**

Yes, Papa. **Tita replied**

That means that, that . . . that . . . . **Mr. Cazembi said**

What is wrong Papa? **Tita asked**

I mean . . . . I doesn't . . . . **Mr. Cazembi said**

Papa, I can still pay. **Tita humbly said**

My son, there is no money with me at this time, and truthfully I cannot come up with your school fees before your exams. **Mr. Cazembi regretted**

Papa, can we borrow from anybody? **Tita inquired**

I have tried all that I could do to see if some of my friends could lend me money but everybody seems to be conscious at this time pending what could be the outcome of the government skirmishes.

Those who know more about such frictions vowed never to loan a single CFA Franc until it is all over. **Mr. Cazembi said**

What should I do next? **Tita quietly said in a low tone**

Have hope, my son, it will one day be all well. **Mr. Cazembi said**

My son, you know your father that he never plays with anything concerning your education; do believe that sooner than later, money will come up for your school fees. The gods of this land will never hesitate to see you through to your final year in that elementary school. Forget about military incursion into governance, they always do that but when they frictions become so wear, statements full everywhere, and so the truth maybe far from reality. Always concentrate on your studies; things will eventually change for the better. **Mrs. Dunduza promised**

Mama, I will have hope and also believe that our Ancestors will see me through in my education. **Tita concurred**

I will see what I can do, our son, before the exams. **Mr. Cazembi said**

Thank you, Papa. **Tita replied**

. . . . Silence . . . .

Did you tell your father about the visit to your headmaster's office, my son? **Mrs. Dunduza asked**

No, Mama. **Tita answered**

My husband, Tita told me earlier today, shortly after his return from school that their school headmaster asked him to come and see him in his office on Monday morning before the start of lessons. **Mrs. Dunduza said**

What for? **Mr. Cazembi asked**

I don't know, ask him he is still here he can tell you everything. **Mrs. Dunduza answered**

Papa, before I left the test taking Classroom today our headmaster told me to come and see him in his office on Monday morning before any lessons. **Tita said**

Why? **Mr. Cazembi asked**

I do not know, Papa. **Tita answered**

It could be . . . . perhaps . . . . the school fees. **Mr. Cazembi guessed**

That could be, Papa. **Tita replied**

. . . . Silence . . . .

His before any lesson statement . . . . kind of concern. **Mr. Cazembi said**

That is just what he said, Papa. **Tita replied**

Did you ever molested him or thrown stones at him after asking you to go home? **Mr. Cazembi asked**

No Papa, never. **Tita answered**

What an invitation! **Mr. Cazembi exclaimed**

I do not know Papa. **Tita said**

Is this the first time of such an invitation by your headmaster? **Mr. Cazembi asked**

Yes, Papa. **Tita answered**

Therefore, it must be for the school fees. **Mr. Cazembi said**

That could be Papa. **Tita replied**

Our son, Tita, make sure you go to his office on Monday morning before any lessons. And answer him truthfully all the questions he would ask you. Did you hear what I said? **Mr. Cazembi said**

Yes Papa. I heard. **Tita replied**

Tita, our son, you have heard your father, try to present yourself to the headmaster as an intelligent students that you are. Do not bother yourself about the Class 4B teacher; that one has came and passed. **Mrs. Dunduza adviced**

What Class 4B teacher? **Mr. Cazembi asked**

He said that the Class 4B teacher forced their headmaster to send him home. **Mrs. Dunduza answered**

A common Class 4B teacher controlled the headmaster? **Mr. Cazembi asked**

That was exactly what he said, my son could you please tell your father about the Class 4B teacher? **Mrs. Dunduza politely said**

Yes Mama. Papa, the headmaster considered my plight after my explanations of the whole situation to him and he was about to allow me to stay back in school and take the test, but the Class 4B teacher who was the Class 4A Test supervisor insisted that I must vacate not only from the test taking classroom but also the entire school premises. **Tita explained**

What a show of wickedness! **Mr. Cazembi exclaimed**

Imagine that type of nonsense. **Mrs. Dunduza said**

Why must he mastermind for the headmaster of the school? Who authorized him to? What a disloyalty? **Mr. Cazembi questioned**

I was surprised Papa. **Tita replied**

Does the Class 4B teacher know you before? **Mr. Cazembi asked**

He must know me because sometimes we do have combine lessons, especially when our Class 4A teacher is absent, but during which we could have combined lessons. **Tita answered**

So, your teacher doesn't normally stay in the classroom? **Mr. Cazembi asked**

He does, but for this third term, this is the only time he was absent from class. **Tita replied**

And he treated you that way? **Mr. Cazembi asked**

Yes Papa. **Tita answered**

In the past, have you ever disobeyed any of his orders? **Mr. Cazembi asked**

No, Papa, I have not. **Tita answered**

There must be a reason for his lashing out on you without provocation, maybe he is one of those who dislike the progresses of intelligent students like you, and so, he must have seen this as an avenue of achieving his aim. Good teachers will not easily send you home during such crucial times like that instead they would ask you to finish the test and/or exams and bring the school fees the next time. **Mr. Cazembi said**

I told the headmaster that I wanted to stay and take my test and that I would pay the school fees and the Class 4B teacher shouted on me. **Tita said**

That's rude, shouting while the headmaster understood your points. Imagine such a ridiculous teacher. **Mr. Cazembi said**

Such a show of ungraciousness by a teacher who supposed to be helpful to students, especially this time it is widely believed that basic primary education is the bedrock of the future for many children, although wisdom never depends on claim, what will be will surely be. Those who had no such opportunities of either attending or finishing elementary education will equally make it in life, sometimes becoming more important men and women. So, if the Class 4B teacher thinks that such method of frustrations could hinder the developments and progresses of such students like you, he is surely miscounting the numbers. **Mrs. Dunduza said**

That Class 4B teacher could be those left behind by the run-away or he could be one of the wicked ones among us who are more head bent on scuttling it for bright kids like our son, especially when his/her parents are poor. On sensing poverty from such kids, 'who rah', he dashes their educational hopes. **Mr. Cazembi said**

My son, since you do not always have closer encounter with him, be witty and whenever he approaches you for any reason show politeness and understanding. Do not ever be the first person to call the shots. As your teacher he has every right to discipline you or even reject you if you do not pay your school fees. He may deem the lack of payment of your school fees as a cheat if he is sincere, otherwise his bitter encounter could be to call the bluffs. Always do respect him and never express any misgivings at him whenever and wherever you see him, either alone or in a company. **Mrs. Dunduza said**

I will always respect him. **Tita replied**

Incline your ears, Tita. Did you hear what your mother just said? **Mr. Cazembi inquired**

Yes Papa. I heard what Mama said, all that Mama said. **Tita concurred**

Again, make sure that you visited your headmaster in his office on Monday as he said, okay. **Mr. Cazembi said**

Yes, I will Papa. **Tita re-assured**

You can now go to bed and get a good night sleep. Sleep your head off. Did you hear me? **Mr. Cazembi cautioned**

Yes Papa, I grudge no pains. **Tita agreed**

. . . . Silence . . . .

Tita went to their inner room where he sleeps with his immediate junior sisters. And his father exchanged few more words with his mother and that was it.

Tita spent the weekend as usual and his parents kept watchful eyes on him to see if he was ever been bothered by the thoughts of the previous Friday, when he was deprived the opportunities of partaking with his fellow classmates for the first time. Tita continued with his normal routine and never seem to be bothered by the activities of the yesterdays. He was more focused on his daily family contributions, especially during the weekend when he most of the times voluntarily partake in the minor family responsibilities like helping his sisters wash clothes, plates etc before embarking on his studies. Tita looked cheerful and happy like his usual safe, and during the evenings he went to their school premises to either play and/or watch soccer which was his most favorite hobby outside of reading and writing. His parents called him closer and cross examined him just to make sure that nothing was bothering his mind, and he passed the entire detective test. So, his parents confirmed his statement of having no grudges which he made one of the previous nights.

CHAPTER TWO

Tita Meets the Headmaster

On Monday morning before Tita finally departed for school his parents reminded him not to forget seeing their school headmaster in his office as he requested. And they reiterated their earlier position that he should present himself as brilliantly as necessary, well dressed and never to give out of point answers to specifically directed questions. They reminded him that he should not lose hope in what could be the purpose of the headmaster's call. They urged Tita to approach the headmaster confidently in his office like a humble brave child who understood his family's conditions. Tita promised his parents that their advices would always be with him and help to present himself more boldly in the presence of their school headmaster in his office alone. He told them that he loved his primary education and must avoid all gambles and unnecessary utterances to those who were in charge, because such could nip his ambitions at the bud. Tita told them that based on other series of questions tossed to him by the headmaster and his immense concern of him, his call could be to prove all heart breaking tongues too wrong. And he left for school having taken his breakfast.

After morning gathering for the school officials' message, Tita headed straight to the headmaster's office and he saw the headmaster in his office. Meanwhile, some teachers who came late were also coming into Mr. Mwata's office to sign in. On seeing Mr. Mwata who was sitting on his main office seat, he offered him a seat in front of his desk, looking at Tita face to face. Tita, immediately he entered the headmaster's office wasted no time in greeting him.

Good morning, Sir. **Tita greeted**

Good morning. How are you today? **Mr. Mwata responded**

I am fine Sir. **Tita replied**

Did I ask you to come to my office during this time today? **Mr. Mwata asked**

Yes Sir. **Tita answered**

When was that? **Headmaster asked**

It was on Friday last week, Sir. **Tita answered**

Could you tell me that your name again? **Mr. Mwata requested**

Sir, my name is Tita. **Tita replied**

Yes! Yes!! Yes!!! Have a seat (pointing at the seat). **Mr. Mwata offered**

. . . . Silence while those teachers that came to work late came in and signed in, and left. Some of the late comers barely looked at him and signed in, and left while the rest of them never cared to notice his presence since he was not any of their class pupils. When it appeared that no other teacher was in late so as to sign-in for the day's duty, the headmaster closed the register he was going through certain records with and calmly kept it aside and got his attention focused on Tita. Meanwhile, like any pupil would do despite his/ her courage and brevity when presented with the option of meeting with Mr. Mwata alone, Tita felt kind of jittery and a little shaky but held his breath so as to retain consciousness. And the headmaster knowing his profession, he used eyes to know a ripped corn husk without been told. Having worked with pupils of Tita kind for years, he understood, how uneasy they felt on meeting with him, especially when he/she has committed an offence or when he/she has not paid his/her school fees. Therefore, to avert the fear that could stroke Tita's being; he immediately assured him that he meant no harm to him as one of his most intelligent students. And their conversation progressed.

Tita how is your father? **Mr. Mwata asked**

He is fine Sir. **Tita answered**

How about your mother? **Mr. Mwata asked**

She is fine, Sir. **Tita answered**

How about your sisters? **Mr. Mwata asked**

They are also fine, Sir. **Tita answered**

Do you know the purpose of your being here today? **Mr. Mwata asked**

No, Sir. **Tita answered**

I called you because of your school fees. **Mr. Mwata said**

Yes Sir. **Tita replied**

Last Friday you were sent home and barred from taken the test. Are my correct? **Mr. Mwata asked**

Yes Sir. You are very correct. **Tita humly answered**

Did you tell your parents why you were sent home? **Mr. Mwata asked**

Yes, Sir. I told them. **Tita answered**

What did your father said? **Mr. Mwata asked**

Sir, he said that he had no money to pay my Third Term school fees at this time, but that he is making every effort to make sure that it will be paid. **Tita answered**

Did you tell him that the promotional exams are barely two weeks away? **Mr. Mwata asked**

Yes, Sir. I did and he told me that the present hazy situation in the country has only reduced his wages but has also forced potential lenders to freeze their assets. **Tita answered**

That's unfortunate. Do you know that without paying your school fees, you will not be allowed to seat for the promotional exams? **Mr. Mwata asked**

Yes, Sir. I know and that is disturbing Sir. Please, I do not know what to do again. Sir, please. **Tita touchingly begged**

Does your father have other brothers and sisters? **Mr. Mwata asked**

Please Sir; I do not understand what you mean. **Tita answered**

I mean, does your father have other brothers and sisters in your family or elsewhere? **Mr. Mwata asked**

No, is only my father from his own mother but my paternal grandfather married about four women. **Tita answered**

Do his half-brothers help him? **Mr. Mwata asked**

No Sir, for school fees like this they don't help him even if they have the money they could give to him. **Tita answered**

Why? **Mr. Mwata asked**

They said that I am intelligent pass their children, so out of greed; they never like to help my father financially. **Tita answered**

Do they have any dispute with your father? **Mr. Mwata asked**

Sir, they could have hidden agendas but presently they do not seem to have any conflicts. **Tita answered**

His half-brothers must be stupid to disregard somebody who is intelligent as you. Maybe they failed to understand that you could add more strength to the entire families. **Mr. Mwata said**

My paternal grandfather's first wife had only female children so he got married to a second wife who also had female children and he got married to my paternal grandmother who had only my father, and my grandfather go married to the forth wife who had seven (7) sons and no female. **Tita replied**

I have seen why your father finds it as difficult to receiving arms from your uncles. I see you as a brilliant child; therefore, I will see what I can do to help you overcome this mess. **Headmaster said**

Yes Sir. Please Sir. **Tita begged**

Without wasting time so that you can go back to the classroom and continued with your lesson. I want you to come to my office on Thursday this week which is about two days today. Do not come to school early, wear your school dress and come directly with your father to my office. You come when you know that lessons are about to start. Did you hear me? Come directly with your father to my office. Is that clear? **Mr. Mwata said**

Yes Sir. **Tita replied**

If you get home after school tell him that I want you and him in my office on Monday morning during first lessons, and if he refuses to come with you I will send you home. **Mr. Mwata said**

I must surely tell him Sir. **Tita complied**

Tita, listen attentively; missing part of your Thursday's lessons is better than chasing you out of the exam hall on the exam day. And this time is during time for review, so nothing so special is going on, only try to re-read your notes and make sure that you understand them more. **Mr. Mwata said**

Yes Sir. **Tita replied**

You can now go back to the classroom, I had already informed your class teacher that I will have a conversation with you this morning, so, he will not punish you for coming in to the classroom late. Should he ask you why you are late, tell him that you were in my office. Go back. **Mr. Mwata said**

Yes Sir. Please thank you very much, Sir. **Tita humbly replied**

Tita went back to the classroom to join the rest of his classmates. On spotting Tita, his class teacher asked him where he had been all this while, and he told him that he was at the headmaster's office and his class teacher told him "go in", and he went and sat on his designated position on his classroom seat. Some of his closer classmates looked at him inquisitively and he blinked, and the others frowned at him and cared less for his presence. He sat quietly in the class and got focused on that day's lesson.

During recreation (a long-break) some of his fellow classmates approached him and asked him why he entered the classroom when they lessons had already started, in fact, his first time of displaying such "teacher never like behavior", and he told them that he was at the headmaster's office. Some of them wanted to know exactly why he was invited by the headmaster but he declined to tell them, and the rest of them suspected that it could be because of his school foes and asked him if he had paid, and he said no, and in their desires to ascertain the purpose of his visit to the headmaster's office;

Tita, what is wrong with you? **Changamire** (He is as the sun) **asked**

Nothing is wrong. **Tita answered**

Then, why did you entered the classroom so late today? **Changamire inquired**

I was at the headmaster's office. **Tita answered**

Doing what? **Changamire asked**

He called me to his office. **Tita answered**

He called you to do what? **Changamire asked**

He had discussions with me. **Tita answered**

You had discussions on what? **Changamire asked**

We had just discussions. Do you remember last Friday? **Tita replied**

They messed with you, right. **Changamire said**

No. **Tita responded**

Have you paid your school fees? **Yerodin** (Studious) **asked**

No, I have not. **Tita answered**

Was it the purpose of the discussions? **Yerodin asked**

Somehow yes. **Tita answered**

What do you mean, somehow? **Yerodin asked**

He also discussed that with me. **Tita answered**

You should know that the exams are around the corner, and therefore you shouldn't chose being messed with all the time. **Yerodin said**

What can I do! **Tita exclaimed**

You tell your father to pay your school fees. **Yerodin said**

I have already done that. **Tita replied**

Is your father dead? **Yerodin asked**

No. **Tita answered**

Therefore let him pay your school fees and get you out of the next shit. **Yerodin said**

Things like that sometimes happen, you just don't know. **Changamire said**

Yes, it does. **Tita responded**

We know that you are brilliant and we don't want to lose you. **Changamire said**

I know . . . . **Tita responded**

You are one of us, do you know that? **Changamire said**

Yes, I know. **Tita responded**

We just want to be with you in class as always. **Yerodin said**

We were just worried that maybe the headmaster don't want you in school any more unless you paid your school fees. **Changamire said**

No. The headmaster already told me that without paying my school fees, there would be no exams for me, although he feels with me. **Tita replied**

Now, we know, we just believe that things will be fine again, and you will pay your school fees. Don't worry, you hear. **Yerodin consoled**

Thank you so much. **Tita replied**

.... Bye ... Bye .... (They said and most of them left) leaving some of his intimate friends with him.

At the end of that school day when Tita reached home his mother was at home as usual this time only with his most junior sister who was busy emulating her mother in the act of local mat weaving like a toddler. And his other sisters went to the stream to fetch water because there was not much water in their local big water pot made up of clay, and his father had not returned from either a job hunt or from firewood collection for sale. On seeing Tita, her mother immediately asked him if he saw the headmaster and Tita said 'yes' he saw the headmaster, thus;

Good afternoon Mama. **Tita greeted**

Good afternoon my son. Did you see the headmaster? **Mrs. Dunduza inquired**

Yes Mama. **Tita replied**

Go inside and put down your school bag and remove your school cloths, eat your food and relax yourself. **Mrs. Dunduza adviced**

Yes Mama. **Tita agreed**

Tita took his time and did as his mother directed him to without further conversations with her. After eating and minutes of relaxation he took his afternoon nap which was necessary because his mother never allowed him to embark on any other thing after returning back from school at the end of the school day unless he had taken his nap. His nap lasted as usual and before he worked up, his sisters had returned from the stream. His sisters were there when the lengthy discussion about his education was going on last Friday night, so, they felt for their brother and reasoned with him and understood the importance of his education. To make sure that Tita never deceived himself and to make sure that the price worth the candle, they twisted him a little to ascertain the truth.

Senior, Tita. **Kalonji called**

Yes, my sister. **Tita responded**

How was school today? **Kalonji asked**

It was fine. **Tita answered**

Were you sent home again? **Kalonji asked**

No, I was not. **Tita answered**

Did you meet with the headmaster? **Kalonji asked**

Yes, my sister. **Tita answered**

Was there any problems? **Kalonji asked**

No, certainly not. **Tita answered**

Was his call for good? **Kalonji asked**

Somehow, yes. He requested to see our father and discuss my nonpayment of this term school fees with him. **Tita answered**

I hope everything will work out fine. **kalonji said**

I hope so, let us watch and see. **Tita replied**

. . . . Silence . . . and his sisters went back to engage themselves in the rest of the day's routine. When his father returned back and after dinner, his mother told his father to ask him if he saw the headmaster as he supposed to, and his father wasted no time in determining whether Tita saw the headmaster for real.

Tita my son. **Mr. Cazembi called**

Yes Papa. **Tita responded**

Did you see the headmaster today? **Mr. Cazembi asked**

Yes, Papa. I saw him in his office. **Tita answered**

Good son. I am proud of you. **Mr. Cazembi remarked**

Thank you, Papa. **Tita replied**

What did he said? **Mr. Cazembi asked**

He wanted to know why I have not paid my school fees until this time. **Tita answered**

Was that all? **Mr. Cazembi asked**

No, Papa. **Tita answered**

What else? **Mr. Cazembi asked**

He told me to tell you that he wants to see me and you in his office on Thursday this week during first lesson. **Tita answered**

Why? **Mr. Cazembi asked**

He said that he wants to discuss my nonpayment of this term school fees with you because he is worried that an intelligent student like me should not easily be tossed out of the classroom while my father is still alive. **Tita answered**

Where else can I go borrowing? **Mr. Cazembi disturbed**

Papa, there is no need to worry, the headmaster indicated that he wants to see you so that he could struck a deal with you on how best to retain me in school, especially during the coming exams. His deal may be for the best interest of all of us. **Tita said**

Have you seen that my husband? His call has some merits. I don't think he is requesting for your presence to laugh and jeer at you. **Mrs. Dunduza said**

I have already scheduled an appointment on Thursday this week. **Mr. Cazembi replied**

Is that Papa? **Tita humbly asked**

Yes, I have. **Mr. Cazembi answered**

My husband, what appointment do you have on Thursday this week? **Mrs. Dunduza inquired**

Do you know Mr. Kakuyun (Arms the people)? **Mr. Cazembi asked**

Yes, my husband. **Mrs. Dunduza replied**

He told me to help him gather palm fruit bunches on Thursday. **Mr. Cazembi said**

My husband I understand your points but please forget about going to gather that palm fruit brunches and concentrate on our son's issue which is so important at this time. Since the money that would be made through that assignment of yours on Thursday will not be closer to paying our son's school fees, however, I strongly suggest that you please cancel your appointment with Mr. Kakuyun and go to the school with our son to see their headmaster. **Mrs. Dunduza suggested**

Seeing the headmaster is important, Papa. **Tita humbly said**

Please, I need time to think this over. Imagine my scheduled appointment on Thursday. I had already . . . . **Mr. Cazembi replied**

My husband, please think over it. **Mrs. Dunduza pleaded**

. . . . Silence . . . . while his father reflected to determine which one of the two alternatives should be accepted by him based on the degree of its importance. While he retrospect, his wife was quite by his side and Tita and his sisters remained speechless. After moments of reflection, he came up with a decision.

My wife this is an understandable reason in your statement. There is no need chasing shadows concerning our son's education, and I cannot say till tomorrow what I can do today because tomorrow may be too far and the opportunity forgone. Therefore, I concur with you to go to our son to his school on Thursday and see his headmaster. But more importantly, I don't want to be messed with. **Mr. Cazembi agreed**

My husband, thank you for your understanding of the importance of our son's education, and I assure you that the headmaster will not mess with you. **Mrs. Dunduza said**

He is our son. But how do you know that the headmaster will not try to mock at me? **Mr. Cazembi queried**

My inner most being assures me of the headmaster's sincerity and concern of our son's education, therefore, his call must be for good. **Mrs. Dunduza responded**

You know that although I may be poor, and that hurts. **Mr. Cazembi touchingly said**

Does being rich mean owning everything? How poor are we? We eat all that we want and nobody and absolutely nobody in this household has one day skipped his/her scheduled meal because of lack of what to eat. We eat our bellies full with good food. What about those who claim to be so rich and their children are wandering the streets begging? Do you call that wealth? Rubbish. **Mrs. Dunduza said**

Some people are accustomed to ridiculing, even when the situation does not call for it. **Mr. Cazembi said**

I understand my husband that some people are so inhuman but some of their utterances reveal their true selves. **Mrs. Dunduza responded**

My wife, you know this type of work I do, sometimes when you disappoint your customer he/she never comes back to you easily, and besides, we are many that do these types of jobs. One customer lost could mean a lot of things. **Mr. Cazembi said**

I know my husband, I understand, but believe that a disappointment of such could be a blessing. This is the first time of been invited by the school headmaster himself, so, I want us to make that could be one time sacrifice. Tomorrow is another day; we cannot spend forever in the headmaster's office. **Mrs. Dunduza responded**

I will go and tell him to hire another person for that job because I will not be able to make it on that day due to circumstances beyond my personal control. I hope he will understand? **Mr. Cazembi contemplated**

My husband, he will definitely understand. **Mrs. Dunduza responded**

I hope he will . . . . **Mr. Cazembi said**

Has he paid you? **Mrs. Dunduza asked**

No, you know me. I do not collect money before the job is done. I either collect money and immediately start work or collect money when the work is done. And I feel stronger that way. **Mr. Cazembi answered**

I love you my husband. **Mrs. Dunduza said**

I love you too. **Mr. Cazembi responded**

Our son, your father has decided to go with you on Thursday. **Mrs. Dunduza said**

Thank you, Papa and Mama. **Tita replied**

Yes, our son. **Mr. & Mrs. Cazembi said concurrently**

Our son makes sure on Thursday that you get all your things ready and we will go and see him. And try to remind me that on Wednesday night so that I will not forget. Did you hear me? **Mr. Cazembi said**

Yes Papa. I will. I must. **Tita happily replied**

I will equally remind you of that. **Mrs. Dnduzau assured**

Tita, did you forget to tell us any other thing? **Mr. Cazembi asked**

No, Papa. I have said all. **Tita answered**

Now all of you my children can go to sleep. Are you happy? **Mr. Cazembi joked**

Yes, Papa. **They all replied at once**

Good night my children. **Mr. Cazembi said**

Good night, Papa. **They all replied at once**

CHAPTER THREE

Tita Finishes Primary School

D ays came and passed, and on Wednesday after dinner Tita reminded his father of their schedule the morning of the following day, and before sleep Mrs. Cazembi recalled her husband's attention on that. On Thursday morning Tita and father after taking their birth, ate together and began their journey to his primary school to see their headmaster in his office because he must be expecting their arrival. Along the way, his father questioned him further so as to know if they headmaster really invited him along with his son to his office.

My son Tita, are you sure your headmaster invited me to his office today? **Mr. Cazembi asked**

Yes Papa, he told me that last Friday. **Tita answered**

Who else was there when he said that? **Mr. Cazembi inquired**

No other person, Papa. **Tita replied**

So it was only two of you? **Mr. Cazembi asked**

Yes, Papa. **Tita answered**

I hope his call is for good. **Mr. Cazembi said**

Our headmaster seems to be a very good person. **Tita responded**

Do you know that if not for this militia group rumors which full everywhere, I could have long paid your school fees? **Mr. Cazembi inquired**

Yes Papa, I know. **Tita replied**

I hate to be asked by outsiders to perform my family responsibilities because, do you know why? They may think that I am a lazy man. **Mr. Cazembi said**

The headmaster knows that I always pay on time at least before major tests but this time something may be wrong, so, he decided to find out why and as well make a deal. **Tita said**

Does he stay alone in his office? **Mr. Cazembi asked**

Yes Papa, he does stay alone in his office. **Tita answered**

Do you know whether he invited other teachers to be present? **Mr. Cazembi asked**

No Papa, he shouldn't do that because this seems to be a personal discussion between two of you in particular. **Tita answered**

I hate embarrassment. Do you like that? **Mr. Cazembi inquired**

I hate to be embarrassed too. It kind of irks. **Tita replied**

I don't want to be embarrassed by the unexpected presence of other teachers excluding the headmaster himself. **Mr. Cazembi said**

Papa, our headmaster from all that I know will be the least of all to embarrass you. He always stands by his words and hates meddling with private affairs. **Tita responded**

I believe you my son. I believe you. **Mr. Cazembi said**

. . . . Silence . . . as they walked barely few steps to the entrance of the school premises. They walked passed and entered the headmaster's office. The headmaster was pleased to see them and he immediately offered them seats after shaking hands with Mr. Cazembi. They passed greetings and the headmaster without been told had memorized Tita's name and he called him by his name as they got seated.

Tita, what is your father's name? **Mr. Mwata asked**

Sir, my father's name is Mr. Cazembi. **Tita politely answered**

Mr. Cazembi welcome to my office. I am Mr. Mwata the headmaster of this school. Your son must have already told you that. **Mr. Mwata said**

Thank you Sir, my son told me. **Mr. Cazembi responded**

I told your son, Tita, to come with you and see me in my office today at exactly this time you are here. **Mr. Mwata said**

My son told me that Sir. **Mr. Cazembi responded**

Do you know why I asked you to come with him to my office Mr. Cazembi? **Mr. Mwata asked**

No, Sir. I have no idea. **Mr. Cazembi answered**

Do you know that your son is an intelligent student? **Mr. Mwata asked**

Yes, I know that he is intelligent, Sir. **Mr. Cazembi answered**

In fact, your son, Tita, is one of the most intelligent and well behaved pupils in this school. **Mr. Mwata said**

I am happy to hear that, Sir. **Mr. Cazembi responded**

Do you know that your son has not paid his school fees for this term only? **Mr. Mwata asked**

Yes, I know Sir. **Mr. Cazembi answered**

So, Mr. Cazembi, why haven't you paid his third term school fees? **Mr. Mwata asked**

Sir, I always pay his school fees on time previously but this time things are different. **Mr. Cazembi answered**

What do you mean by 'things are different'? **Mr. Mwata asked**

Sir, it is because of this rumor everywhere, my customers are no longer willing to spend for the type of jobs I do. **Mr. Cazembi answered**

What rumors? **Mr. Mwata asked**

Sir, I mean, the federal government rumors. **Mr. Cazembi answered**

You mean the rumors of the militia group and the federal government on power tussles? **Mr. Mwata asked**

Yes, Sir. **Mr. Cazembi answered**

There are rumors that the militia group staged an aborted coup d'état and are planning to topple the federal government and are being backed by the Prime Minister. And that the militia group vowed to oust the President, and that the President in defense of himself and the country has setup a manhunt squared so as to fish out the real culprits of the said aborted coup. Does that affect your earnings? **Mr. Mwata inquired**

I now understand. This rumor has stopped me from making a single CFA Franc, Sir. **Mr. Cazembi said**

What type of work do you do for a living Mr. Cazembi? **Mr. Mwata asked**

I am a laborer Sir. **Mr. Cazembi answered**

That is a pity. **Mr. Mwata said**

But Sir, in the previous years before this time things have not been so hard. Is the President currently doing badly? **Mr. Cazembi inquired**

Obviously, the President has not been doing badly but sometimes he could face opposition from those who are either enemies of progress; believe that they could outperform the president while in the office; for selfish aggrandizements, and those suffering from 'quick wealth syndrome' despite the costs. This incumbent president since his election into office has not been doing bad. At least human basic needs are within the affordability of the common man. Those controlling unguided arms and ammunitions should sometimes be so careful. **Mr. Mwata said.**

I hope the militia group should call off their mission for the benefits of the people like me because this rumor has edged me. **Mr. Cazembi responded**

Mr. Cazembi. Do you know that this school does not allow any of its pupils who have not paid his/her school fees to sit for either test or exams for that term? **Mr. Mwata asked**

No Sir. **Mr. Cazembi answered**

That's exactly how it works in this school and that is the rule. **Mr. Mwata said**

I have done all that I could but nobody is willing to even lend money out. **Mr. Cazembi responded**

So, do you want Tita as intelligent as he is to miss the forth coming exams which start after next week? **Mr. Mwata asked**

No Sir. What can I do? **Mr. Cazembi answered**

Tita will you like to miss your promotional exams? **Mr. Mwata asked**

No Sir. Please Sir. **Tita humbly answered**

Mr. Cazembi. Do you see that your son is willing and determined to be in school, and he doesn't want to lose? **Mr. Mwata asked**

I understand that Sir. But what can I do? **Mr. Cazembi answered**

Mr. Cazembi. Is there any way you could come up with the money on the morning of the first exam day, that is, before the start of exams? **Headmaster asked**

Sir, to tell you the truth I have exhausted all my avenues. There is no hope of coming up with such amount of money. **Mr. Cazembi answered**

The best thing therefore should be to send your son Tita home and tell him to forget about the promotional exams. **Mr. Mwata said**

Please, Sir! Please, Sir!! Please, Sir!!! I will pay. **Tita pleaded**

We just don't have that type of money anywhere now or even in a month time. Oh! **Mr. Cazembi touched**

Mr. Cazembi, I see your son as an intelligent and brilliant pupil, and having gone through his academic records this is the first time he delayed in paying his school fees on time. As a believer in the growth and development of our people and the preservations of our various good traditions as transferred to us from our ancestors, I want your son to continue with his chances in life since, you, his father want him educated in the cultural way, and he Tita has accepted to make his dreams and your aspirations come true by putting in all his efforts academically to work so as to achieve academic excellence in this school. I truthfully hesitate to deprive you, Mr. Cazembi, and your son, Tita, that opportunity of attaining the desired academic heights and reaping the fruits, and may our ancestors be my witnesses. **Headmaster sincerely said.**

What can I do Sir? **Mr. Cazembi asked**

Mr. Cazembi considering the present situation of things and the hazy atmosphere, I came up with an amicable solution that could be of most benefit to you and your son in particular and to all of us in general. There is fear and suspicion that this militia group mercenary into the federal government polity may last longer than anticipated, in that case it could be kind of hard to this present job anomie on your side to go away unless there is a change of career. So, I have decided to offer you a helping hand by lending you money to pay for your son, Tita's school fees, not only for this school term but for also some other times when it could be as difficult for you to raise his school fees. Do you accept my proposal? **Headmaster said**

Yes Sir, as long as it is within allowable limits. **Mr. Cazembi replied**

Starting from this term I will cover your son's school fees with no strings attached. No interest and/or late fees attached. I am not going to give you the money at hand, rather I will pay his school fees from my salaries and whenever you get the money within the relevant or succeeding term you pay me back. I mean, when I paid this Third Term school fess, you will pay me back first term of next school year, and should I also pay his first term of next year school fees, you will pay me back second term of next year. I envisioned that it is the only remedy to deal with the current job crises and avert dis-enrolling your son from school. So, what do you decide? **Mr. Mwata said**

Sir, I want the deal. **Mr. Cazembi replied**

Can you raise the money at the needed times? **Mr. Mwata asked**

Yes Sir. I am sure I will. **Mr. Cazembi replied**

I want to assure you that based on the present situation of things, I mean, the political climate, war certainly is not eminent because that seems to be the only obstacle that could stood on your way of coming up with the repayment as at when necessary. The militia group does not have the stronger power yet; after all, they are not dealing with a fool. **Mr. Mwata said**

Thank you Sir, **Mr. Cazembi appreciated**

Mr. Cazembi I see you as a hardworking man and you are still young with strength. I am convinced that you will make it. Besides, you have a very good son by your side that looks promising; please do not allow him to slip off. Train him the good ways at home and always instruct him like a good father. Again, our communities, country, is in need of such almost spotless students like Tita your son. **Headmaster said**

I understand the importance Sir. I will also give him the best of instructions. **Mr. Mwata assured**

We should not allow the method of education of these days as seen in schools to ruin the good traditions of our people. We should always combine education of this nature with moral values because at the end our traditional values remain paramount. **Mr. Mwata adviced**

Sir, despite what is learned in schools, our moral traditions stand undiluted and they remain our flesh, blood and bones. **Mr. Cazembi responded**

Do you have any other thing to tell me? **Mr. Mwata inquired**

Sir, you have proved beyond all reasonable doubts that you are surely one of the best persons of your tribe. Your ability to draw from our Ancestors has made you a person to reason of. You are a complete blessing to this land and your foot prints on this soil will never be easily erased. Your education signifies only hope, progress and the continuity and sustenance of the needy like me. In the past and until today, there have been countless stories of how our people who acquired western education later betrayed their people both at home and elsewhere whom they were indeed educated/ trained to help and assist. And most of the times they forget about our traditions and prefer the more inhuman ways in matters that desires moral purity. You have also enlightened me the more on the future of tomorrow based on the present political chaos being generated by the militia group. I couldn't have known what next to do without your clarifications.

I sincerely appreciate your acceptance of my son, Tita as your son also. Your understanding of his efforts and academic achievements so far is enough for me to go home with. Truthfully, never before in all the days of my son, since he first entered primary school have I received such a warm and promising welcome from such an important personality like you. Your remark of him has made me a proud father more determined to expense more energy so as to see him through in all his educational endeavors. He has been a good son so far, and I do believe that he heard all that you said today so that tomorrow he will also make your advice part of the custodian of his days. Again, Sir I am pleased and proud of you, and I use the name of all my family members to thank you on this day invoking the spirit of our Ancestors and God to be with us all. Tita my son say thank you to the headmaster for he has saved you from the stinks. **Mr. Cazembi responded gratefully**

Thank you so much Sir! Thank you so much Sir!! Thank you so much Sir!!! **Tita happily said bowing his head on the headmaster's table**

Yes my son. I am happy for you. I want your success academically and wise. Always keep on maintaining your academic excellence. **Headmaster said**

Thank you Sir. **Mr. Cazembi said**

It's all right. **Mr. Mwata said**

Tita you can now join the rest of your classmates. **Mr. Mwata instructed**

Yes Sir. **Tita replied**

Mr. Cazembi it is nice having you in my office today, you really care for your son's academic success. **Headmaster said**

Yes Sir, my son is so important to me and he is the only son I have just like myself. **Mr. Cazembi responded**

That was just exactly what he said. **Mr. Mwata said**

Tita reached his school bag and stood up from his seat and was about to leave the headmaster's office.

Mr. Cazembi, you are now free to go, just keep our agreement in mind. **Mr. Mwata said**

I will always remember that Sir. I give you my words. **Mr. Cazembi responded**

Mr. Cazembi stood up to leave the headmaster's office and them shake hands.

Have a nice day Mr. Cazembi. **Mr. Mwata said**

I will. Thank you Sir. **Mr. Cazembi replied**

Please, thank you Sir. **Tita said**

You are all welcomed. **Headmaster said**

Tita and his father left the headmaster's office simultaneously. As they went outside the headmaster's office Tita flashed his father a very bright happy looking face, and his father smiled and called him "my son, lucky boy". As they worked passed Tita's classroom block he gently touched his father's hand and told him that "there is our classroom", and his father looked towards the direction of the classroom, and Tita told him "bye bye Papa. I will be home soon", and left and entered his classroom.

Meanwhile, when they were coming, on passing through the classroom blocks and heading towards the headmaster's office Mr. Cazembi was jerking his head looking from one side to the other, staring at teachers because he thought that they teachers may have heard information about him and could laugh at him for his inability to pay his only son's school fees. And on entering the headmaster's office he was somehow nervous but composed because he thought that the headmaster could use a little trick to lure him to face the mass number of teachers who could be present, so, he first looked around immediately he entered just to make sure that it was all clear.

When Mr. Cazembi returned home, he broke the good news to his wife and their daughters and they were all happy and his daughters started jubilating saying "Tita! Tita!! Tita!!! We are so happy for you, is really you". Before Tita returned home from school that day, they prepared a special food for him so as to tell him that he has done the family proud.

When Tita returned from school his mother gave him a cheerful welcome and petted him, and on spotting him home his sisters jubilated once again calling, shouting and when they were happy jubilating some of their available family members came outside and stared at them in bewilderment while some of them approached them to ascertain what happened. His sisters were proud of him that his academic performance had helped paved his way to the highest level of basic elementary education. They confessed that without his academic efforts it could have been so difficult for him to be promoted without taking the necessary and needed promotional exams, and could have meant either repeating class 4 or dropping out of school very close to the finish line. They told him that he could now be in school without worries since his school fees had been taken care off.

Tita intensified his efforts to always be on top of the class without hassles since their school headmaster has reduced impediments like that of the Class 4B teacher. He maintained his excellent position while in school without falling back due to overconfidence. Meanwhile, his sisters were always pleased with him although some of them were deprived the opportunities of basic primary education for his sake, they held nothing against him. They understood the family situation and joined their mother in learning the local mat weaving business because although market was scarce mostly due to the insurgence, they did believed that surely after their brothers settlement, things could change for the better, and they could relocate to the towns/cities for better business opportunities, that is where mats sell more.

His parents worked relentlessly to make sure that they sponsored him through in school, at least to ensure that he got elementary six, and subsequently took his First School Leaving Certificate Examination (FSLCE) so as to receive his First School Leaving Certificate (FSLC) which was widely regarded and accepted. And having reached an accord with his headmaster, it all depended on them to make sure that they never reneged on that although the headmaster been so humane could allow him to be in school while they pay him back all his money later, but "once beaten, twice shy and Heaven surely helps those who help themselves". During that time in his country somebody with FSLC could get work in certain companies, a work that his/her salaries could be enough to satisfy basic family needs. In those years in this Central African country such a certificate was better than the first degree of today from accredited higher institutions like universities, polytechnics, colleges of education, and teachers training colleges respectively, depending on areas of specialization although it is gradually becoming a common symptom.

In those days those that never finished elementary school did also landed on good jobs as long as the person reached up to elementary four and as long as he/she had family connections, but his own scenario was different because his parents had no such connections that could buttress him should he failed to finish his primary education. All his uncles and nieces were all locally based and were just been introduced to the towns and cities where major companies/industries were located at.

Tita stayed in school and successfully finished his education to primary six, and when the result of his FSLCE came out he was on top of the class, he made a 'Distinction'. Tita was proud of his academic achievement and filially loved his parents and his headmaster the more. He achieved his first dream of passing through elementary six because his parents never reneged on repaying their school headmaster. They always reimbursed him on any CFA Franc spent on Tita's school fees. Immediately after the posting of their FSLCE results Tita rushed to the headmaster's office and bowed low before his presence and thanked him while in a celebrating mood, and the headmaster was so pleased because Tita had once again proved that he was capable of been trusted.

Tita later rushed home and broke the news of his excellence once again to his parents, and sisters, and they were full of joy and merriments. They all thanked God and their Ancestors for their intermissions which provided a sponsor for their children and had also aided him in making a 'Distinction' in his FSLCE. A grade mostly made by geniuses. His parents scheduled a visit to the Headmaster's House in the schedule at the school premises at the Teachers Quarters. The headmaster accepted to receive them on the scheduled date. Before the scheduled date his mother went to the market to buy things for the preparation of food that would be presented before the headmaster as a token of their appreciation of his immense help, so his father emptied his pocket so as to facilitate the purchase of the food items. On the schedule date Mrs. Dunduza with the help of her fellow husband's clan woman, Mrs. Kafe` (Quite) and her daughters' prepared delicious food, and they carried it along with them and with her husband and Mr. Changa

(As strong as iron) their kinsman to the Headmaster's House at the Teachers Quarters in the school environ. His father had already managed to purchase a bottle of hot drink that he went along with.

The headmaster having already been informed of their coming invited about two people from his village, and also few other teachers who lived at the Teachers Quarters on school compound. And those invitees were all seated before the arrival of Mr. Cazembi and his family and their accompanists. They were happily welcomed at the Headmaster's House and Mr. Mwata's wife and children helped them to bring down their basins of food from their heads. They exchanged greetings and inquired about each other's health conditions. And Mr. Mwata introduced his invitees to Mr. Cazembi who also did same. Mrs. Dunduza handed the basins over to the headmaster's wife, Mrs. Yamro (Courteous) and Mr. Cazembi handed over the bottle of hot drink to the headmaster. They thanked the headmaster and his family for their supports.

Here is a bottle of hot drink as a token of thank you, Sir. **Mr. Cazembi said**

Is this for me alone? **Mr. Mwata asked**

Yes Sir that is the little I can provide. **Mr. Cazembi replied**

That is nice of you. **Mr. Mwata said**

. . . . Silence . . . .

Here is the little food I prepared for your good loving family (pointing at the food). **Mrs. Dunduza said**

Heehi! Is all of this for us? **Mrs. Yamro exclaimed**

Yes Ma, it is for you. **Mrs. Dunduza responded**

What prompted this nice show of appreciation? **Mrs. Yamro asked**

Sir is such a good man. **Mrs. Dunduza answered**

This is so nice of you. **Mrs. Yamro said**

Mrs. Yamro called her female children to come and send the gifts in, and she immediately followed them inside and instructed them to bring out some quantities that will be used to serve the visitors and their invitees. Her daughters wasted no time in doing as their mother instructed them to. And while eating and enjoying the meal Mr. Mwata called Tita and told them that he was the best among those that took FSLCE, that he got a 'Distinction'. He told them that Mr. & Mrs. Cazembi were Tita's parents, and that he came to know them, especially Mr. Cazembi when his son Tita was having school fees difficulties. That he was the only one left without payment of school fees among his classmates and was one day bared from taken the test during his third term in elementary 4. "So, I looked at Tita's record and discovered that he was such an intelligent student who deserved to be retained in school, and besides, that was his first time of paying his school fees late. Hence, I invited him to come see me in my office the following day. After seen him in my office I also invited him and his father to my office, and they honored my invitation. After discussions with Mr. Cazembi, I saw his predicament and decided to offer him a helping hand, and we agreed on the terms that I should pay his son's school fees whenever he could not come up with the school fees on time, and that he would pay me later, and he accepted my offer and we reached an accord. Thereafter, I began to cover for his son in the areas of school fees when necessary through to his primary six".

The headmaster continued that "this young man you are looking here (pointing at Tita's father) is a truthful person. There was never a time he hesitated on paying me back all my money as was used to cover for his son's school fees. With such families like him, I hope the best of our professions must continue to be manifest. Based on my encounter with certain families, our people surely prepared to work with those in our profession". His invitees were surprised, and they thanked him for his philanthropic spirit and urged him to continue to do such a good work as long as he had, especially that time that their country was drifting gradually from grace to grass. And they commended Mr. Cazembi for inspiring the headmaster the more because some people like him could not offer such helps because of the fear of been manipulated, but with such fulfillments of agreements, others like Tita could equally benefit.

Mrs. Yamro thanked Mr. Cazembi and family for their show of gratitude because 'some kids on seeing their FSLCE result posted could back away and turned their back on my husband, but Tita's case was different, he proved that he deserved the help that he received. In addition, some parents could on hearing that their sons result had been posted and that he made a 'distinction' could equate themselves with my husband and instead discussed a more important thing. In your case you have proved beyond all reasonable doubt that you deserved the helps that you received. You have truly passed the litmus test with the lucky ones. Tita your son has great potentials which when well guided by you his parents and his father in particular must yield the desired results, and subsequently lift the veil of poverty from your heads if any. But allowing him to do as he deserved having achieved a recommendable elementary feet could have devastating consequences and far reaching effects. Tita, in every of your future options in life choose wisely as you have always does. Please, my child do not allow what you do not know much about to rule your conscience and dominate your being, and as well control your existence".

Mr. Cazembi expressed his appreciation to the headmaster and his family and told them that "I do not know where to start thanking you sir for your goodness and kindness to my family, for letting this poor thing see his dreams come true and for making part of my family's aspirations a reality. When I had lost all hopes, you rekindled my hope again, when I was in a friend to none of my customers you employed me, and when no one offered to give me loans, you loaned me money. Sir, your show of concern to my son, Tita, in particular and my family in general will linger in my memory to eternity. Your attitude towards me and my family has proven that you are a staunch believer of our tradition which abhors invoking the spirits of our ancestors in vain whenever men/women of the same tribe like us are engaging in any form of agreements. Mrs. Yamro has also helped to enlighten me the more that you have a reasonable wonderful family bonded by the same spirit of ever willingness to aid and assist the likes of my son Tita who could be the pathways in the bush tomorrow. I also want to thank your fellow teachers who are here today, and as well implore them to always emulate the headmaster and in their daily dealings with their students because Mr. Mwata surely leads by example. "Please, our teachers do not try to subvert the principles, ideologies and ethics for which the headmaster has set forth, instead strive to copy from him and even endeavor to be better if you can. This headmaster has definitely redefined some of our people's notions and believes, especially in this section of this country. So, many a time, some people do not want to identify themselves with teachers, especially because of the ways they inhumanly treat their pupils, some of them fail to allow such excellent ideals to excel. My gratitude is also extended to people from Mr. Mwata's home town for creating an enabled environment for the upbringing and sustenance of such a man of his people. Again, thank you Sir for your immense understanding and help".

Mr. Changa thanked the headmaster for his belief in the development and progress of his people no matter how small because "truthfully the young shall grow and the growth is today as I am looking at all of us. You have paved the way for my relatives and fellow kinsman's son, Tita, it is now left for him to draw from our Ancestors and to continue to live an exemplary life. To him that much is given, much is also expected. Our headmaster, Sir, you are a great gift to this section of our country, to this poor village that deserved to be treated and mended with traditional medicine. With people like you, we have hope that the current crises by the militia group will adequately be taken care of, we have hope of staying in this village as encompassed by our tribes because we have no other places to call home. We have hope of one day earning again like the yesteryears before the current tussles with the President and the rest of his government-militia group connection. This community deserves more of you and wishes you happy more days in our mist. My you stay and retire in our beloved community as the headmaster of our small primary school with your family".

The headmaster accepted all their 'thank you' messages and re-assured them that he would always do what was necessary to assist any student like Tita to achieve his/her elementary school dreams. "Tita, having passed through the first stage of your educational ladder, they journey may not end here. You could eventually be enrolled in the secondary school and perhaps subsequently in the university. In all your educational endeavors always make sure that you remember your hard work during your primary school years". Mr. Mwata reminded his father that based on his job status and earning power, it was not necessary that his son Tita must attend secondary school, 'him Tita could start somewhere like learning a business, handwork etc after which he can enroll himself and continue from where he stopped. He is still a young boy and to tell you the truth, in the next eight (8) years he would still be of average age to start from year one in the secondary school". The headmaster stressed that contrary to the widely held notion that someone of about 25 years of age was a little advanced to start secondary school, the truth is that even those in their thirties and forties could start secondary schools as freshmen. White people or can I say Europeans and other educational advanced countries that our people thought that they made it early in life in schools, "some of them are more older than you take them to be". In their own land a person of Tita's age from such a 'well-to-do' families could start work shortly after primary school and re-enrolled himself/ herself in school after a reasonable number of years of work, and/ or when he/she must have gotten married and/or with children.

In those foreign countries they most of the times 'take their own destiny into their own hands'. They do not like to be frustrated out of their heart desires, and are determined to put in extra efforts so as to achieve their basic aims although some of them are complete loots but those their days are numbered. Therefore, Mr. Cazembi the ball is now on your curt, it now all depends on you whether you can afford his education to the secondary school level. I have played my own part. If you have no money or anybody to help sponsor him through the secondary school, please, do act wisely as usual because I will not like to hear that this intelligent young boy wasted away due to lack of support". Mr. Mwata explained to them that the current political debacle which had led to serious security issues in their country were been taken care of by the federal government although the militia group had been patrolling certain remote villages warning the inhabitants to stay off the federal government and also spreading false rumors. "There is every indication to believe that this economic caricature imposed by the 'hit and run' forces will not lead to a full scale conflict whereby inhabitants will be forced to run helter scatter, scrambling and scampering". He told them to continue to move about their normal duties and never to confront assumed rebel forces, because confronting them could have fatal consequences.

At the end of the headmaster's statement, some of the teachers buttressed his call for calm and tranquility and further urged them to be more concentrated as usual. One of the teachers reminded Tita that in the absence of his father's financial strength to send him back to school, this time the secondary school, he Tita should always understand that the rest depended on him. "Tita, you can still be where you want to be in life without much hassles, always be of help to yourself whenever necessary". Finally, Mr. & Mrs. Cazembi wished them well and they stayed some few more minutes and left the Headmaster's House at the Teachers Quarters.

At home Tita joined his younger sisters in contributing to the family routine while also reading his books when he had time. He stayed quietly and peacefully with his sisters and his parents, and there was never a time he went out to cause problems due to show offs. He continued to humble himself showing optimum respect to all those who deserved. For him to apply for admission into the nearest secondary school in his ward he had to wait for at least one month as approved by their Board of Education (BoE). So, he continued to hope that maybe his father could come up with the offer of getting him enrolled in the secondary school so as to further his education beyond the secondary school level. As days rolled by, his father continued to search for work assiduously, only working whenever there were offers, and his mother continued to make every effort to ensure that he ate well because "good health supersedes any other thing". Towards the end of the required period for application for admission to the nearest secondary school, and having discussed everything concerning that with his wife, so, one night his father made it very clear to him that the option of going back to school was no longer feasible because of circumstances beyond his control. His father expressed regrets but assured Tita that he could still make it in another field of endeavor, after all, education to such levels were not the end of everything.

Our son Tita. **Mr. Cazembi called**

Yes, Papa. **Tita replied**

Incline your ears. **Mr. Cazembi requested**

Yes, Papa, I have. **Tita replied**

I don't know how you will feel. **Mr. Cazembi said**

What is that Papa? **Tita humbly asked**

My son, your father have taken a thorough screening of myself and discovered that I cannot afford to send you to the secondary school. You understand that I am the only son of my mother, and certainly nobody helps me when I am in such a financial distress. **Mr. Cazembi said**

Yes, I know Papa. **Tita replied**

Your mother and I have decided that you will not enroll in the secondary school this time because we truthfully cannot afford to pay your school fees. You know how hard it was before you finished your primary school. The economy is still like that and even worse because the militia group is slapping people anyhow, and things are deteriorating by the day. So, I do not know how long it could take me before I could come up with your school fees, so, please my son do reason with us. **Mr. Cazembi said**

I understand Papa. **Tita replied**

I know how it pains to tell a brilliant son like you to stop at the elementary school level although you have gotten your FSLC which was our primary arm. Had it been that militia group stayed off the economic route, you could have used your FSLC to at least start work somewhere in the town with the help of our willing relatives, but unfortunately, things have partially gone out of hand, and the used to be available works are no longer there for people with FSLC even if their parents have connections. More so, your entrance to the secondary school could have been much easier. **Mr. Cazembi said**

No problems Papa. What am I going to do next? **Tita humbly inquired**

I will get with some of my friends and relatives that have those that are either in trade, crafts etc and implore them to give me a helping hand. Getting them to be off assistance to me could take a while, therefore, Tita, our son, you must excises patient. **Mr. Cazembi said**

I will have patient, Papa. **Tita assured**

What type of work/trade will you like? **Mr. Cazembi asked**

. . . . Silence—as Tita took himself memory lane.

I prefer to learn trade. **Tita answered**

What type of trade my son? **Mrs. Dunduza asked**

Mama, I mean, trade like the selling rice, beans and those things that are used to cook them. **Tita answered**

Why did you choose such a trade? **Mrs. Dunduza asked**

Mama, it is because I believe that everybody eat rice and beans a lot. **Tita answered**

That is a brilliant idea. A lot of people eat that, and that implies good trade. **Mr. Cazembi said**

It will make good trade, Papa. **Tita responded**

You choose well my son. **Mr. Cazembi remarked**

Yes, Papa. **Tita responded**

Do you have any other choice like; learning hand work as a Bicycle Mechanic, Block Layer, Block Molder etc or other trades like selling Cattle, Cows, Goats, Sheep, and Butchering etc? **Mr. Cazembi inquired**

I like the one I choose, Papa. **Tita replied**

It is alright; I will get with some of those I told you about and see what they can say. **Mr. Cazembi said**

Yes, Papa. **Tita replied**

You stay in the house and continue to do as you have been doing. Do not bother yourself, I will find something new for you to do in place of the secondary school. **Mr. Cazembi assured**

I have no problems Papa. I have accepted the changes. **Tita replied**

My good son, you always understand our predicaments. **Mrs. Dunduza said**

Yes, Mama. **Tita replied**

My finding you a new thing will not take too long, you hear? **Mr. Cazembi said**

Thank you, Papa. **Tita replied**

I hope you are not worried? **Mr. Cazembi asked**

I have no problems, Papa. I am fifty-fifty. **Tita answered**

You can now go to bed all of you. **Mrs. Cazembi said**

They greeted them as usual and went in for sleep.

Thereafter Tita continued to spend time at home with his sisters, going to the soccer pitch in the evening during good weathers and sometimes helping his father to finish his jobs, especially during bush fallow clearing periods for the farming season. He was of immense help to his parents during his little stay at home prior to his moving to the towns to learn his desired trade. Meanwhile, his father was busy asking his friends and relatives who could offer him help in training his son the rice and beans trade. At a certain stage one of his relatives from the same community accepted to tell his son to take Tita to the town and train him in the rice and beans etc trade which was flourishing at that time. Tita's father was more than pleased to get a relative, Mr. Mutope, (Protector) who could help him at those tough times. His relative promised him that he would send for his son Mpyama (He shall inherit) and that he would be back in month's time to negotiate with Mr. Cazembi so that his son Tita could be taken along with him.

When Mr. Cazembi returned home he disclosed everything to his wife who thanked God and their Ancestors for their provision of a new path way for their only son, especially during the time when getting someone to assist them was harder than 'bending a steel rode with mere hands'. Tita was later informed that one of his relatives had accepted to train him in the 'rice and beans' trade, and he was happy to join such a trade.

CHAPTER FOUR

Tita Goes To Town

After few days Mr. Mutope sent for his son who promised to visit home in one of those month ends, especially during the months that they had reduced volume of transactions. Mpyama made good his promise of coming to see his father and as well abide by his directives. When his son returned, they sent for Mr. Cazembi and luckily he was at home that day and he arrived at his relative's house without delay, and they all exchanged greetings and later Mr. Mutope asked him to explain everything to his son, Mpyama, and Mr. Cazembi told him all about his son Tita. Mpyama was so impressed by Tita's performance and he told Mr. Cazembi that "since he is the only son, there is no need passing through the rigorous school years. The best thing at this time is to learn trade so as to assist when needed. "When he applies his knowledge and understanding to trading, he will equally excel because it is the same thing as been in school and performing excellently".

Mpyama used himself as a perfect example because he had FSLC at the time when it was still more useful and not many people had it at that time, and still he envisioned the future and set it aside and learnt the rice and beans trade. And he said that "today what forced me out of further education is gradually proving to be a reality". At the end Mpyama accepted whole heartedly to go back to town with Tita in a week time with no strings attached. He also promised to settle Tita at the end of the agreed six (6) years of service with him and with Mr. Cazembi contributing about 25% of the money needed to settle him. Tita's father immediately went back home cheerful, and in the night of it Tita was informed of the decision made by his would be boss.

Tita, our Son. **Mr. Cazembi called**

Yes Papa. **Tita answered**

I have just reached an agreement with Mpyama the son of my relative Mr. Mutope. **Mr. Cazembi said**

Yes, Papa. **Tita replied**

You are to return back to town with him in a week time. No delays are anticipated. **Mr. Cazembi said**

Yes, Papa. **Tita cheefully replied**

We agreed that you spend six years with him. Does that sound good to you? **Mr. Cazembi asked**

Yes Papa. **Tita answered**

He said that six years was necessary for you to learn the business well and also stand better chances of starting your own. **Mr. Cazembi said**

Yes Papa. It is good Papa. **Tita replied**

He promised to settle you at the end of the six years with me providing about twenty five percent (25%) of the settlement money. Truthfully, he offered me the best deal so far. **Mr. Cazembi said**

That is good, Papa. **Tita replied**

He also has FSLC that he took years back and left it to join trade as you are about to do. **Mr. Cazembi said**

Really Papa! **Tita replied**

Since ever he started this trade he has been doing a lot of good things in their family, not building houses everywhere or embarking on other unending material acquisitions, but he has always been there whenever needed, contributing whenever necessary and he never disappoints his parents and relatives. **Mr. Cazembi said**

That is nice of him, Papa. **Tita replied**

He is also a staunch believer of our tradition like his father. You will go to the town with him and he will not disappoint you. Did you hear me? **Mr. Cazembi adviced**

Yes Papa. **Tita replied**

Make sure that you get your cloths washed before next week Friday and get them well packed. I will buy another bag for you tomorrow so as to accommodate your cloths. **Mr. Cazembi said**

Yes Papa. I will do. **Tita replied**

That is all that I wanted to let you know about. **Mr. Cazembi said**

It is alright, Papa. **Tita assured**

Tita left with his sisters as usual to have a good night sleep.

Tita got all his cloths washed with his sisters who most of the times did his cloth washings unless he volunteered to wash them by himself. His sisters helped folded his cloths for him and packed them before his departure date. And his mother gathered certain farm produce that he would be traveling with. On the night prior to Friday, his father called him and advised him for the last time before his departure.

Our Son, Tita. **Mr. Cazembi called**

Yes, Papa. **Tita answered**

Your journey commences tomorrow. Are you ready? **Mr. Cazembi inquired**

Yes Papa. I am very much ready. **Tita responded**

Have you packed all your needed things? **Mr. Cazembi asked**

Yes Papa. **Tita answered**

Are you sure? **Mr. Cazembi asked**

Yes Papa. I have done all my packing, and my sisters also helped me did that. **Tita answered**

Good son. **Mr. Cazembi remarked**

Thank you, Papa. **Tita replied**

My beloved wife, do you have anything to tell our son before he goes to bed prior to his departure tomorrow? **Mr. Cazembi inquired**

Yes my husband. **Mrs. Dunduza responded**

You tell him. **Mr. Cazembi said**

Our son Tita, take a good look at every one of us. **Mrs. Dunduza requested**

Tita stared at all of them

I promise you as your mother that nothing and absolutely nothing will ever happen to us. We will be here until you return from your journeyman ship. **Mrs. Dunduza said**

Yes Mama. **Tita replied**

Our son, Tita, take a good look at every one of us. **Mrs. Dunduza requested the second time**

Tita stared at all of them again

I promise you as your mother that nothing and absolutely nothing will ever happen to us. We will be here until you return from your journeyman ship. **Mrs. Dunduza said the second time**

Yes Mama. I believe that. **Tita touchingly replied the second time**

Our son, Tita, take another good look at every one of us. **Mrs. Dunduza requested the third time**

Tita stared at all of them the third time like a kid that feels for his parents.

I promise you as your mother that nothing and absolutely nothing will ever happen to us. We will be here until you return from your journeyman ship. **Mrs. Dunduza said the third time**

Yes Mama. I believe that Mama. **Tita replied the third time**

Our son, Tita, hold your ears with your fingers. **Mrs. Dunduza requested**

Tita held his ears with his fingers. The right hand fingers for the right ear and the left hand fingers for the left ear.

You are the only son that we have. Please, do not disappoint us. Always strive to make us proud as your have being doing. We are all that you have. **Mrs. Dunduza pleaded**

Yes Mama, I know. **Tita replied**

Our son, Tita, hold your ears with your fingers. **Mrs. Dunduza requested**

Tita held his ears again with his fingers.

You are the only son that we have. Please, do not disappoint us. Always strive to make us proud as your have being doing. We are all that you have. **Mrs. Dunduza pleaded**

I will Mama, I promise to make this family proud. I will Mama. **Tita assured**

You have heard what your father said about your would be boss when you get to his house and shop in the town always stay where he asked you to stay, and do not be disloyal to him. You know how old he is and he is not yet married because he wants to balance himself well before marriage, therefore, try to be careful on how you relate with outsiders. Was he in a hurry he could have gotten married long ago, I know what most women want and he surely got that. Concentrate on what he teaches you and like an intelligent person try to remember those things well because they are the bases of your learning the trade. Should there be any conflict with you and another person, please, our son do not result to physical combat always report every misunderstanding to him and never act without his consent in such crucial issues. Again, you have seen how his relationship with his co-traders, do not try to instigate them through the use of gossiping. Answer only those that they asked you and tell him whatever bad you saw against him but do not fabricate stories so as to buy his conscience. As you leave here tomorrow to the town with him, the spirit of our Ancestors and God will guide you safely to your destination and will also be with you all until your apprenticeship has peacefully and successfully come to an end. **Mrs. Dunduza advised**

Mama, I will never do anything so as to tarnish the innocent image of this family while in the town. I will do everything possible to work amicably with my boss and shall avoid any act of gossiping. When with my boss, I promised to put all my knowledge to work so as to learn this trade so well, and six years is enough for me to know the trade well. And I believe and hope that nothing will happen to you all until I came back from the town when I must have learnt my trade finished. **Tita assured**

We are always with you. **Mr. Cazembi said**

Yes Papa. **Tita replied**

Our daughters', your only brother, Tita, is leaving for town tomorrow as we have been saying. Do you have anything to tell him? **Mr. Cazembi inquired**

Senior Tita, I hope you have heard all that our parents said. We have no other brother except you and we will not like to hear bad stories about you while in the town learning the trade. Always make sure that you respect your boss and also always be sincere to him. Do not try to become the boss yourself but rather be loyal to your boss. You have seen how hard it was when you were in the primary school to sponsor you through, always bear that in mind. A good son is the proud of his parents and a bad son is a total disgrace to the family. We are your sisters, so, we expect you to assist in the alleviation of our own standard of living when you became your own boss. Always behave as our parents have instructed you while with your boss in the town. We your sisters, we will truly miss you while you are absent from home. Have a safer journey. **Kalongi sorrowfully said**

I have heard all that you said my sisters and I want to re-assure that I will always do whatever that is necessary to be with you whenever needed when I became my own boss. Do not allow the thought of me to distract you; always engage yourselves in various good assignments whenever necessary. I will miss you, my sisters too. **Tita touchingly replied**

Our son, you have heard your parents as well as your sisters, there is no need for more instructions. Go with . . . . His is your blood relative, please, never chase shadows or indulge yourself in the pursuit of vain glory. Strive to be like your boss unless he is stealing and/or involving in ritual activities, when either becomes the case, we ask you to deviate and return back home by any true means, but I your father I doubt that. **Mr. Cazembi said**

Yes Papa. **Tita replied**

You all can now go to sleep. **Mr. Cazembi said**

On Friday morning minutes after breakfast, his father took him to Mpyama who was ready sitting with his parents waiting for their arrival. When they arrived they exchange warm greetings, and Mpyama said that there was no need to waste time. He ask Tita few questions just to know if his father gave him a hint of what was involved in the trade he was about to begin learning.

Tita. **Mpyama called**

Yes Sir. **Tita answered**

I heard that you came out with a 'Distinction' in the FSLCE. **Mpyama said**

Yes Sir. **Tita assured**

Congratulations. **Mpyama said**

Thank you, Sir. **Tita replied**

Did your father told you that this rice and beans etc trade will last for six (6) good years? **Mpyama asked**

Yes Sir. **Tita answered**

Did he tell you that he will provide only 25% of the money needed for your settlement? **Mpyama asked**

Yes Sir. He did. **Tita replied**

Do you understand that you are my relative? **Mpyama asked**

Yes Sir. I know. **Tita answered**

I do not expect to have any problems with you whatever. **Mpyama asked**

Yes Sir. **Tita answered**

Are you aware that I am not married? **Mpyama asked**

Yes Sir. **Tita answered**

Do you know that I am not a small boy at this age for marriage? **Mpyama asked**

Yes Sir. **Tita answered**

I earned this through my effort, truth, sincerely, abstinence and dedication to duty. And obviously, I want you, my relative, to take a similar position like mine and even perform better because the foundation had already been laid for you. **Mpyama said**

That's obvious my brother. **Mr. Cazembi said**

I want to make it very clear to you in the presence of your father and my parents. From the time I became like you as an apprentice to this day, I have never given myself up to a woman, perhaps a prostitute for that matter. And my restraints on pursuing passionate appeals have eventually made my day, which is why I can afford to help you today; otherwise things couldn't have been so easy. As a business man, a trader in particular, I meet a lot of girls, ladies women, you name them and I interact with them and discuss with them but purely on transactional basis. I do not spend all my fortune to have sex with them because I am not ready yet to get married. As a boss I can buy gifts of considerable worth to girls, ladies etc of my choice because as at this time I have the CFA Franc to do that but am not infatuated with that yet. But as an apprentice, I could not afford that because all the money belonged to my boss, and should he discovered that I engaged in such things instead of saving them, he would surely send me home, and I could equally lose my chances in life because 'opportunities may come but once'. And when I was serving my boss there was never a time I called in girls either to his house or his shop and had any sexual relationships with them, and never did I dashed out all my boss food stuffs in order to answer a 'wealthy guy'. More so, the responsibilities of cooking what my boss ate resided solely with me, and there was never a time I saw all his money and decided to poisoned him out so as to acquire his assets and began to own them. And finally, I never through the use of gossips set my boss up so that he could meet his untimely death in the hands of his enemies for me to appear clean and be in charge of his inheritance. I promise to always treat you as a blood relative while in town. If you do not find favor with me due to whatever reason, tell me and I will bring you back home. **Mpyama said**

Thank you Sir, I will not disappoint you Sir. **Tita assured**

You have said all, there is no need for more worries, and he who has ears let him hear. **Mr. Mutope said**

Thank you very much my brother I have heard your instructions to my son, Tita. I hope he must behave himself because I do not know any other place to be so assisted if not here. Should he ever decides to disgrace himself he will come home and suffer like me and only eats when there is food, and if he ever misbehaves and comes home, he cease to be my son. **Mr. Cazembi said**

Tita, when you get to town with your brother do stay well with him and always respect him because I give you my word, he will never teach you the bad ways. His is such a nice boy. **Mrs. Mwanze** (Protected) **boss mother said**

Yes Mama. **Tita replied**

Before mid-day of that day Tita and Mpyama left village for town. They arrived in his boss residence after few hours on the road because Mpyama leaved in one of their state major cities which were not too far from home. And luckily the then political climate was not tense in that area of town. Tita settled with his boss and after few days, he took him to his shop and introduced him to some of his fellow traders who were on the same market lines with him. His boss followed the normal procedures of introducing a new apprentice to existing bosses as well as apprentices, and he called them and gave them their necessary things respectively and Tita was accepted by them and he began to be part of them. those other bosses told him that as an apprentice, he was expected to follow the rules as already explained to him by his boss and there was no excuse on that 'no fist fight for customers, just calls'. And the leader of the apprentices told him that, they never tolerate conflicts between apprentices and that any misunderstanding between him and a fellow apprentice must first be reported to his boss for necessary action, and "you cannot go into another boss's shop either to fight a fellow apprentice". And they said that they appreciated each other and always worked united to ensure each other's success. They said that "their market line apprentices abhor looting of their boss money because that jeopardizes their general interests and cast aspersions on them". Tita promised them that he would abide by the rules, and that he would not do anything contrary to the wishes and aspirations of his boss as his apprentice and other bosses as a market line apprentice. Tita's boss told them that his apprentice looked reasonable and that he was his blood relatives.

Tita stayed with Mpyama his boss peacefully and continued to learn the trade. He gradually became acclimatized to the township environment and as well got used to their lifestyles. He got focused and dedicated to his trade more than any other thing with absolute reverence to his boss who never employed any tricks to hurt his feelings. During his early years with his boss, he was taken to their village town meeting and also introduced to the people from his communities that lived in the same city with them. And sometimes Mpyama with him paid visits to some of his boss village people who reside in the town as well as his friends both married and unmarried. Some of their people in the town with them accepted Tita whole heartedly and always urged Tita to take things easy because 'block by block a house is built, and the journey of many miles starts with a single step'. Meanwhile, his boss had already warned him of the dangerous nature of the city where they resided in. According to his boss, some apprentices like Tita used to sleep in their shops after business hours before the start of the conflicts between the government and the militia group, but since they crises started, nobody sleeps in the shops after business hours anymore because government security guards could kill them thinking that they were the rebel minded militia men. His boss also told him that, they used to close sometimes late in the evening, but since ever the start of the chaos, they no longer close shops so late so as to be able to get home on time to avoid been run-down by either by government forces or militia group.

His boss instructed him before his full service in the shop that never a time should he ever try to close late for the day's business in his absent because doing so would be so risky, despite the merits of it. He also instructed him not to wander in the night for any reason whenever he was absent, and to develop cordial relationships with customers because they were the business stimulus as well as catalyst without them their trade was doomed to failure. In his words 'customers are the only reason why we are in business, without them, we sell no goods, and our trade goes under, but with them, our business flourishes and we get to where we are going'. He further warn him never to engage in any form of conflicts with their fellow 'yard residents' because doing such could lead to unavoidable combat because some of those sharing compound with them came from different places, and may be difficult to be pacified. Besides, he warned him to eat only what they cooked because they were only two and that he could provide what Tita would always eat while at home.

Tita obeyed all his boss rules and never tried to manipulate him detrimentally. He avoided all unwanted contacts with females and never yielded in to undue pressure from persistent girls, ladies etc who always came-by, pretending to be customers but with the sole intent of falling in love with him. He also consistently avoided the tactics of sharing girls with his fellow apprentices either in the same market line or elsewhere. Some of the apprentices had a system of introducing a fellow apprentice who refused sexual contacts with girls through a process known as 'team sex'. During some of the holidays before his settlement, his boss sometimes visited the village with him because been the only son of his parents it was necessary to keep his parents lively and healthy. And whenever they visited home, his boss would buy things for him to give to his parents as well as food that would serve them until they returned back to the city and beyond.

Mpyama provided all his basic needs to him and warned him never to involve himself in the business of outsmarting customers which had became the order of those days because such could backfire, and he advised him to save his stipends as accumulated from fringe benefits-selling un-returnable items a little above the supposed selling price. Tita always ate to his satisfaction both at home and in the marketplace, sometimes he called those selling moi moi (food made from beans that are either wrapped with broad leaves during boiling or small empty milk canes) etc and purchased as much as he wanted in the presence of his boss using the money his boss always gave to him for marketplace feeding, and his boss would never be worried. Throughout his stay with his boss there was never a time his boss frowned at him or spent unnecessary hours with any lady in his presence. His boss sometimes told him that he would only get married in his late forties which could be barely few years after Tita's settlement.

CHAPTER FIVE

Tita Settled

One year prior to Tita's settlement (end of six years of learning the trade) and in one of Mpyama's travel home, he informed Tita's parents that their son was about to finish learning the trade therefore, his father Mr. Cazembi should be getting ready so as to be able to provide his own portion of the 25% settlement money as previously agreed. His boss disclosed to them that Tita had been doing so good so far and that he had never misbehaved even for one day, and that he had already understood how the business work, and that "by the end of his sixth year, he has learnt everything a couple of times more, and will be more positioned to stay on his own comfortably". He told them that since Tita started learning the trade under him, there had never been a time any of his things was missing and that Tita had always been financially responsible and up-to-date. "Tita knows the numbers and has not fallen prey to playing with any of the assets entrusted to him".

Mpyama told Mr. Cazembi that his own portion of the settlement money should be ready at least one month before the end of Tita's sixth year in the trade. And that as soon as Tita completed his required number of years, he would waste no time in coming home with him for settlement. So, they should expect him home with Tita, days or weeks after his service end date, thus, there was no need wasting time on accumulating their own portion of the needed money. His boss made it known to them that "the best thing after leaving trade is settlement without delay so that the apprentice could go ahead and start his/her own, because delaying could result to forgetfulness, especially if the former apprentice was allowed to spend years before giving him money to start his own. Early start would ensure that the former apprentice continued from where he stopped without going through a rigorous process of refreshment, and it will help to retain his/her customers whom he had already known when with his/her boss and that promotes his/her business, and it reduces the chances of unnecessary shop closure due to ignorant and lack of knowledge of the could have been known commodity prices. And it offers the new trader the chances to be well positioned in a market line that will attract more customers thereby offering him the opportunities to excel and prosper". He told them that in about five (5) months time, Tita will start looking for a shop of his own in the same market that his own is situated because their marketplace is where most people come to purchase, and that since ever he started doing business in that market it had all been good market seasons. And he inquired to know whether Tita's father could come up with his own portion of his son's settlement money when necessary.

Sir, did you heard what I said? **Mpyama inquired**

Yes my brother, I heard you. **Mr. Cazembi replied**

Can you come up with the 25% in about one year time? **Mpyama asked**

I will see what I can do. **Mr. Cazembi answered**

So, you want me to believe that you can accumulate that amount before the said settlement time? **Mpyama asked**

Yes, I will come up with that amount. **Mr. Cazembi answered**

Sir, when I get back to town, I will let my brother Tita know that his settlement is assured based on also his father's assurance. **Mpyama said**

Yes, tell him not to worry, since you have almost done everything, there is no much left, only finishing touches. **Mr. Cazembi replied**

Sir, I will surely let him know. **Mpyama assured**

It is now about five years since my son Tita joined you as his boss in the trade, therefore, I deem it wise and necessary to say that six years is not one day, so at the right time, if "I am lifted up and thrown down" the my 25% portion must surely come out of my pocket. I cannot disappoint him now that I am still young and vibrant. **Mr. Cazembi said.**

Sir that is all I want. **Mpyama satisfied**

Mpyama was happy and satisfied by Mr. Cazembi's assurance because he hated a situation whereby after bringing out such huge amount of money to settle his servant, the servant's father declined to make good his own promise of providing his own portion of the money. His boss became convinced that Tita been the first of his relatives to receive such opportunities after he started his own should not prove to be a wasted effort, or a situation whereby people would start blaming him for not settling his servant who was as well a relative appropriately. Mpyama could settle Tita with all the needed money but Tita been the only son should be forced to retrospect because "most of the times 'only sons' do wander deeper into the pit of shirt, they always wallow in the worst stinking mess behaving as if they are doing the right things". So, his father contributing the 25% would act as a deterrent to Tita.

Mpyama spent hours with Tita's parents in their house, and Tita's mother made 'quick food' that was served to their son's boss because they were not expecting him. Before Tita's boss left, he told them that their minds should be glued on their discussion, and he gave money to Tita's sisters and mother, who joyously accepted the money.

Sir, you stay well with your family, I will now be on my way. **Mpyama said**

Thank you so much my brother, I will always appreciate your help. **Mr. Cazembi replied**

There are no problems, sir that is certainly why we are relatives 'one palm washes the other, vice versa, and no condition maybe permanent'. **Mpyama said**

Thank you for your understanding. You are really a blood relative of mine, and your sisters have also know that. **Mr. Cazembi replied**

Sir is surely what we can do for each other. **Mpyama said**

My wife, my brother is about to leave. **Mr. Cazembi said**

Thank you so much my brother-in-law. Without you it could have been hard on us. We appreciate your help so far and will always do. I am so pleased to welcome you in our house and to hear that your brother Tita is doing very fine. The news of his good behavior is enough for me. When you go back to town please do great him for me. Tell him that we are all well and hearty, and that he should continue to concentrate on his trade as he has been doing. As you go, the spirit of our Ancestors and God will guide you safely home. Tell him that his father is making every effort to ensure that he starts on his own as soon as his boss confirmed that he has learnt a lot of the trade. Greet your parents etc for me when you get home. Again, thank you, and may it be well with you. **Mrs. Dunduza said**

I will extend your greetings and assurance to him, Ma. **Mpyama replied**

Thank you so much Sir. Greet him for us also. **Kalonji said**

I surely will. **Mpyama replied**

Thank you my brother. **Mr. Cazembi said**

Sir, see you next time I visited. Bye and have a nice day. **Mpyama said and left**

See you. **Mr. Cazembi replied**

Mr. Cazembi accompanied Mpyama a fraction of a mile and they departed.

Meanwhile, barely after one year of Tita's stay with his boss and based on the assurance and information from his boss and others on Tita's behavior, his father started saving money little by little despite the fact that the 'hit-and-run' militias were on every side of the major streets thereby forcing the economy on a consistent downward trend. Mr. Cazembi's piece meal by piece meal savings were necessary to at least raise a sizable portion of his own share of 25% needed for his sons settlement. As at the time of his son's boss last visit to their house in the village, his father had already accumulated about 45% and was working had to increase the amount. Mr. Cazembi knew that he could raise another 5% before the end of the year prior to his settlement and does not know how else to raise another 50% that would make the money complete. And he does not like to drain his wife's pocket because his wife's money always act as a buffer for feeding the family and attending to other emergencies that could not easily be postponed, and things were very hard for so many families in the village, therefore, the possibilities of borrowing such amount of money was no longer there. He continued to contemplate weighing all options.

When Tita's boss returned back to town he was pleased to see that everything was in place where they always supposed to be. Tita was in the house when he returned on optional market day but Mpyama never liked to run seven (7) days a week business, so he closes his shop on Mondays because he believed from his business indicators that Mondays selling yielded the least of profits because those that travelled home during the weekends always returned with enough food that could serve them on Mondays, after which they began to approach their own side of the market. Mpyama told Tita that he went to their house and that he saw his parents and brothers and sisters.

Tita, I went to your house. **Mpyama said**

How are they Sir? **Tita asked**

They are all fine. **Mpyama answered**

Did you see my parents? **Tita asked**

Yes, I saw them. **Mpyama answered**

How are my parents? **Tita asked**

They are fine. **Mpyama replied**

Sir, did you see my sisters? **Tita asked**

Yes, I saw them as well and they are all fine. **Mpyama answered**

I discussed about your coming settlement with your parents, and your father assured me that he would be ready for that. **Mpyama said**

Thank you Sir. **Tita replied**

He made me understood that he has been making all the necessary efforts so far so as to be able to contribute his own portion of your settlement money. **Mpyama said**

Yes Sir. **Tiata replied**

Your mother was happy for you, she told me to tell you that you should not worry because of them because they are 'healthy and hearty', and that you should always concentrate on learning the trade as usual, and that your father is making every effort so as not to disappoint you on the settlement date. **Mpyama said**

Yes Sir. Thank you very much sir. **Tita replied**

Was there any problems during my absent? **Mpyama asked**

No Sir, everything went normal. **Tita replied**

After taking his birth and eating and resting, Tita gave Mpyama the account of his business transactions in his absence. And as usual Tita gave exact and accurate accounts of how the business went and never tried to use one of the last minutes opportunities offered to him before his settlement to dodge money around, defraud and/ or manipulate his boss financially and materially. Tita's sincerity and accountability so far made his boss to further believe that Tita was determined to be useful and as well important to his parents, sisters, and relatives and who else, because although he seemed to be a brilliant guy who made 'Distinction' in his FSLCE, he could turn out to be a market fool, a pure trade moron, and a transaction nonentity because "sometimes those who are academically intelligent turned out to be complete idiots outside the field of education, and sometimes completely useless inside the field of education". Besides, Tita had proved furthermore that he was determined to continue with the business that he had chosen as his career path, and not meddling with his boss assets in his absence was another assurance that he preferred to be completely settled by his boss and not be chased away and asked to start his own trade from the money stolen from his boss.

In about a month of Mpyama visit, Mr. Cazembi decided that the best way of out of his 'contribution predicament' was to pledge a portion of his land to willing pledgees so as to raise the needed amount of money to complete the one he had already saved. He reasoned that pledging a plot of land could take months considering the spate of crises going on in their country, therefore, for him to get willing pledgees he must 'bring out the said portion of land' and approach them early. Mr. Cazembi was not used to either pledging or selling land otherwise he could have done that to send his only son in particular to the secondary school and university and the others in general to the primary school, especially his first daughter. He believed things like land should not be easily given away for any reason because reclaiming them could be difficult. And before the advent of colonialism when most of their people depended on agricultural produce 'no one was going about hungry'. While he understood the importance of education to him such importance was merely 'secondary' so, he believed in the gradual process of transitioning from the stage of 'traditional education' to that of 'cultural education', completing one section of cultural education before the other simultaneously. Since his son was also the only son, Tita could reclaim the pledged land as soon as he began to make his own money after settlement.

To get the attention of potential pledgees, Mr. Cazembi having discussed that with his wife began to approach those he thought that could accept to pay for the land and hold it until when he could pay them back and have his land released back to him. He circulated the news among those who could be pledgees and waited for their response. Months passed without getting most of them accept to pay for the land, more so, he understood the consequences of early pledge that if care was not taking the money could gotten squandered away but that depended much on the nature of persons. Mr. Cazembi was not that type of man who believed in eating it all at the nearest 'Cheap Mammy Bar'. He knew his duty to his only son and was determined to fulfill his promise to him, and more so, the money meant for his son's settlement was a 'no go area', that could only be used for what it was meant for. And Mrs. Dunduza his wife was not a woman who spent it 'all at once' in the market buying expensive food items, jewelries and other unnecessary things.

As the time for Tita's settlement was fast approaching with no hope getting any pledgee in site, because all of those who promised to take the would be pledged land into consideration were yet to confirm their interest and as well pay because 'whosoever pays first gets the farmland'. As he kept on believing that his son would not be disappointed he continue to toil and labor, putting aside a little portion of his wages just to complete the already accumulated amount of 50% of the required 25% from him. And his wife kept on working as usual to make sure that she continued to give her husband the necessary back up, and their daughters continued to emulate their most senior sister and their mother who never showed them the ugly ways. Some of those Mr. Cazembi reminded about the said portion of land for pledge, bluntly told him that they could not bring out any CFA Franc considering the current situation of things as at that time, and some of them told him that their minds where on it.

Only about one month before the complete six years of Tita's service as an apprentice, one man, Mr. Nogomo (Prosperous) who does not like to say a lot of things and who was known to kept to himself and only speak when necessary, came to his house in the evening, and he was surprised to see the man in his house. They exchange greetings and he offered his visitor a sit to seat down.

Mr. Cazembi there is no need to waste time on the purpose of my visit. I remembered that one time ago you came to me with a pledge of land offer. Am I correct? **Mr. Nogomo inquired**

Yes Sir. You are correct. **Mr. Cazembi replied**

Has the portion of land been pledge? **Mr. Nogomo asked**

No Sir. I am still looking for pledgees. **Mr. Cazembi answered**

Is the portion of land fallowed? **Mr. Nogomo asked**

Yes Sir. I did not work there last farming season. **Mr. Cazembi answered**

Is it good for next season's farming? **Mr. Nogomo asked**

Yes Sir. If not for the pledge I could have worked there next farming season. I give you my word. **Mr. Cazemi replied**

I believe you. **Mr. Nogomo said**

I am sure Sir, very sure. **Mr. Cazembi replied**

How much did you say the amount you need was? **Mr. Nogomo asked**

Mr. Cazembi told him the requested amount in CFA.

Is that all you need? **Mr. Nogomo asked**

Yes Sir that is all I need. **Mr. Cazembi answered**

Do you have another person whom you promised to pledge the land to? Do you have a special person of interest in mind? **Mr. Nogomo asked**

No Sir. I placed the portion of land on a 'first come, first take' basis. **Mr. Cazembi answered**

Mr. Nogomo reached down his pocket and brought out bundles of CFA Franc well banded with small rubber like ribbons.

Take this money Mr. Cazembi. **Mr. Nogomo offered**

Mr. Cazembi accepted the money with enthusiasm.

Count it. **Mr. Nogomo said**

Yes Sir. **Mr. Cazembi replied**

He took the money and got focused on counting the money while Mr. Nogomo looked on. After counting the money, he told Mr. Nogomo the amount.

Is it complete? **Mr. Nogomo said**

Yes Sir. It is complete. **Mr. Cazembi replied**

Please, Mr. Cazembi, there is no need to hurry, just take your time and recount the money again. **Mr. Nogomo said**

It is alright Sir. **Mr. Cazembi replied,** and concentrated on recounting the money while Mr. Nogomo waited for him to finish and after recounting the money;

It is exactly the amount I requested Sir. **Mr. Cazembi said**

So, it is complete? **Mr. Nogomo asked**

Yes Sir, it is complete. **Mr. Cazembi answered**

I couldn't have brought this money for the said portion of land earlier than now. What next is left? **Mr. Nogomo inquired**

The next thing now is to write the agreement and look for witnesses for the avoidance of doubt, Sir. **Mr. Cazembi responded**

As you know, Mr. Cazembi I am not that type of man who believes in reaping off, enriching me through the weakness of the poor, and/or inflating money owed so as to get wealthy. I give you my word, unless the mistake comes from your own side, I shall remain infallible on this. Therefore, there is no need for outside witness, may our Ancestors and your wife and children be the witness. **Mr. Nogomo assured**

I understand what you mean Sir, and I take your word for it. **Mr. Cazembi said**

Do you have pen and paper since that method has become the order of the day just for formality sake. **Mr. Nogomo asked**

Eh . . . m . . . . began to look, trying to call his wife to go and look for pen and paper.

Never mind Mr. Cazembi, I think I came here with pen and paper. **Mr. Nogomo said**

Good of you Sir, you have truly spared me the hassles. **Mr. Cazembi replied**

Mr. Nogomo reached his other pocket and brought out a plain sheet of paper with pen.

Mr. Cazembi, do you know how to write? **Mr. Nogomo asked**

No Sir, I did not attend Sir, I did not . . . that time I mean, things were . . . . **Mr. Cazembi answered**

Do not worry yourself, I can write the agreement. **Mr. Nogomo said**

Thank you Sir. **Mr. Cazembi replied**

What is the name of the place where the portion of land is located at? **Mr. Nogomo asked,** as he began to write. And Mr. Cazembi told him everything about the said portion been pledged and Mr. Nogomo wrote accordingly. After writing the agreement, the visitor read it and told him;

I am done writing the agreement; please call your wife and any of your daughters. **Mr. Nogomo said**

Yes Sir, I will. **Mr. Cazembi replied**

Mr. Cazembi called his wife and Kalonji who appeared came without wasting time from the kitchen where they were busy preparing for dinner.

Yes, my husband. **Mr. Dunduza answered**

Stay here two of you, and listen to what Mr. Nogomo has to say. **Mr. Cazembi said**

I just reached an agreement on a particular portion of a farmland with your husband and father respectively. I have finished putting the agreement into writing, and I want your presence so that you could be a witness to this while I read it to you all. **Mr. Nogomo said**

Yes my husband-in-law. **Mrs. Dunduza replied**

Mr. Nogomo read the agreement in their local language.

Did you understand every content of this agreement? **Mr. Nogomo asked**

Yes Sir, we did. **They all responded at once**

Sign here Mr. Cazembi, your initials only. **Mr. Nogomo said**

Yes Sir. **Mr. Nogomo said,** and signed at the place designated for him

Take this Mr. Cazembi, (gave one copy to him) that is own copy. **Mr. Nogomo offered**

Yes Sir. Thank you Sir. **Mr. Cazembi accepted**

This is my own copy (raised his own copy). **Mr. Nogomo indicated**

You did well Sir. **Mr. Cazembi said**

Thank you all. **Mr. Nogomo cheerfully responded**

Mr. Cazembi and his visitor exchanged more few words with the visitor, and Mr. Nogomo assured him that he would not be in need of the money he used to pay for the portion of farmland for considerable number of years despite the situation in the country because he needed more land for farming, especially when all his sons had gotten married and have started bearing children, therefore, there was need for more farmlands so as to see what they could eat, especially the younger ones that their children are still small, and that "although most of them live in the towns, the one that stayed back with him at home needed more backup. Since he chose to stay with us his parents, he deserved to feed well with his family as well". And the Mr. Nogomo told him that should he had such a portion for pledge again, he would be more than willing to comply depending on the amount, and Mr. Cazembi made it known to him that he never liked to either pledge or sell land but considering the situation of things "when the preferable is not available, the available will be preferable", and that should there be another opportunity for that, he would let him know. Mr. Cazembi expressed his gratitude to him for answering his call when he had almost lost hope of revival, and promised him that he would be the first to be contacted should such show up again.

Sir, when can I go with you and show you the portion of farmland? **Mr. Cazembi asked**

Next weekend during the evening. Is that okay with you? **Mr. Nogomo inquired**

It is fine Sir. **Mr. Cazembi replied**

Before that time, I will tell my last son's wife to be around so that she can go with us to the place. **Mr. Nogomo said**

It is good Sir. **Mr. Cazembi replied**

I hope I have spent enough time with you; I will be going please, make sure that you do not forget part of our discussions. **Mr. Nogomo said**

I will keep that in mind. Thank you so much Sir. **Mr. Cazembi replied**

See you next time. **Mr. Nogomo said,** and left his house

Have a nice day Sir. **Mr. Cazembi replied**

As soon as Mr. Nogomo left, Mr. Cazembi rushed back to his seat and sat down and slumped and took a good breath in and out, like if to say his class teacher asked him to 'breath in and out' after messing in the classroom. He stood in his seat still for a couple of minutes and later called his wife to show her the money brought over by Mr. Nogomo the man who he pledged the portion of farmland to. And he told his wife that 'this completes the money, as I already told you that I needed only 50% of my own portion of the 25% for our son's settlement money'. Mrs. Dunduza heaved a sigh of relief and told her husband that "I now feel at home because since ever you told me about what was left of the money, I have been wondering on how we could come up with the rest of the money, and nicely, today all the money has been completed. After their conversations, he took the money and put it where the rest of the money was. He had no fear of hiding the money because his daughters were still afraid of meddling with any amount of cash that was not given to them by their parents, and his wife was the last woman to ever gamble with their son's opportunities.

At exactly the promised time by Tita's boss, Mpyama returned home with him one afternoon while Tita went directly to his father's house after their arrival from the town to Mpyama father's house. Tita was instructed by his boss that his settlement would take place after two days in his boss house there in the village, and that Tita should inform his parents so that they would be there on time during the late afternoon hours. When Tita reached home his parents were perplexed because Tita had added little weight and looked healthy, hearty and cheerful, and his parents and his sisters were so happy to see him once again after about two years of none visits to home. On seen him they rushed out and hogged him calling him as they used to call him and asking him;

Our son, Tita, welcome home. **Mr. Cazembi said**

Thank you, Papa. **Tita replied**

How is your brother? **Mr. Cazembi asked**

His is fine Sir. **Tita answered**

Did you come home with him? **Mr. Cazembi asked**

Yes Papa. **Tita replied**

How was the township? **Mr. Cazembi asked**

No problems, Papa. **Tita replied**

You have physically changed! **Mr. Cazembi exclaimed**

Yes Papa. **Tita replied**

Our son, we are so happy to see you back home. I will go and prepare something for you to eat because you have travelled a long distance to home. **Mrs. Dunduza said**

Thank you, Mama. I am not hungry, I ate before coming back. **Tita replied**

Is what you ate before coming home from the town still in your stomach? You must eat something. **Mrs. Dunduza said**

It is alright, Mama. **Tita replied**

Welcome home senior Tita, welcome, we are very pleased to have you back home. Senior, you have gained more weight. **Kalongi happily said**

Come! Come!! Come!!! Let us go and cook something for him to eat.

His mother called his immediate junior sister while the rest of her sisters stayed with him asking him questions while he answered.

Before Tita left the township for home, his boss gave him a substantial amount of money to buy things for his parents and sisters as presents which he would given to them when he returned home, and Tita made good selections of certain items which he purchased for them without purchasing fake things and pocketing the rest of the money. The following day after his return he brought out a couple of bags that he returned from the city with and distributed those gifts among his parents and sisters who were so pleased to accept them. His parents wondered how he came up with such presents and he told them that his boss gave him money to purchase things for them prior to their travel home. Therefore they accepted their son and the presents without further questions.

Tita also told them that he came back with a bag of rice and half-bag of beans and other things to cook them with, and those things were still at his boss house, and that he would take them the next day when they meet for his settlement.

In the night of that same day Mr. Cazembi with his wife contemplated how they could go to Mpyama the following day without anything. His wife told him that they were taken aback, therefore, there was no way she could rush to the market and purchase the necessary things and prepared them within the shortest time frame available. His husband said that there was no need to bother her because Tita's boss already knew that the given time could not allow them to come to his house with any form of presents. Her husband convinced her that what their son came back with could reach up to 60% of the said 25% settlement contribution, an indication that 'our son's boss do not demand any other thing from us, therefore tomorrow we go and see him just like that". His wife understood her husband's point of view and agreed to bother herself less, 'after all, his boss is also his brother".

At the said time Tita and his parents and his immediate junior sister arrived at Mr. Mutope his relative's house. They passed greetings and got seated.

Welcome Sir. **Mpyama greeted**

Thank you my brother. **Mr. Cazembi said**

How are you my sister? **Mpyama asked**

I am fine, Sir. **Kalonji replied**

Sir, I hope you all know why I asked you to come? **Mpyama asked**

Yes, my brother. A scheduled errand does not take the crippled by surprise. **Mr. Cazembi answered**

Sir, Tita has completed his six years of service; it came to a completion three weeks ago. **Mpyama said**

Thank you my brother, I am happy to hear that. **Mr. Cazembi replied**

I have known your son, Tita, for years and he has always proved beyond all reasonable doubt that his is able and capable of been his own boss. He has learnt the trade like a reasonable person, understanding the entire things that he was thought, been able to maintain a stronghold in my absence and always gave an accurate and complete account of his stewardship. He never tried in any way or by any means to maneuver me neither does he caused problems for me both in the house and in the shop nor planted any iota of evil against me. He had served me well and therefore he deserved my settlement of him in full by merits. **Mpyama truthfully said**

I am very grateful, my brother. **Mr. Cazembi replied**

I paid for his shop before coming to the village with part of his settlement money and everything is now in place for him to start on his own as soon as the rest of his needed money is given to him. Having spent years with me and having convinced me that he is not only a good relative but also a trusted one, I will also offer him free one year accommodation in my house since I am not yet married after which he can go and live on his own. **Mpyama said**

I am very grateful of you my brother. **Mr. Cazembi replied**

Tita after here today: do you want to continue to live with me in the town? **Mpyama inquired**

Yes Sir. I appreciate that Sir. **Tita answered**

You have heard him. **Mpyama said**

Yes we did. **Mr. Cazembi agreed**

Tita, you are no longer my apprentice, you are now my brother as usual, so our further relationship depends on mutual understandings and corporations. While we live together in the town, you are not expected to contribute anything unnecessarily but you can buy whatever you like as long as there is an accommodation for them. You know the rules on external relationships that still hold. **Mpyama said**

Yes Sir. I understand. **Tita replied**

Mpyama went in and came out with a small waterproof of CFA Franc, and kept it by his side.

Sir, where is your 25% of the settlement money? **Mpyama asked**

My brother, here is the money (brought out the money). **Mr. Cazembi answered**

Please give it to Tita. **Mpyama said**

Mr. Cazembi gave the money to his son Tita.

Tita took the money from his father and slowly counted it, and told them how much it was.

That is exactly what I asked you to contribute for Tita's settlement. **Mpyama said**

Yes, my brother. **Mr. Cazembi replied**

Mpyama brought out the money in the small waterproof and gave it to Tita's father, and his father accepted the money.

Please Sir, count it. **Mpyama said**

Yes, my brother. **Mr. Cazembi said,** and focused on counting the money, and after counting the money, he told them how much it was.

Yes Sir that is exactly the amount I gave to you because fifteen percent (15%) of the money was used to pay for Tita's shop accommodation in our market line because he was lucky to get a shop in our busy line, it was not like that before. Sir, there was no way we could have missed that extraordinary opportunities, and more so, with my presence in that market-line your son is sure to be successful despite the odds. **Mpyama said**

Thank you my brother. **Mr. Cazembi replied**

Sir, give that money to Tita, and Tita count it. **Mpyama said**

Yes Sir. **Tita said,** and collected the money from his father and counted it, and told them how much it was.

That's right. **Mpyama acknowledge**

You are correct my son. **Mr. Cazembi said**

Tita, my brother, you now know how much you have with you. **Mpyama said**

Yes sir. **Tita replied**

Will that sum of money be enough for you? **Mpyama asked**

Yes Sir, it will be enough. **Tita replied**

Are your sure that, that amount of money will be enough for you? **Mpyama asked again**

Yes sir, this amount will get me all that I need everything considered. **Tita replied**

Tita, if that sum of money with you will not be enough for you, please, tell us right here, right now. **Mpyama requested**

This sum of money with me will certainly be enough for me. **Tita assured**

Henceforth, you are your own market line boss. Always make use of that money and do not hesitate to ask me any questions that you may have. **Mpyama advised**

Thank you so much sir. **Tita replied**

I am very grateful my brother, thank you. **Mr. Cazembi said**

I am very pleased my brother-in-law, thank you so much for your immense help. **Mrs. Dunduza said**

Thank you Sir. **Kalonji said**

You are all welcomed. **Mpyama replied**

Mpyama's, family members that were there to witness the settlement were all pleased and some of them said in low tones that Mpyama had done everything for him. And before they left his boss asked them to remember to carry his bag of rice etc that he left with him. Mpyama also told him to spend at least one week with his parents before returning back to town while he himself returns back the following day because it was almost market biggest season. Mr. Cazembi never knew how to continue to thank Mpyama neither does Mrs. Dunduza because he had surely lifted what could have turned out to be a veil of shame from their faces. It could have maybe taken longer than necessary for Tita to find a place for learning his heart desires had it been that they never had a blood relative already in the business. Tita's parents thanked all Mpyama family members present, and they departed for home. Meanwhile, before their departure Tita promised to continue to abide by the rules and never to disgrace either his boss or his parents.

Tita returned home with his parents and sister and spent about one week at home before returning to his former boss house in the township. Before he went back to town, he made it known to his parents that his boss was the best blood relative outside of his parents and sisters he had seen. He told them that his boss never denied him any single thing that he deserved and that there was never a time he had any form of conflict with him or taught him the evil way. As he was about to go back to town his parents cautioned him and he reiterated his promise to them.

His parents warned him that since he had become his own boss he should be very careful of his dealings financially and how he engages in those business transactions that could yield optimum results, and that he should continue to follow his brother's footsteps because he would not try to defraud the money back from Tita when back to his house in town. They also made it known to their son that Mpyama offer of free accommodation for such number of months was a very big added advantage. Finally, they brought it to his attention that they pledged a portion of farmland so as to complete their required 25% contribution although they added 50% of their savings to that. His sisters advised him of the need to continue to be obedient to his former boss as well as dedicated to work because "to him that much is given, much is also expected". Tita reiterated his promise to them and told them that he would do every necessary thing within his reach to be with them whenever needed both physically, financially and materially, and that nothing would ever make him to back off from them.

CHAPTER SIX

Tita on His Own

On a Monday afternoon, Tita returned back to town to Mpyama's house, his relative and former boss. Mpyama was at ease to see him back to his house to stay for the promise one year and as well opens his own shop which was almost open having put everything in place for its normal operations. Mpyama observed Tita to see whether he had worries staying in his house but Tita appeared undisturbed and determined to carry on from where he stopped. After his return, Mpyama told him to relax for at least two good days before going for 'whole sale' purchases of the commodities from the outside market that he would eventually retail in his shop since it was almost market largest season that attracts the highest number of customers, during which even if someone's shop was kind of empty he/she would still sell his/her merchandise. Tita concurred to Mpyama suggestions and said that he would go for such 'whole sale' purchases in about four (4) days time. Meanwhile, Tita inclined his sense of reason to ascertain if Mpyama needed him in his house in truth, and he discovered that Mpyama never minced words, so, his 'yes' was his 'yes' and not to buy anybody's favor or appear to be a very good person. What Mpyama cannot do for you 'he would simply tell you that he cannot do that for you', and never 'out of fear swallows a hurt knife'. He concluded that Mpyama having bared his mind in the presence of his parents etc, it was left for him to buy exactly what he was sent to the market for. Consequently, he decided to use the immense opportunities offered to him by the one year free accommodation to save more money that would also make him become 'a big boss' (those with more than average amount of money invested in their shops).

Tita knew that it was only a complete fool who couldn't read the clear and visible hand writings on the wall that would not know that Mpyama had done everything for him financially and in kind, adding the monetary value of the one year accommodation to the entire money given to him amounted to far more than he promised to settle him with, and besides, Mpyama did not disclose to those at present during his settlement the exert amount of money involved in the prepaid shop rent. The truth was that the said 15% by his former boss was actually about half of what was used to prepay for the shop rent. Furthermore, all the money saved by Tita during the apprenticeship was with him, Mpyama never asked him to return a single CFA Franc, although he sometimes saw all the money but he never for one day either warned Tita against that or questioned him on why such a substantial sum of money. The money saved by Tita as an apprentice was even more than the 25% required of his father which his father endeavored to contribute. So, putting everything together, Tita started his own trade at a very comfortable level far more than most of those starting that type of trade at that economic critical period and perhaps previously.

Prior to the start of his own trade Mpyama asked him whether he used any portion of his settlement money for any reason on the few days he spent with his parents at home.

Tita. **Mpyama called**

Yes Sir. **Tita answered**

Did you return back with all your settlement money? **Mpyama asked**

Yes Sir. I have it with me. **Tita replied**

Did you happen to spend any portion of it for any reason while at home or on your way back? **Mpyama asked**

No Sir, I had no need for that. **Tita answered**

I will be going for a 'whole sale' purchase on the day we usually go. **Mpyama said**

Can I go with you Sir? **Tita asked**

Yes, you are so free to join me. **Mpyama agreed**

Yes Sir, I will go with you, sir. **Tita responded**

Do you understand that you do not need to put all your money in business at the same time? **Mpyama asked**

No Sir. **Tita replied**

As a new starter, you will go with at least half of your money, and after the initial 'whole sale' purchase, you can continue to purchase later. This is necessary because if you use all your money at the same time, it could create a burden and maybe too difficult for you to handle considering the amount of money you have. I have not seen a place where such amount of money or even half of it could be used in one 'whole sale' purchase by any starter. So I suggest that you spend only about 35% of your money at this initial time so that you can easily handle it. it is also important to purchase in a considerable quantities for retail to avert the attention of existing greedy bosses in our market line who may think that you have come to the market-line to 'challenge them', and it also allows you to handle your trade effectively and manage it efficiently. **Mpyama advised**

Sir, I understood what you mean, I will certainly do as you said. **Tita agreed**

You should know that it is better to be much more focused on your business than telling every inquisitive mouth how much money you were settled with. Please, know that the unusual economic downturn has created undue hardship for many people including fellow former apprentices who could have long been settled, and some shop owners are today managing to stay afloat, therefore, like before, and speak very wisely. **Mpyama advised**

Sir, I will be very careful of my utterances. **Tita promised**

I harped on the condition of your continued stay with me here while in the village. Do you remember that? **Mpyama asked**

Yes sir, I still remember. **Tita answered**

So nice of you, one more thing, you are not expected to contribute to any form of feeding or provision of other basic needs while in this house until after my promised one year of accommodation has elapsed. But you can buy what you want as a youth. Did you hear me? **Mpyama inquired**

Yes Sir. Thank you so much. You have truly done a lot of good things for me. You are the best person I have in this township and also as a relative of such. **Tita cheerfully said.**

That's all that I wanted to let you know. **Mpyama said**

Thank you Sir. **Tita replied**

On the agreed outside market day, Tita got all his things ready and went for the whole sale purchase with Mpyama, and they went to the market early so that he could purchase all that he needed as a new starter 'who opens his own shop for the first time, Mpyama reduced his own purchases to less than one-tenth of what he normally purchase so as to monitor how Tita does his purchases and as well help him carry his goods to the loading spot so as to avoid been maneuvered by 'truck pushers' who sometimes made away with buyers goods when unmonitored. Tita took his time to do his purchases and limited his purchases to exactly about 35% of his settlement money. He bought all that he needed based on only on his personal preferences without Mpyama's masterminds. They spent time in the outside market making sure that they never rushed anything to avoid purchasing merchandises in whole sale that its retail prices could summarily turned out to be less than the whole sale purchase prices, because when that happens Tita's business immediately goes under because he will only be on debt instead of making profits. And they never purchased items that Tita was not sure of its retailing so as to avoid the issue of 'uncertainty principle' (a situation whereby there is no sure accurate method of prediction). Tita purchased all that he needed and with the help of his former boss, he carefully conveyed them and loaded them on vehicles going to his market destination.

When they arrived at their market selling spot, he and Mpyama unloaded his merchandise into his shop, and since they returned late from the outside market they left the items on the floor of his shop without arranging them in place. Mpyama also left his small purchased items in his own shop and they closed for that day and went home. The following day Tita and Mpyama returned back to their market line and Mpyama helped him to put those things they purchased from the outside market in their proper places. They staked the bags of rice and beans well on the floor of his shop, and the other items were carefully staked on shelves. Later Mpyama invited other shop owners available that deal on such businesses and asked Tita to tell them that he had started his own trade in that market line. Tita did exactly as he was instructed to do, and the invitees were also given their basics as written in their Bylaws.

They accepted all their necessary things and wished Tita well in his business in their line of trade as his own boss. Mpyama spent time with him after the departure of that rice and beans shop owners and he was there when customers began to enter Tita shop and did retail purchases. Before he left Tita's shop he wished him well and invoked the Spirit of God and their Ancestors to bless his shop as well as its contents and also to guide and protect him as he traded as his own boss.

Tita became the master of his own trade, making business decisions mostly by himself and always seeking for answers on relevant business questions from his former boss. He combined intelligent, knowledge and prudency to his day to day business activities, and he followed Mpyama's instructions without trying to do as he wished which could nip his business at the bud. He gradually continued to increase the amount of money invested in his shop as was instructed to him by his former boss and Mpyama's advice continued to yield the desired results. Those customers who had already known him relocated to his new shop for retail and partial whole sale purchases respectively, and they were happy that he had became his own boss because 'sometimes becoming someone's own boss never come easily' because there were so many odds on the way for apprentices that only those who chose self discipline could prosper. Mpyama never backed away from him after opening his own shop, he continued to visit his shop from time to time to see how businesses were moving and as well instruct him more if need be. And more so, Mpyama continued to go to the outside market with him until after he made sure that Tita had fortified his own shop with his settlement money—a huge investment for sure.

While in his brother's house, Mpyama never force anything on him so as to allow him time to always be out on time at his shop because as a new starter he needed to convince customers that he was always available for business and therefore must be there when necessary. Mpyama many of the times does the basic house cleaning and other routines like cooking etc while Tita 'goes to his shop for business; Mpyama remained unperturbed by Tita's gradual rise in business strength and never indulges him in any form of clandestine activities whatsoever so as to bring Tita down. Mpyama continued to abide by his words and never for once 'eat back his vomit'. Mpyama accommodation of Tita gave the young shop owner a good start and as well busted his business more than some of those who had already spent years in the business.

Tita became dedicated to his business and never gambled with his sole opportunities in life because "if a blind man fails to grab a big snail that his/her foot touches, his/her own could be over". He avoided all unnecessary contacts and continued to put more time to his business spending all the necessary hours in his shop, returning and been at home when needed. He avoided the temptations of early contacts with the opposite sex because in towns/cities, whenever 'you become your own boss them ladies etc begin to love you mostly for money and little for marriage. And those 'unfortunate preys who never retrospect before embarking on such relationships get drowned and sink really deep', but those that listen to the 'voices of reason' never regret their decisions. He also avoided forceful 'win over' of customers which could instigate him with common apprentices and other shop owners, and he never played the fool of sharing his shop consumables either on credit to those 'once in a life time customers' or 'the wealthy beggars'.

CHAPTER SEVEN

Tita Lives on His Own

Tita continued to be loyal to Mpyama who never hided the appreciation of him, and who continued to buttress him in whatever nice way possible. Tita walked the streets of the township free and was never for one day attacked by the opposing forces to the government, and those in their market line continued to cherish him. Before the end of the promised one year free accommodation, Tita had made good money that could rent him any room of his choices within the relevant areas of town. In the eight to nine month of staying with his former boss, he told him that he was about to look for a room of his own. Mpyama reasoned with him and promised him that he would equally help him on that, and that had it been that there were more vacant rooms left in the place that he rented, it could have been a nice thing two of them staying in the same compound. Mpyama told Tita to continue to focus on his shop and only look for outside room for accommodation when necessary.

Tita continued with his business and also continued to search for his own rooms for rent during none shop days. He adopted the philosophy of Mpyama who never opened his shop on Mondays. Meanwhile, Mpyama had gone to one of the most quiet and peaceful places in town to look for accommodation for Tita. On consistent searching, he found a room located in a very friendly street, a nice inexpensive place, conducive for a young man. Tita later found an accommodation at another section of town that 'attracts a lot of ladies on their bikinis', an expensive room meant for those that 'are either from wealthy families or that has spent years in business as their own bosses'. When Tita disclosed that to Mpyama, he objected to that, and told Tita that it was so early for him to start mingling with such people, especially considering the nature of family that he originated from. Mpyama convinced him on the need to distance himself from the stinks of the town gullies 'because their stains smell so bad', and could ruin good morals and destroy traditional family lineages. Mpyama later presented him with the offer of the room he had found for him based on the location, serenity and conduciveness nature of it. Tita was pleased, and he accepted the offer without hesitation, and that was during the tenth month. The owners of the room said that it would be available in the eleventh month, so, Mpyama demanded for the required rental amount of money from Tita so as to pay for the room and as well secure it. Tita without hesitation gave the needed amount of CFA Franc to Mpyama, and before the end of the tenth month, they went and paid for the room, and Tita also inspected the room and approved of it without coercion.

At the end of the promised twelve months, Tita moved-in to his own room with the help of Mpyama. Tita purchased all that he needed to stay on his own and as well positioned them in his own room. The following day after his moved-in, Mpyama visited him and spent hours with him, and Tita's residency was a stone throw from where he lived. In the afternoon of that day Tita cooked food that they eat together, thereafter; Tita became almost independent from Mpyama his blood relative, but he continued to visit Mpyama during some weekends while Mpyama continued to monitor him so as to ensure that he never wandered into the streets in the nights to grab 'shit things home'. And he continued to visit Tita's shop when necessary so as to show him his relentless supports. Tita in his own room never attempted to convert his room to a brothel, whereas there were occasional visitors from fellow traders but he was conscious of his involvements, never to have dealings with those who could stick into his palms and never got washed off again. He made his room a safe place of abode because 'unverifiable encounters could end him in the militia group's trap and ripped him of all his belongings for safety, or he either joins them or loses one or both of his limbs'. To be on a safer side, he continued to work with his boss who was more acquainted with the township lives. The extra burden of taken care of himself which became necessary having moved into his own room never prevented him from been an efficient trader-been at his shop always when necessary.

While on his own his business continued to flourish and he continued to fortify his shop making sure those basic merchandise mostly needed by customers were always present for their purchases. He continued to be a reasonable trader by saving most portions of his profits for continues buying and selling. After about one year of his own accommodation, he took permission from Mpyama that he wanted to travel home and see his parents and sisters etc. Mpyama approved his request without delay and told him that he was always free to travel home to the village whenever he deemed it wise and necessary, but that he should not make consistent home travels part of his business routines because by so doing he could lose 'expensive customers' (those customers that buy large number of items per purchase). Mpyama promised to watch after his shop in his absence.

Tita who was 'in the money' (making good profits) bought expensive things for his parents, and tried to show them to Mpyama but he told him that 'Tita you are free to buy whatever you want/ desire for your parents and sisters etc, only make sure that you made such purchases from your part of profits, so, next time there is absolutely no need to show me such things'. Tita thanked him, and the following day Tita travelled home to his village with other things like a bag of rice, sizeable quantity of beans etc.

Tita was received at home with jubilation by his parents and sisters. Their hearts were filled with joy and they were all full of merriments, and some of their family members came out to join them in celebrating Tita's first home visit since ever he started his own business. Some of the rest of their entire family members' whole heartedly welcomed him and wished him well. In the morning of the following day after his return he handed over to his parents and sisters all that he bought for them, and in the evening of the same day, he shared rice and beans etc to all the relevant mothers in the entire family as was customary in many of the Central African Nations. His parents were so happy that their only son had made it to self sustenance since he could stay alone and come home that big even to the point of knowing that the rest of the family members also deserved his kindness. They inquired from him to know if he was still staying with his brother, Mpyama, although they had already been informed by close sources that he had found his own living accommodation months ago. Tita told them that he spent twelve months at Mpyama's room and that before the end of his stay at his house, he helped to secure a conducive place for him and that since about a year ago he had been living in his own room. They asked him how long it took him to open his own shop, and he told them that he spent only about three days after departure from the village, after which his shop opened. And that Mpyama helped him a lot to ensuring that he could stand on his two feet without slumping. Tita disclosed to his parents that what his brother did for him never stopped at those things that he promised in their presence, because Mpyama never wanted him to spend his own personal money buying food items and other basic house needs for a complete period of twelve months.

They asked about his relationship with Mpyama since ever he moved out of his room. And Tita sincerely told them that he had been relating with his former boss well more than like before, "sometimes when I am not around like now, he looks after my shop to ensure that nobody meddles with it, and also visits my room to make sure that it remained locked until I returned back from my travel. He has always been such a good person to me and despite all the CFA Franc that I make, he cares less to either demand or borrows money from me, such a nice man". He made it known to them that it was because of him that he never moved to the roughest and most expensive area of the cities because he objected to that with reasons.

His sisters asked him more about the township and he cheerfully explained on their concerns and they also queried him to know if women were in such a business, and he told them that women were certainly in such businesses, especially those that either their tradition and/or culture allowed for that. His other family members received all his gifts with enthusiasms and urged him to continue with such show of unity and oneness without slumber. He also handed good gifts to some of the youths of his entire family members and they were more than happy to have him in their mist.

Tita did not waste much time at home in the village as he spent only four days before returning back to the cities. Before, he went back to the city he went to Mpyama's house to see his parents and other family members, and they were all glad to see Tita gradually becoming a more responsible person in their bloodline in particular and the community in general. At Mpyama's house Tita behaved as a witty and reasonable person by giving a certain amount of money to his former boss parents and to also the little kids who were there when he came. Meanwhile, before Tita went back to town his father told him of the need for her sister to learn 'female cloth weaving' which she had indicated interest in after her elementary three which she brilliantly completed. And his parents told him that they had found a place where she could learn that in one of the surrounding villages. Tita without wasting time gave them money to support her sister as needed and also money to his other sisters for their own local mat business, and more so, he gave a reasonable amount of money to his parents respectively. They warned him that he should first consider how much that was in his pocket before making monetary expenses, and he told them that he was conscious of what he was doing. Prior to his departure, his parents advised him to always emulate his brother, Mpyama, who had proven beyond all reasonable doubt that he was all time ready to assist him excel and prosper, and that finding his own living room accommodation and opening his own shop should not in any case hinder him from approaching Mpyama for reasonable and good advices. They told him that "our son, Tita, now that you are on your own always draw from your brother so as to avoid any last minute mistakes. Mpyama started cooking before you therefore he has more broken pots. Be with him, and he will never disappoint you". Later Tita returned back to town to continue from where he stopped.

Tita's visit rekindled his parents hope and as well lessoned their daily burdens for the first recommendable time since his sponsorship started right from the primary school. His home coming revived his parents, re-energized them, rehabilitated them, restructured them, re-inspired them, and gave them more comfortable hours of sleep in the nights. They could now dose away and wake up when necessary without been bothered with such questions like "what will my children eat tomorrow? There is no money or food left in here; I am getting tired of this nonsense; what am I going to do? And his visit brightened his sisters chances of attracting home well doing/well to do people because they were sure to get married in the future, and considering the situation of things during that time, 'young men and indeed vibrant young men want to get married to those who have promising and/or established family backgrounds', especially those from good families. And it also increased their opportunities of going to the towns to sell their mats should they ever chose to, and fortified their most junior sister with a lot of materials to learn her own handwork well.

Tita back in the township continued to focus all his attention on his trading business relentlessly. He continues to seek advices from Mpyama who always proffered solutions to any of his problems both businesses related and others. Tita's business continued to flourish and always taken the upward trend, and he continued to make his parents advises and traditional religious beliefs the custodian of his actions keeping morality at the forefront of all his dealings. Like Mpyama who never invited any female friend in his presence for any form of pleasure while he was resident in his room. Tita avoided insatiable pleasurable wants and instead believed that at the right time and only when necessary he would get married to a woman of his choice without nursing around women genitals as if to say 'he is waiting for a new born arrival'. He knew that Mpyama's lack of adherence to the passionate world had not only made him a complete man but had also made him a "man whose yes is his yes and his no means only his no". He continued to send things to his parents whenever necessary and continued to be visiting home as time permits and always providing his family with all their needs, and without forcing them to go for purchases on credits in the village which most of the times 'disgraces a poor family'. Tita never relegated respecting and listening to Mpyama's advises to the background as he continued to be his own person in control of his conscience.

One day as Tita was returning back from the market after closing work for the day, one young man with his bible approached him. Tita knew that there were such people around but he was yet to fathom out why the young man chose him as the target of preaching that late evening.

Good evening sir. My name is Sokoni (Came from the sea). **Sokoni greeted**

Tita continued to walk home pretending not to hear his greetings.

Good evening sir. **Sokoni greeted again raising his voice**

Tita remained unshaken and continued on his way home.

Good evening sir. **Sokoni shouted,** and came so close to him

Who are you? **Tita asked**

I am a preacher sir. **Sokoni answered**

Yes: what can I do for you? **Tita asked**

I came with the word of God. **Sokoni answered**

What word of God? **Tita asked**

Word of God from the bible, sir. **Sokoni answered**

Please, I am a traditionalist and I prefer my own way of knowing God. **Tita said**

Are you a pagan? **Sokoni asked**

What is a pagan? **Tita answered**

Sir, pagans are those who believe in the African Traditional Religion as was left to us by our Ancestors. **Sokoni said**

Why? **Tita asked**

Sir, it is because our Ancestors lived under sin and were not sanctified by the innocent blood of the only son of God that came to deliver this world from their sinful nature. **Sokoni said**

Who among men shall deliver our Ancestors that had passed away uncountable number of years ago? I ask you who among men delivers them? **Tita asked**

Our savior, the only son of God was sent to come and do that, sir. **Sokoni answered**

I have heard of that, but I cannot abandon my traditional belief because of such stories as compiled and written by your holy book. **Tita said**

Sir, I am one of his messengers. I came to share this word with you, and also deliver you from your pagan beliefs so that on the last day all of us could cheerfully join the chariots to Heaven, where we will live and suffer no more. **Sokoni replied**

I have no time to discuss further with you today, please, I am just returning from a place I have spent hours in. I need to be home. **Tita pleaded**

Sir (pointing at the bible), this is the only true home. Whosoever that does not believe in this shall perish. So, this is the only time, truly, the only opportunity for you to repent from your sinful ways. I am here to assist you to enter heaven. **Sokoni insisted**

Is this the only true way to a utopian Heaven? **Tita asked**

Yes, this is the only true way to Heaven, and there is no other way. **Sokoni answered**

What of other religions? **Tita asked**

They must also accept the teachings of the bible and our savior, the only son of God for them to be accepted in Heaven. **Sokoni answered**

This world is much larger than you all could comprehend. This world is a pluralistic place and therefore people should be allowed to choose, and not to force any religion on them because one day such cunning use of force could backfire. **Tita warned**

Sir, for this world to be saved they must accept the bible, and there is no time because the savior cometh soon. We are fast approaching 2000 years which is the finish line, and so, the savior cometh soon. **Sokoni replied**

Again, I have no time for your rabbles, especially at this time. So get out of my way. **Tita warned**

Where do you live sir? I can come to your house. **Sokoni inquired**

I don't accept uninvited visitors to my house. **Tita replied**

God is important in our lives, and this bible is here to prove that. **Sokoni said**

I have no time for you now. **Tita replied,** and walked fast and distanced him.

Repent! Repent all ye that are heavily burdened and I shall give you peace. This is only the time you have. Repent . . . . !! **Sokoni continued to shout**

The following day after the encounter, Tita went and narrated everything to Mpyama who laughed and told him that he had been encountering such people many times on his way back home, especially from the shop. Mpyama also told him that they sometimes knocked at someone's door uninvited with bibles in their hands. Mpyama wondered whether that was the first time of encountering such people, and Tita admitted that he has had such encounters with them, especially when he was an apprentice and shortly when he started on his own but that he declined to give them the opportunities of exchanging words with him. Tita said that "when I was living in your house they used to come, but I denied them the opportunities of entering your room, so, the normally backed out and went". Mpyama warned him never to allow such people to approach so close to his house, especially their females because most of the times when you proved 'hard to get' they would use their female preachers to engage you, and once that happens all your assets could be committed to their care and poverty could begin to chase you around again. Mpyama advised him to hold firmly to his traditional beliefs because 'new brooms sweeps clean' and that 'the end will surely justify the means', and that 'the path to the Truth lies only in your dealings with fellow human beings because by so doing you will surely know who is cheating who'.

Tita drew from his experience while under the full supervision of Mpyama and decided to stick with his traditional beliefs because 'stiffer punishments of the sinful offender make African Traditional Beliefs a pagan religion, but only time will tell'.

CHAPTER EIGHT

Tita Had a Visitor

As days passed by Tita continued to avoid unwanted contacts with the so called protestant preachers who filled every streets of the towns/cities. One none market day Tita was sitting in his room relaxing and heard a loud knock-a real bang, on his door, he was surprised who that could be because the bang came with greater intensity. Tita gradually opened the door and instantly saw a beautiful young woman with bible in one of her hands, and on seen him she flashed a tantalizing smile at him and asked him;

Please, sir. My name is Sanga (Came from the valley). Can I come in? **Sanga asked**

Who are you my dear lady? **Tita answered**

I came to you with good news. **Sanga said**

What good news? **Tita asked**

Offer me seat and I will shear with you the good news. **Sanga answered**

As Tita continued to look at her and interact with the lady, he continued to be more attracted to her.

Come in and don't waste my time. **Tita said**

Thank you, sir. **Sanga replied,** and sat down and was about to open her bible

Now, that you are sited. What is the good news? I hope you did not come in here to tell me anything about the book of yours or ask me to repent? **Tita asked**

No sir, try to understand sir. **Sanga answered**

Understand what? **Tita asked**

I want you to understand that there is not much time left for you to give your life to our savior the only son of God. This is the only time you have to do that sir. **Sanga answered**

I am tired of that nonsense, please if that is the good news do get up and get out of my room. **Tita said**

Sir, I came to deliver you from your sinful ways. **Sanga replied**

I said get out of my room. **Tita said**

Sir, before I leave I want to show you something. **Sanga pleaded**

I said get out of my room now. **Tita insisted**

Can you read sir? **Sanga asked**

Yes, I can read. What has that got to do with getting out of my room? **Tita sternly answered**

Please, come closer to me and I will show only one thing meant for you and you alone, and after that I assure you that I will leave your room. **Sanga said**

Tita went closer to her and she open a certain section of the bible where she kept a little leaflet, and as Tita was been filled with the sweet saint that oozed out of her beautiful body, she said 'look at this sir', and as Tita mopped at that, she gently touched him at the back with his breasts and caressed his neck with her finger nails, and instantly electric shock arrested Tita's private parts and his entire body began to vibrate requesting for more. Tita continued to mope and the lady asked him;

Sir, have you seen where I am pointing at? **Sanga asked**

M . . . m . . . mm . . . . **Tita answered**

Do you see it well sir? **Sanga asked**

Mm . . . mm . . . . **Tita answered**

Are you sure you have seen it well sir? **Sanga asked**

Mm . . . mm . . . m . . . mm . . . . **Tita answered**

The lady waited for a while and Tita never seemed to dislike the urge been transmitted to him from the lady. When he finally left the lady's contact, the lady asked him;

Did you understand what I showed you? **Sanga asked**

M . . . m . . . mm . . . . **Tita answered**

Do you still need my presence in your room? **Sanga asked**

Mm . . . mm . . . mm . . . . **Tita answered**

I want you to be saved. Do you need me to be saved? **Sanga asked**

Mm . . . m . . . mm . . . mm . . . **Tita answered**

Can I go now? **Sanga asked**

No, you can stay a more little, stay a more little, a more . . . . **Tita answered**

The lady stayed in his room for a couple of hours and preached to him while they exchanged conversations, and before the lady left she handed him a pamphlet of the Assemblies Mission and promised him that she would always come by to make sure that he repented completely so as to enter Heaven, and Tita agreed to corporate with her.

Meanwhile, one night when Mpyama was out of town, Tita, while in his new location defiled his former boss advice of always avoiding the nights until the hazy situation in their country finally boiled down. He went to the 'other side of town' where half dressed ladies came out to hang around in the night and watched them.

And as he reached the 'hot zone' one of those ladies spotted him and rushed him and wrapped her right hand around his neck and pecked him a couple of times and took him to the corner.

Baby, my name is Jaga (Outsider). What is your name? **Jaga asked**

Mm . . . mm . . . . **Tita answered**

Sweet baby: what is your name? **Jaga asked**

Mm . . . mm . . . mm . . . . **Tita answered**

So, you don't have a name? **Jaga insisted**

My name . . . . My name . . . is . . . My name . . . . is Tita. **Tita replied**

The lady intensely continued to caress him while Tita stood still, transfixed without rejecting any of her moves.

What do you do for a living? **Jaga asked**

Mm . . . mm . . . m . . . . **Tita answered**

Where do you work? **Jaga asked**

I am a shop owner. I . . . own a shop. **Tita answered**

On hearing that he owned a shop, the lady gradually reached his pants and gently touched his balls and waves engulfed Tita.

Where do you live? **Jaga asked**

Mm . . . mm . . . mm . . . . **Tita answered**

Where do you live? I mean your house? **Jaga asked again**

Mm . . . mm . . . . I live down there (pointing his hand towards the direction). **Tita answered**

Do you live alone? **Jaga asked**

Mm . . . mm . . . mm. **Tita answered**

Do you live alone? **Jaga asked again**

Mm . . . Yes. **Tita answered**

The lady gently placed her mouth so close to his ear and softly said;

Take me home now.

Mm . . . mm . . . mm . . . . **Tita replied**

Take me home now. **Jaga said,** and massaged him the more.

Mmmm . . . Mmmmm . . . . Mmmmm . . . . **Tita shaked and wetted his underpants with fluid**

After reaching partial climax he came to his senses and reached his pocket and gave the lady a certain amount of CFA Franc, and the lady insisted that she wanted to be with him. Pretending to accept Jaga's offer, Tita ran away from the place to his room, while running the lady looked at him and laughed.

As time progresses Sanga continued to show up in his room with her bible preaching to him and developing a more cordial relationship with him, but to completely get hold of him was a little difficult because he was afraid that Mpyama could uncover his secret dealings. After about one and half more years in his new location he told Mpyama that he wanted to relocate to another section of the town, that he no longer found his residence any more conducive. His boss suspected foul play and objected to that. Meanwhile, during one of the occasions Mpyama had already caught Sanga in Tita's room preaching to him. When the lady left Mpyama nearly slapped Tita, the first encounter of such nature and he warned him to put pack his reproductive genital were it rightly belonged and wait for the right time to do that, and that if he insisted on marrying he should look for a good woman and marry out rightly without flirting. Mpyama tried to pacify him to continue to live in the place he secured for him, but he insisted that he must relocate 'having tasted the sweetness of it' the best thing was to join them. Tita disobeyed Mpyama for the first time and went close to the 'hot-zone' to reside. Before he finally packed out of his former residency Mpyama had already informed his parents on Tita's involvements with those he bluntly refused to accept and accommodate. Tita's parents sent an SOS and warned him never to vacate his former place of residency for any reason and that he should always emulate the precepts set forth by Mpyama his brother.

His father knew everything about Tita's former residence because at the second year of securing his own living accommodation he brought him to the place and he spent one complete month before going back to the village, and his father had also visited there a couple of more times since after. As the argument heated on why Tita should remain in his present location of residency, Mr. Cazembi paid him an unscheduled visit so as to convince him on the need to remain where he lived. Despite all the pressures from his parents and Mpyama, Tita insisted that he must pack out of for good, and later he promised his father that he would not pack out again, and he eventually packed out of his former residence to a place where Mpyama's eyes could not easily reach. Tita having disobeyed all that contributed to his well-being and progress retracted his steps from Mpyama's room, although he occasionally visited him, and gradually began to disappear from approaching his shop. As time went on, and Sanga continued to visit his room Tita started contemplating on joining the 'New Crusaders of Heaven', the Assemblies Mission. Mpyama was still enveloping Tita, so Tita thought that should he continue to distance himself from his only true relative in town, there could be drastic measures so as to keep him on check. So, Tita dealt the final blow by relocating his shop to another location, disappearing completely from the view of Mpyama. On sensing the danger around the corner Mpyama visited Tita and tried to make him reason so that he could not end up been laughed at in the end because there was no other true salvation than that of 'a friend in need who is a friend indeed'. He warned Tita that although the militia group were been gradually crushed by the government forces, there was still reason to believe that their country was in crises. In that case he Tita needed to be himself again and continued to display exceptional qualities. Tita listened to his entire plea and when he left, Tita continued to follow those ladies at the back and continued to wallow into a pit of shit-local latrine.

Having betrayed his solemn promise to his parents, sisters and relatives, Tita began to act like a 'lost domestic animal that visits any house it hears the voices of similar animals thinking that it is where it certainly belongs'. Tita's self arms length option from all and sundry gave Sanga the needed opportunity to strike him really hard. As he continued to visit for preaching, one early night she knocked at Tita's door as usual and Tita initially thought that it could be a real danger, so he never wanted to open the door but on hearing of her voice "Tita, is me, please darling open the door", he went and opened the door and the lady rushed in immediately and shouted "close the door! Close the door!! They are after me". Tita instantly closed the door and the lady stood still and told him that a couple of guys started chasing her as she was passing along Tita's street, and that those guys vowed to kill her that night. Tita was surprised because of the reemergence of such dangers.

Sir, what am I going to do now? **Sanga asked**

This is serious! **Tita exclaimed**

It is already night. **Tita said**

Yes sir. **Sanga replied**

Can you stay here until they go? **Tita asked**

They vowed to kill me, sir. **Sanga answered**

Do you mind spending the night here? **Tita inquired**

Sanga stayed for a couple of seconds before answering.

I wouldn't mind, sir. **Sanga replied**

You can stay here until tomorrow morning, you here. **Tita said**

Yes sir. Where am I going to put my bible? **Sanga inquired**

Place them on the table. **Tita said**

Sanga slowly worked closer to the table and placed his bible and sat on the seat.

Tita exchanged few more words with her which she cheerfully with smiles canvassed with him.

Are you hungry? **Tita asked**

Yes sir. **Sanga answered**

What would you like to eat? **Tita asked**

What do you have sir? **Sanga answered**

I have cooked rice and I have soup with 'amala'. **Tita said**

I will eat rice sir. **Sanga replied**

I will go and bring that out. **Tita said**

I can help you with that, sir. **Sanga replied**

Never mind, just don't bother yourself. **Tita said**

I will help you on that sir. **Sanga insisted**

Tita showed Sanga the pot of rice and she used plates to bring out the quantity that will satisfy her and maybe Tita and positioned that for them to eat.

Dear, you go ahead and eat. I will eat amala. **Tita said**

No sir, I put this for two of us. It is because of you that I put this much. **Sanga replied**

Tita took his own position and ate with Sanga. After eaten she staked the plates neatly in their designated location ready to be washed in the following morning. During bed time;

Dear, you can go to bed if you want (pointing at the bed for her). **Tita said**

Yes sir. **Tita replied**

Do not wait for me to go to bed; I will sleep on this mat here. **Tita said**

Sanga pretended as if she never heard what Tita said. Shortly, Sanga took her position on the bed, and as Tita lay on the mat, Sanga called him;

Sir, why do you prefer to sleep there? **Sanga asked**

Nothing, I will like to sleep here. **Tita replied**

Are you avoiding me? **Sanga asked**

No, certainly not. **Tita answered**

I want to sleep with you. **Sanga said**

No not at all. **Tita replied**

I will come and join you over there. **Sanga said**

No, just go to sleep. **Tita replied**

Sanga got up from the bed and went to Tita and bent on him and joined him.

No. not like that, this mat is too small for two of us. **Tita protested**

I need you sir. **Sanga said**

Mm . . . mm . . . . What? **Tita asked**

I need you on bed sir. **Sanga insisted**

Mm . . . mm . . . m . . . . This mat is too small. **Tita said**

Sanga gradually hooked him and held him tight on her breast and continued to request.

Come to bed darling, come to bed. **Sanga requested**

Mm . . . mm . . . mm . . . on bed! **Tita replied**

Come to bed darling, come to bed. **Sanga insisted**

Having turned Tita on, he sluggishly got up and they left the mat and got themselves entangled on the bed. Sanga continued to turn him on, and she pulled off her dress and braze allowing all her body to be touching Tita's. At the point when she knew that

Tita had been consumed passionately and could offer no more resistance, she gradually told Tita to undress himself and he complied and she removed her paints exposing her womanhood to Tita.

Darling, do that with me. **Sanga said**

Mm . . . mm . . . **Tita replied**

I need you, enter me now. **Sanga requested,** and felt Tita's manhood with her fingers, and Tita immediately penetrated her and enjoyed the night with her. And after having enough of him, they slept off. Before they slept off;

Darling, tomorrow you will go with me to our church, you hear. **Sanga said**

I will . . . . **Tita replied**

Darling, tomorrow we go and see our church members, you hear. **Sanga said again**

I will . . . . **Tita replied**

Darling, tomorrow we go and see our pastor, you hear. **Sanga said**

I will . . . . **Tita replied**

Darling, tomorrow, you join the Assemblies Mission, you hear. **Sanga said**

I . . . . I will . . . **Tita replied**

In the morning Sanga assisted him in washing the plates and doing other relevant things and after which they ate breakfast and headed to the Assemblies Mission.

CHAPTER NINE

Tita Joins AM

Tita was taken to the Assemblies Mission (AM) compound and subsequently introduced to its members. Sanga gave testimonies after which she asked Tita to step forward and face the congregation as was normal under such circumstances. And Tita reluctantly did as he was directed and the congregants were full of praises. Sanga said that 'this young man you see standing here, is my brother in the lord, and he has just decided to seek the way to the Father who is in Heaven. He has decided to forgo the pagan way which prevented our ancestors from entering heaven before the coming of the only son of God. I spoke to him and told him the whole stories of the truth of the bible and he decided to abandon his previous ways, and even forget about his trade and come and worship with us today. It is my view that this my darling brother's visit will not end here today, after today he will continue to join us for worships as one of us and as a member of the Assemblies Mission". Sanga told pastor Lasana (Poet) that it was now left for him to introduce their new convert to the rest of the congregation. The Assemblies Mission pastor said thus;

Halleluiah! Halleluiah!! Halleluiah!!!

Amen! Amen!! Amen!!! **Congregants responded**

Praise the lord. **Pastor Lasana said**

Halleluiah **Congregants responded**

Praise . . . the . . . lord. **Pastor Lasana said**

Halleluiah **Congregants responded**

Praise . . . the . . . living lord. **Pastor Lasana said**

Halleluiah **Congregants responded**

This young man you see standing here is today the anointed one of us. **Pastor Lasans said**

Yes. **Congregants responded**

He has chosen to see the way of salvation. **Pastor Lasana said**

Yes. **Congregants responded**

He has come to be delivered from his sinful ways. **Pastor Lasana said**

Yes. **Congregants responded**

We will not disappoint him. **Pastor Lasana said**

No, never, not at all. **Congregants responded**

In our mist he shall find salvation. **Pastor Lasana said**

Yes. **Congregants responded**

This young man has been looking for safety. **Pastor Lasana said**

Yes. **Congregants responded**

Today he has found safety; the door of Heaven has been unlocked for him. **Pastor Lasana said**

Amen. **Congregants responded**

He has decided to abandon his parents, brothers and sisters and relatives and join the cross to Calvary-a burden of proofs. **Pastor Lasana said**

Yes. **Congregants responded**

He has decided to abandon his shop and come to us. **Pastor Lasana said**

Yes. **Congregants responded**

Today, you will open your eyes and see God Himself. **Pastor Lasana said**

Amen. **Congregants responded**

While the pastor was busy ranting praises, Tita got transfixed and was just looking at the congregation, staring at them without uttering a word.

Young man, my dear brother in the lord, please tell your brothers and sisters here your name. **Pastor Lasana said**

My name is Tita. **Tita replied**

What brought you here to the Assemblies Mission? **Pastor Lasana asked**

Assemblies! **Tita exclaimed**

Yes, brother what brought you to the Assemblies Mission? **Pastor Lasana asked again**

I like to be a member. **Tita answered**

Amen! Amen!! Amen!!! **Congregants responded**

Praise the lord. **Pastor Lasana said**

Halleluiah **Congregants responded**

Did you hear what this young man just said? **Pastor Lasana asked**

Yes. **Congregation responded**

Have you accepted us in your mind? **Pastor Lasana asked**

Yes. I have. **Tita replied**

Amen! Amen!! Amen!!! **Congregation full of shout of praises**

Tita, have you accepted the Assemblies Mission in your mind? **Pastor Lasana asked**

Yes, I have. **Tita replied once again**

Tita, have you accepted to follow the teachings of the bible? **Pastor Lasana asked**

After millions of years! **Tita exclaimed**

Yes, my brother. Have you accepted to abandon your pagan ways and follow the way of the lord our savior as the only true way? **Pastor Lasana asked**

Yes, I have, but . . . **Tita answered**

Brother, there is no need for 'a but', have no fear. **Pastor Lasana said**

Yes, I have. **Tita replied**

Amen! Amen!! Amen!!! **Congregants responded**

Today, we have received you and accepted you as one of us. You are now a member of the Assemblies Mission, here in this congregation. We are now your parents, brothers, sisters and relatives. We are bound by oath to be one and only one, so we always strive to see to the benefits of one another. We provide for ourselves, always giving to the needy because the Lord brings and takes. As a new member, I will assign you to our dear sister in the lord Sanga, she will continue to help you with the teachings of the bible and also aid you in understanding it, and as well be of assistance to you in any other related issues as it pertained to the Assemblies Mission and the way of salvation (immediately the pastor made mention Sanga as Tita's aid, passion waves again passed through his tube but this time just as a reminder). **Pastor Lasana said**

The pastor took him on a little praises;

My fellow brothers and sisters, please join me to say, Welcome to Tita to the Assemblies Mission. **Pastor Lasana said**

Tita, you are welcomed to the Assemblies Mission. **Congregation shouted**

Tita say praise is to the lord. **Pastor Lasana said**

Praise is to the lord. **Tita replied**

Tita say halleluiah. **Pastor Lasana said**

Halleluiah. **Tita imitated**

Amen! **Congregants responded**

Tita, say amen. **Pastor Lasana said**

Amen. **Tita said**

Halleluiah **Congregants responded**

Your membership of the Assemblies Mission is hereby confirmed, and after Sanga will acquaint you with our programs of events. **Pastor Lasana said**

After that day, Tita began to live a more secretive life keeping to himself and seeking advice from Sanga in particular and other church members. Although he was still somehow dedicated to his business but the 'passion curve' was gradually eating deeper into his skin. He continued to attend church during their church days with occasional attendances of ordinary session days. To make sure that Tita became hair to toe member of the church, Sanga continued to offer him herself allowing him to control her body as much as he wanted. Tita continued to empty his spermatozoa while Sanga continued to occasionally sleep with Tita at least once a week, especially during his none work days.

Tita became gradually engulfed by his church members and he gradually started contributing financially to the church. He began to display unusual behavior to his parents, sisters and relative, especially his former boss who continued to do everything within his reach to return him to who he was. As months gone by, Tita's deep rooted ties continued to penetrate deeper into the soil of the Assemblies Mission. One day Mpyama went to his shop and saw a good number of people praying with him in his shop. Mpyama stayed off course until after the prayer and dismissal of what seemed to be a prayer meeting; Mpyama asked Tita what was going on.

Tita: what is happening? **Mpyama asked**

Those are our church members. **Tita answered**

Why were they here? **Mpyama asked**

They came to pray. **Tita answered**

They came to pray for what? **Mpyama asked**

I told them to come and pray here, sir. **Tita answered**

Pray here for what? **Mpyama asked**

I needed prayers. **Mpyama answered**

You needed prayers for what? **Mpyama asked**

They are my people. **Tita answered**

They are your people for what? **Mpyama asked**

They are the only people I want. **Tita answered**

The only people you want for what? **Mpyama asked**

They are my only parents, brothers, sisters and relatives. **Tita answered**

Your only brother . . . ? **Mpyama asked**

Yes, I have that right. **Tita answered**

Your only brother . . . ? **Mpyama asked again**

Yes, my only parents, brothers, sisters and relatives: and what about that? **Tita questioned angrily**

Tita, calm down, calm down. **Mpyama pleaded**

I cannot do without them anymore. What have I done wrong? **Tita stammered**

Tita, calm down, my brother please calm down. **Mpyama pleaded**

No, what have I done wrong? Answer me. **Tita asked meanly**

Tita, it is not that way, you still have opportunities, in fact, the time to chase them off your back. **Mpyama said**

Not that way. So, you don't want to answer me. **Tita replied**

Those Assemblies Mission members can destroy your youth and make things so hard for you. **Mpyama said**

I said not that way, sir. **Tita replied**

What way is better? **Mpyama asked**

What have I gained? **Tita sternly asked**

Tita, my brother you have gained a lot of things from your cradle to the time you became completely financially independent, there have been reasonable people who are so willing to help you succeed in life. **Mpyama answered**

Is that what I have gained? **Tita asked**

What else do you want to gain? **Mpyama answered**

If not for one thing, I could have ordered you out of my shop, sir. **Tita said**

You Tita, ordered me out of your shop? **Mpyama surprised**

Yes Sir, I don't know why you are still here. **Tita replied**

Tita is something wrong with you? Are you crazy? **Mpyama asked**

You crazy pass sir. **Tita angrily replied**

Tita, me (pointing at himself) Mpyama crazy passed? **Mpyama asked**

I want only the Assemblies Mission members, only, yes, only. **Tita answered**

So, you don't want us anymore? **Mpyama asked**

I have been saying that. **Tita shouted**

Tita, listen attentively; I can get this people of your back if you want me to. I can stop them from coming to your shop and your room to disturb you. Do you want me to stop them? **Mpyama inquired**

Don't ever try that. Stopping . . . **Tita shouted**

Why? **Mpyama asked**

Tita immediately left his shop and went out leaving Mpyama alone inside the shop. While the skirmish was going on the passerbies' customers and other shop owners were busy looking at what was going on.

CHAPTER TEN

Mypama Visits Pastor Lasana

Having noticed how Tita was morally dwindling, Mpyama took it upon him to try once more to get Tita off the hook. He immediately made an unscheduled visit to the pastor of the Assemblies Mission, and pastor Lasana duly welcomed him and accepted to speak to him. Mpyama explained everything to pastor Lasana, and Lasana told him clearly that they never forced Tita to become a member of their church, that one day him Tita was introduced to the church by one of their female members and Tita from his heart accepted to become a member of the Assemblies Mission. And that at Tita's age nobody could take such decisions for him, 'he Tita can definitely speak for himself'. Mpyama applied all the necessary methodologies to getting the pastor renounce Tita and released him. But pastor Lasana bluntly refused having envisioned the merits of it that Tita was certainly with substantial amount of CFA Franc-wealthy for sure; at his age that could give the church a good lift. So, pastor Lasana instead asked him to come back on his none market day so that Tita could be around to deicide for himself.

Pastor Lasana informed Sanga of Mpyama's visit to him and instructed her to hint Tita on the purpose of Mpyama's visit. Sanga smiled and told pastor Lasana that Tita could not easily cease to be a member of the Assemblies Mission, and the pastor congratulated her for such a 'fatty capture' and also urged her to continue to do everything within her reach so as to ensure that Tita remained a loyal and faithful member of the Assemblies Mission because 'getting hold of business gurus like that take days of nights vigil, and once they are ours, we shouldn't let them go so easily".

On the scheduled day, Mpyama arrived on time before Tita. Pastor Lasana in the mist of few official members of the Assemblies Mission disclosed to Tita that Mpyama his former boss and as well his blood relative came for him;

Tita. **Pastor Lasana called**

Yes, Pastor. **Tita replied**

Do you know this person (pointing at Mpyama)? **Pastor Lasana asked**

Yes Pastor. **Tita answered**

Who is he to you? **Pastor Lasana asked**

He is my former boss. **Tita answered**

What do you mean? **Pastor Lasana asked**

He thought me my trade. **Tita answered**

Is he related to you? **Pastor Lasana asked**

Yes somehow. **Tita answered**

How related? **Pastor Lasana asked**

He is my relative, a blood relative. **Tita replied**

Do you know why he is here today? **Pastor Lasana asked**

No, not at all, pastor. **Tita answered**

He came for your sake. **Pastor Lasana said**

Yes pastor. **Tita replied**

Mpyama. Could you please tell him why you are here? **Pastor Lasana requested**

Mpyama explained why he came for Tita that as long as the township was concerned he was the only person in a position to answer all queries about Tita's whereabouts because it was him that brought Tita to the township from the village, sponsored him and supported him until he became somebody of importance. And that Tita came from a very poor family and that his parents and sisters depended much on him. Mpyama said that "I took all the pains to make sure that Tita as my blood relative never pick food from the dustbin. I did all I could to ensure that he is who he is today. Should anything happens to him, I am the only one to be blamed for, and so, I want my brother Tita back. His parents are Traditional Families who have being living exemplary lives, and their only son Tita was brought up that way and he has been following such Ancestral ideologies without flaws, making truth, unity, oneness, sympathy, tolerance, spirit of brotherhood and sisterhood, and morality his watch words and the custodian of his days". Mpyama said that he knew that Tita could be regarded as an adult because he had money and had chosen to gamble around with it to the merits of 'fine weather friends' and those who are head bent on littering the streets with stains. After his appeal for the release of Tita from the Assemblies Missions;

Tita did you hear what your brother and former boss said? **Pastor Lasana asked**

Yes pastor. **Tita answered**

What do you decide? **Pastor Lasana asked**

He is not here for me. He must have come for another purpose, not to take me away from this . . . the . . . not me. **Tita answered**

He said you should let go the membership of the Assemblies Mission and return back to your parents. **Pastor Lasana said**

I have warned him that the members of the Assemblies Mission are my parents, brothers and sisters and as well my relatives and he doesn't seem to hear that. **Tita replied**

He said that he cares for your safety? **Pastor Lasana said**

That is not true; he must be making a mistake. How old does he think I am? Indeed, I have come of age to make personal decisions and choices. **Tita replied**

In this congregation we do not ask members to leave or force them out, members are allowed to choose either to stay or to leave although we have rules which we do follow. As it was said earlier it remains your choice to continue with us, but if you need our assistance so as to continue with us, we will be more than happy to assist. **Pastor Lasana said**

I don't need Mpyama in my life anymore. You people here are my witnesses. I here and now ask him to please stay off my back. **Tita warned**

What about your parents and sisters in the village languishing? **Mpyama asked**

I don't care anymore. I have gone deep with them and I cannot turn back. Do you remember the 'other side of town'? What about it? I deserve. **Tita replied**

Has it been so long that you defile the traditional moral code of conducts? **Mpyama asked**

Yes sir, it has. **Tita answered**

Who knows how many? **Mpyama asked**

I need many more, I aren't going to quit doing that with them. That is all I want. You know one thing sir; I can't be like you, too tough sir, too tough. **Tita answered**

So, you (pointing at Tita) ate that shit. **Mpyama astonished**

Yes, I did and I have being eating that for a while now, and that makes me a bad person, doesn't it? **Tita replied**

Tita I don't believe you. **Mpyama said**

Believe it now, please, don't come here to disgrace yourself again for my sake. I know what is good for me. You can go ahead and lock your doors forever. We shall see how it will all end. Who needs you after all? **Tita replied**

Tita, are you referring to me? **Mpyama asked bewildered**

Yes, I am referring to Mr. Mpyama, Pastor you tell him not to come here again to speak to me for any reason. I don't want him anymore. Imagine that, all these things imagine that, I couldn't have, I suppose . . . **Tita warned**

Do such restrictions make me a bad man, Tita? **Mpyama asked**

Yes it certainly does. I want it my way, there in my own room, here with . . . that is all I want. You know, I can't stay without that anymore, so there is no need coming for a rescue. I started that and I want that, and I still want that and I will continue to do that. **Tita answered**

Mpyama got up and nearly slapped Tita

Mr. Mpyama respect yourself. Tell him to respect himself here. Don't ever try it; otherwise you will instantly see my response. **Tita shouted**

So you will fight me Tita? **Mpyama asked angrily**

Don't force me to otherwise I wouldn't mind. Do you know one thing? It has been years since you put me under your shadow, no passion, no pleasure. I have done that, and you stay away from me. I don't need you anymore. **Tita insisted**

Tita, you, disrespects me again? **Mpyama asked**

I have done that. **Tita answered**

As the exchange of words never seemed to end, the pastor pleaded for calm and calm was restored;

There is no need to force a horse to drink water. Tita has bared his mind to you, and that is what we are here for. He has made it known to you that he deserves his independent and has the right to make choices and as well choose by himself without interferences. **Pastor Lasana said**

That is all I want pastor, and I want this type of person to stay away from me. **Tita replied**

Mr. Mpyama you have heard what your brother Tita said, therefore, there is no need trying to wriggle water out of a stone. I want to use this opportunity to appeal to you to please give Tita the chances he deserves to be with us and get out of his sinful ways. He has made his decision and we are proud to say to him once more 'Tita welcome back'. **Pastor Lasana said**

Thank you, pastor. **Tita replied**

I have no grudges against him, he is only cutting off his fingers one by one, and at a certain stage all his fingers will be gone, and he suffers leprosy. Tita you have been infatuated with the sweetness of evil fruits, but be you careful so that you will not go down the drain of history as a young man that saw to his own ruin. Our Ancestors were here before, they are here today, and they will continue to be here with all mankind. I cannot force you to go contrary to your heart desires and aspirations, but hear me, 'too many spoons spoil the broth'. I have no regrets for my past, my present and my future because 'if you make your bed, you lay on it'. Since you have understood this place that I have spent years in more than me, may it continue to be well with you, but do not ever come back to me when you must have biting this shit more than you can chew because I will never ever be considerate again. I give you my word. **Mpyama said**

You are no longer my brother and my relative. I have found my people and I now belong with them. **Tita replied**

Nice of you, 'Distinction' boy, they are many here, even your mama age mates are willing to absorb you in, be very careful. **Mpyama warned.**

I want it my way, and what about it. That is my business Mr. Mpyama. How many times have you seen me in your room-your heaven, or your shop? And you kept on visiting me, disturbing and distracting me. I'm done with you. **Tita replied**

I speak no further. **Mpyama said**

No, continue to stay and talk. **Tita shouted**

My brother in the lord, the Assemblies Mission wishes you safe journey back to your destination and I ask the only son of God our savior to touch your heart so that you will accept salvation. **Pastor Lasana said**

Very stingy man! **Tita exclaimed**

Mpyama got up and left.

Having exhausted all efforts to reclaim Tita back while in town, Mpyama allowed him to continue his way because consistent efforts to draw him away from his congregation could result to a potential threat to Mpyama's life which could have disastrous consequences, therefore, Mpyama played cool and avoided further confrontations with Tita and gang. Tita became completely married to the Assemblies Mission and began to speak their dialect based on the 'bunch of evidences' as written in the bible. Tita became madly in love with Sanga and began to accept other female passionate offers as were recommended by her. As years gone by, Tita continued to be present in the Assemblies Mission, giving monetary and material donations as well as helping the needy on church basis.

CHAPTER ELEVEN

Tita Declared a Born Again

As time progressed, Tita was officially declared a Born Again Christian (BAC) by the spiritual branch of his Assemblies Mission, and he was recognized as having completely abandoned all his former evil ways and became one of the elect of God Himself. Special church service was held in recognition of Tita as a Born Again Christian which was attended by all important members of that Assemblies Mission church. Tita provided all that was used for 'Offertory' (monetary donation time after which, the reception of Holy Communion) that day he was delighted to be so recognized by their Spiritual Council of the Assemblies Mission (SCAM) of their branch. He received a lot of congratulations from both males and females of his church. Tita invited some of his closest friends to come and witness the declaration, and most of them came with gifts of different nature to the church.

Tita gradually began to avoid his family responsibilities and never cared as usual to visit home to see how his parents and sisters were doing and as well gave them money to tackle their basic responsibilities. Previously, before he became married to the church he usually sometimes sent money home through his former boss who was always so willing to accept his messages and deliver to his parents at home in the village. After two years of Tita's settlement he never stayed six months without visiting home, and whenever he visited he gave them more than enough money for feeding and miscellaneous expenses. His parents waited for about one year and Tita was yet to either show up or send them the needed message through Mpyama his brother whom his parents trusted absolutely. As their eyes were glued on the streets waiting for Tita's message, information reached them that Mpyama came home to the village. On hearing the news of his arrival Mr. Cazembi hurried to see him the following day. After series of discussions with him he told Mr. Cazembi that Tita had become encompassed by one religious organization called Assemblies Mission, and that he had tried all he could to withdraw him from the congregation but his son vowed tooth and nail to continue his membership with the Assemblies Mission.

Welcome home my brother. **Mr. Cazembi greeted**

Yes Sir. **Mpyama replied**

How are the township people and business? **Mr. Cazembi asked**

They were all fine before I left them, and business is going good. **Mpyama answered**

Did you see my son? I have not heard from him for about one year now. I don't know what the problem is. **Mr. Cazembi inquired**

I did not see your son Tita before coming home sir. And he has not come to either my shop or my resident for about more than one year now. **Mpyama answered**

Are you sure he is still alive? **Mr. Cazembi asked inquisitively**

Based on my inquiries from outside sources, I believe he is still alive. **Mpyama said**

Are you sure? **Mr. Cazembi worried**

That is what they said. **Mpyama replied**

Indeed, I am afraid. Oh my only son! Where have you been?
Mr. Cazembi said

Sir, please take it easy. You know I will not lie to you. **Mpyama
consoled**

Yes I know that. **Mr. Cazembi replied**

I know where his shop is and also where he lives and I am the
person who took him to the township. Sometimes I eavesdrop
around his side to know if he still exist, so, I indirectly saw him
before coming home, and he was healthy. **Mpyama assured**

Mr. Cazembi took a deep breath in and said;

So you saw him?

Yes I truly did. Do you remember the last time you visited him
concerning the church thing? **Mpyama asked**

Yes I recall. **Mr. Cazembi answered**

Tita insisted and joined the Assemblies Mission, and last time
I heard that he was officially declared a Born Again Christian, and
even before that time he has been avoiding me and others of such
nature and has wholly committed himself to the absolute care off
his church. **Mpyama said disturbed**

So, Tita my only son insisted on abandoning our traditional
beliefs to join the church? **Mr. Cazembi said in aware**

Yes sir, Tita disgraced me and made a fool of me and went his
way. He has joined the Assemblies Mission. **Mpyama replied**

Tita took such a decision despite all that I instructed him which
he promised me on my last visit to him that he would never do such
a thing. **Mr. Cazembi wondered**

Tita betrayed me. He dined with a particular woman without
my consent years ago in his own living room after which he
became a complete devil to himself and hurries only after sexual

gratification, and today Tita posses' great danger to our family line and community at large. Tita had contacts with prostitutes of the 'other side of town' and after that they lured him and slept with him and introduced him to their Assemblies Mission having been initiated into their own world. **Mpyama said**

On my last visit I asked him to tell me the truth about his affairs and he denied that. So, Tita has poured dysentery shit on my face. He has made me an object of ridicule before the presence of the people of our community. Tita my only son has completely abandoned me, preferring the ways of the prostitute as his best choice. Tita! Oh Tita! Tita!! **Mr. Cazembi felt dismayed**

Sir, there is no need to worry yourself, since he is still alive and as well healthy, he could one day retrospect and trace his way back home to his village people. Last time I confronted their pastor and he invited Tita who appeared before my presence with the pastor and few other church officials inclusive. I explained everything about Tita to them and told them that I wanted him back, and they asked Tita to decide, he totally denied me and nearly fought me. He told me to my own face that he desired me no more and had no other parents, sisters and relatives than their Assemblies Mission church members. "I have done everything I could to make him reason with me using his brilliant and blameless past as examples, but he bluntly refused to listen to me because he has felt the sweetness of the ladies underpants, and that seem to have encaged his mind". **Mpyama said**

Tita, 'so long a letter'. What a disgrace? What a disappointment? Oh my son, a coward? **Mr. Cazembi said**

Can you manage until he looks back sir? **Mpyama asked**

Yes my brother, I have some money saved from the money he has been giving to us so far. And last time, I visited him; he gave me a huge sum of money perhaps out of fear. Thus, we can manage. **Mr. Cazembi answered**

I am happy to hear that. Again, please sir. Do not over thought yourself about him, he is no longer a small child, and maybe he has his own purpose in life. **Mpyama pleaded**

It is alright my brother. I have committed him to the hands of God and our Ancestors. Since he has accepted that hydra headed religion which I warned him against. I told him to continue to emulate his brother and he declined and instead went his own way. Let us watch and see. **Mr. Cazembi said** and got up and left

Tita continued to combine his business with church services and morality, dignity and integrity with sexual pleasure. He became part of the Assemblies Mission's alpha and omega. As a young man with money, the church saw in him an avenue to enrich them and as well eat all their heart desires as it pertained to staple food. He was way far distanced from his family members at home in the village and seldom cared to ask of them. Every time his hop was full of members of his church, some as customers, some as grabbers, and some as beggars while the rest were sexual predators who always sniffed around to offer him to his satisfaction-maybe more.

As messages continued to stream from his parents in the village to him, one day he travelled home to see his parents and as well warned them on the need to either join him in his new faith or forget about him. He never cared to buy things for them as like before and he relegated the gifts meant for his sisters to the background. Tita arrived home to the bewilderment of his parents and sisters. Tita was received at home without reservation from either his parents or his sisters, but unfortunately, Tita came home with only a waterproof containing his bible, nothing more, nothing less, and some money in his pockets.

He arrived home late in the evening when his mother had almost finished dinner. He passed greetings with his parents and sisters who welcomed him as usual but this time with prying eyes. In the night of it after dinner his father called for him and also asked his sisters to be present.

Tita our son welcome home. **Mr. Cazembi said**

Thank you. **Tita answered**

How are you? **Mr. Cazembi asked**

I am fine in the lord. **Tita answered**

How is business? **Mr. Cazembi asked**

Business is moving according to our lord's wishes. **Tita answered**

What happened? It has been years now since you forgot about us. Is there any problems? **Mr. Cazembi inquired**

Everything is fine in the lord. **Tita replied**

Were you sick? **Mr. Cazembi asked**

No, I was fine in the lord. **Tita answered**

Will you shot up your mouth? What do you mean by fine in the lord, fine in the lord, lord, lord, everything lord? All that I have asked you, you answered in the lord. What does that nonsense mean? **Mr. Cazembi stammered**

Papa, if I may call you . . . **Tita said**

(Cuts in) what else will you call me? Am I your mate? **Mr. Cazembi surprised**

Do you understand that things have changed; things are no more as they used to be. In my previous visits home since I became my own boss, I came home with a lot of goodies but today I came without anything because I have chosen the only road to salvation. **Tita said**

What road to salvation my son? **Mr. Cazembi asked**

You see this thing (opens his waterproof and brought out his bible) is the only true way to salvation. **Tita answered**

Tita shot up your mouth. What are you trying to tell us? Are you crazy? Have you gone out of your mind? Look at this foolish boy. What is exactly wrong with you? **Mr. Cazembi angrily said**

Sorry to say that, in this book lays all my hope and in the Assemblies Mission do I have all my relatives. **Tita replied**

What Assemblies Mission? **Mr. Cazembi asked**

As you can see, I am now a Born Again Christian, a true elect of God Himself chosen by Him to win lost souls for Him so that at the end all of us will join Him in Heaven sharing the bliss. **Tita answered**

Tita! Tita!! I still don't understand what you mean. Do you mean that . . . ? **Mr. Cazembi said**

I mean that I am now a Born Again Christian and a strong member of the Assemblies Mission of my township branch. **Tita replied**

When did you join them? **Mr. Cazembi asked**

It has been a while. **Tita answered**

Didn't we agree when I last visited you that the church thing should be over until when the time is right-after a careful and thorough evaluation of their activities? **Mr. Cazembi asked**

Unfortunately, there was nothing I could do, I needed them, and so I joined them for my own good. **Tita answered**

You Tita, my only son betrayed me. You Tita betrayed me! Tita you betrayed me!! **Mr. Cazembi stammered**

Yes I had to. They out of my lustful desires for more became part of me, and surely, I can't again do without them because I need that. **Tita said**

What lured them to you, Tita my son? What made you do that Tita? **Mr. Cazembi confided**

I defiled Mpyama's orders and went out of my way to look at their naked bodies and was subsequently attracted by them, so I couldn't resist the urge thus I gave in, and I have no regrets because I continue to need them. **Tita replied**

Prostitute! Prostitute!! Prostitute!!! You are a complete disgrace to yourself, to your parents and your sisters, and to the entire community. You needed them—what a shame! You went out of your way because of your lustful desires to have sex with prostitutes, and you have become an absolute nonsense and you are happy about that. **Mr. Cazembi annoyingly said**

I have seen the way to salvation. **Tita replied**

Look at you! Look at you!! You have only seen the way to hell. I vowed before your presence when I last visited you that if you ever out of passionate jealousy mess yourself you will cease to be my son. You joined the Assemblies Mission to have that with them all, wide bastard. **Mr. Cazembi said**

No, that is not how it works back there because there are rules that must be followed as the true elect of God. We love each other and are always of help to each other. We have rules and we obey them. **Tita replied**

Why didn't you continue to emulate Mpyama as I warned you earlier? Why? **Mr. Cazembi asked**

Mpyama is his own person, and he is so stingy a person. I know what I want, so, I needed to walk away from him to get what I wanted, hence, I became a Born Again and he doesn't like that. **Tita answered**

You know that we depend on you, and that you are the only person that we can turn to as the only son. **Mr. Cazemi said**

I am going back to town tomorrow, first thing in the morning. **Tita replied**

You can go back this night if you want, silly being. **Mr. Cazembi said**

My son that is not the way it supposed to be. Your father loves you so much, and he does not want to lose you. Since you are now a grown up, you could have joined a church in error but there are still chances for you to recall and abandon the congregation and be yourself again. You are our only son who supports this family financially and materially, just think about that and consider our plights. **Mrs. Dunduza pleaded**

I have made my final decision and can't easily turn back. I have been declared a Born Again and that is all I want. I don't need any of you anymore. **Tita replied**

My son, our son: are you Tita? Are you sure that you are Tita our son? Tell me that you are Tita. **Mrs. Dunduza said crying**

Mama, I am Tita, but I am now on the lord's way. The members of the Assemblies Mission are now all I have and all that I care for because I have chosen with them. **Tita replied**

Tita so you have abandoned your parents and sisters and family responsibilities because of a particular Assemblies Mission somewhere in town. I do not believe you yet. **Mrs. Dunnduza said**

I have told you the truth and unless you people repent, I will have nothing to do with you all anymore. I want them and that is all I want. **Tita replied**

Tita does it mean that you have abandoned us after all these years and all these efforts. Do not allow me to be angry at you. **Mrs. Dunduza warned**

My wife forgets about the foolish wild boy who went all out to the 'other side of town'. **Mr. Cazembi said**

Please, Papa, you should mind the way you talk to me. I am no longer a kid do you know that? **Tita warned**

Tita, Tita, are you referring to me your father that way? **Mr. Cazembi angrily shouted**

You can't do anything. If you ever try me, I will show you this night. Try it and see. **Tita said** and got posed to return his father's punches if any.

Tita, you must fight me this night. Tita I must deal with you this night. **Mr. Cazembi responded** and got up from his sit

Tita angrily got up from his seat and walked to throw his father the first blow.

Tita are you challenging me? Are you about fighting me? You must fight me this night. It is either you kill me this night or I kill you. Two of us, one must go done this night. **Mr. Cazembi angrily said**

I'm ready for you. You are no longer my father. Dare I and I will deal with you this night? I don't need you, I am ready for you. **Tita sternly replied**

Mr. Cazembi immediately rushed and grabbed his well sharpened sword and was about to pierce Tita with it and his wife and daughters restricted him and pleaded with him to let Tita live, and Tita wanted to venture outside and her sisters restricted him. As the tempo died down, Tita's mother began to cry.

Tita! Tita!! I don't think it is you because if it is you, you have disgraced me. Tita have made a mockery of me o . . . o . . . o . . . o . . . Tita has disgraced me o . . . o . . . o . . . o . . . o . . . Tita has rejected me o . . . o . . . o . . . o . . . Tita has abandoned me o . . . o . . . o . . . o . . . o . . . Tita has betrayed me o . . . o . . . o . . . o . . . o . . . o . . . Tita my son is gone o . . . o . . . o . . . o . . . Where else can I see Tita again o . . . o . . . o . . . o . . . o . . . Tita you have abandoned the womb that bored you o . . . o . . . o . . . o . . . Tita have forgotten my pain o . . . o . . . o . . . o . . . o . . . As she continued to cry her daughters came to her assistance and began to shed tears while pleading with her to stop crying.

Senior Tita, you should have stayed back in town and continued to enjoy your mess instead of coming back home to the village to cause problems for everyone. **Kalonji said**

Senior Tita, next time don't ever come back home to start this type of nonsense. **Nyahuma said**

After been restricted by his wife and daughters Mr. Cazembi angrily went inside to their inner room. Tita never cared to console anyone. He barely passed the night and in the morning he departed.

Tita back in town never cared about his parents at home again, and he continued to avoid any contacts with Mpyama. Tita gradually dedicated all his belongings to the Assemblies Mission. After few years of his disregard to his parents and sisters, Kalonji one of his sisters got married to a business man who lived in another city. And when Tita was informed of the day of her pride price, he disowned them all and reiterated his decision that he never knew them again unless they were prepared to join him in the pursuit of the true way to heaven. Tita continued to lose the contents of his shop piece by piece while been the guy in town for all scheduled church bazaar. As time progressed Tita dealt the final blow by disassociating himself from the rest of his community members, especially those in the town with him because he regarded them as infidels and pariahs. Tita stopped visiting anyone of his community members and other extended family relatives who refused to accept his idea of 'born againism'. He stopped attending meetings of any sort that could offer him the opportunities of an unavoidable contact with those he refused to mingle further with.

Meanwhile, after the marriage of Kalonji things became relatively alleviated to his parents and other younger sisters because she got married to a good family that 'understands what it means to be an in-law; that it is a mutual relationship between different family members". So, Kalonji's marriage deviate the eyes of his community from looking further at him as a fool who declined to understand the importance of parenthood which 'is still so vital in Central African Nations'. All invitations by his community members and relatives to attend their occasions and ceremonies were turned down by him as long as the inviter does not accept his religious philosophy. Those who were closer to him and who did not like 'given in' warned him on the dangers of shouting praises in the middle of ladies in their bikinis, and he debunked them with a mere wave of hand and told them to either appreciate him or totally avoided him.

CHAPTER TWELVE

Tita Devoted

Tita lost all intimate contacts that refused to accept his membership with the Assemblies Mission and kept at arm's length any of his tolerated friends, relatives, and community members who ever dared to question his luxurious expenses and donations to his church. Tita fall in absolute love with the bible and with many female members of his church. And there was no time that passed without the agglomeration of certain members of his church in his shop. As Tita paid more attention to the church than concentrating more in his shop, his shop value started to decline.

Tita began to spend more time in the reading of his bible in their parish thereby relegating his business to the background and, and his customers began to complain to nearby traders about his none commitment to his shop as usual. His customers asked what was wrong with him and those of his fellow traders who cared explained to them that he had became a Born Again Christian and that he took his church thing seriously also. On gradual skipping of his shop, his major customers began to back away, and turned to those who could be available during important business hours, because customers dislike shopping in a place that do not take their significance into considerations. And for any business to flourish despite how small, 'customers remain the pivot under which such businesses balance without which such a business goes under'. Considering the location of his shop only those who are always available were the only ones who could make the day, and since he had no apprentice any selling opportunity lost was final unless the customer decided to repeat the following days or left a message that he/she would be back on another day.

Tita was later offered the option of preaching to their Sunday school children by pastor Lasana, and he willingly accepted the offer with grace and without putting other things into consideration. Meanwhile, Tita after refusing to call it quit with his Assemblies Mission's abracadabra, he changed his work days from that he emulated from Mpyama. He started working on Mondays and staying off on Sundays. He was so good at preaching that those kids loved to listen to him preach to them and gradually he began to preach to them during other different days thereby further reducing the number of hours spent in his business per day, and its effect began to show in his assets values as it pertained to his shop. Although he still had some money, it was falling fast below the expectations of his peers and some of his close alleys began to question his whereabouts, and urged him to retrospect and rethink because if he continued the way he was moving, things could eventually got out of hand. They advised him that there was never a time they asked him not to spent time at his church but that he needed to concentrate more on restructuring his shop and always been there when needed so that his customers could be retained and those who had already gone out could be lured back. Tita debunked their advices and told them that he preferred the way of himself, that they should allow things to move the lord's way.

Tita became infatuated with preaching the bible and began to extend his preaching to township communities, and as he continued to preach, combining his brilliancy with eloquent outsiders loved to listen to him, and he was later involved in delivering sermons in their church. As he got encysted with the duties of consistent preaching thereby forgetting his daily business responsibilities and with no person nearby even his church members to cover for him in his shop, while on church assignments, consequently, the contents value of his shop nosedived and Tita was caught unawares. Tita almost lost all, leaving only merchandises with value for his daily feeding and perhaps the payment of his rent. Mpyama sent messages to Tita warning him on the dangers involved in his recalcitrant attitude that had resulted to the almost complete loss of his merchandise forcing him to fall back from grace therefore running faster the road to poverty. Mpyama made it known to him that becoming a beggar with bible clinched in his hand was not the best solution because to secure his portion and felt better was the most important aspect of his life. He begged Tita to abandon self betrayal, self annihilation, self banishment, self imposition of immorality, self abandonment, self disgrace, self disregard, and self debasement and return back to himself and as well better his conditions.

Tita refused to listen to Mpyama's advice and continued to wallow in the abyss of destruction, despair, chaos and anarchy. Tita never made any other effort to resuscitate himself, rehabilitate his shop and remained committed to his business. The cancer worm of religious passion had already eaten deeper into Tita's moral fabrics and there was no other option left for him than to obey the rule of the game. And having portrayed himself as a wealthy person before his church members prior to his asset dwindling, he would feel dismayed begging for money outside of the Assemblies Mission's approved order. And having out of his own carelessness and gluttony for what he does not know much about dedicated his time to the 'Cult of Blood and Flesh', he deemed it unwise to ask for financial assistance from his fellow traders either in the same market line or those he knew in the market. He continued to dislike Mpyama although he could decide to give him a second chance should he truthfully back off the congregations mess.

Tita continued to manage his shop, selling when he could and using his meager profits for feeding, house rents and other minor basic needs and also continued to contribute to women of his church when he could. Tita stopped listening to messages from home and never cared to ask of anyone at his home village again. Meanwhile, after his 'near contact conflict' with his father he seldom visited home, and whenever he visited, Mr. Cazembi like a father continued to tell him to come out from the Assemblies Mission and come back home, while his mother continued to plead with him to recall their hardships in the former days and have a rethink but Tita bluntly refused to pay heed to the advises, and he cared less to visit Kalonji.

In one of the occasions when he visited home to the village, his father sent for some of his kinsmen and when they gathered;

My kinsmen welcome. **Mr. Cazembi greeted**

Thank you, the son of the soil. **Kinsmen responded at once**

I sent for you. **Mr. Cazembi said**

We have come. **Kinsmen replied**

You all know that a toad does not run in a broad daylight in vain, it is either something is chasing or it is chasing something. **Mr. Cazembi said**

Yes very clear. **Kinsmen replied**

I call you all because of Tita my only son. **Mr. Cazembi said**

Yes. What happened? **Mr. Oronde (Appointed)**, kinsmen spokesman asked

Tita is no longer with his parents, sisters and all of us. He has abandoned us. **Mr. Cazembi said**

Where is he? **Mr. Oronde asked**

He should be around. **Mr. Cazembi answered**

Call him, his presence is needed before you tell us anything about him. **Mr. Oronde said**

Tita! Tita!! Tita a . . . a . . . a . . . **Mr. Cazembi called**

Are you sure he is around? **Mr. Oronde asked**

Yes, he ought to be around. **Mr. Cazembi replied**

Tita! Tita . . . a . . . a . . . a . . . **Mr. Cazembi called again**

Tita your father is calling you, go and see why he is calling you. **A woman voice said in the backyard.**

Are you sure he is hearing you? **Mr. Oronde asked**

I have raised my voice to the highest level, unless he had gone out, but I doubt that. **Mr. Cazembi answered**

Tita sluggishly came out from the outside and stared at them

Yes. **Tita asked**

Our kinsmen here want to see you. **Mr. Cazembi answered**

Yes? **Tita asked standing up**

Sit down. **Mr. Oronde said**

I prefer to stand up. **Tita replied**

Sit down my son, sit down. **Mr. Oronde said**

I want to stand up. **Tita replied**

Will you sit down, my friend? **Mr. Oronde pleaded**

No, I want to stand up. **Tita insisted**

It is either you sit down or we go for you. **Mr Oronde insisted**

I prefer to stand up. **Tita head bent**

Please, my kinsmen, there is no need to abandon me, stay and listen to my complainant against him. **Mr. Cazembi said**

Tita or whatever is your name. Sit down immediately or we force you down ourselves. **Mr. Oronde warned**

Tita slowly sat down and Mr. Cazembi told his kinsmen everything about Tita from the time he was in school to the time he got settled and through to his present time;

Tita. **Mr. Oronde called**

Yes sir. **Tita answered**

Did you hear what your father just told us about you? **Mr. Oronde asked**

Yes. **Tita replied**

Did Mr. Cazembi your father lie against you? **Mr. Oronde asked**

No. **Tita answered**

So, he told us the truth? **Mr. Oronde asked**

Yes, he said the truth. **Tita answered**

Mr. Cazembi we can now back you up. **Mr. Oronde said**

I cannot lie against my only son, and you all know me. I do not phrase against innocent people. **Mr. Cazembi said**

Tita, do you understand your position as the only son of your parents? **Mr. Oronde asked**

Yes I do. **Tita replied**

Why have you chosen to abandon your parents and your sisters? **Mr. Oronde asked**

I did not abandon them. **Tita answered**

Why have you chosen to neglect your parents and sisters? **Mr. Oronde asked**

I have parents and sisters in the Assemblies Mission, and I have always been with them. **Tita answered**

Do you mean your own parents and sisters in the Assemblies Mission. **Mr. Oronde said**

I mean them in the Assemblies Mission. **Tita replied**

So, who are Mr. Cazembi and Mrs. Dunduza to you? **Mr. Oronde asked**

They are no longer my parents in the lord. **Mr. Oronde said**

And your sisters? **Mr. Oronde asked**

They are also no longer my sisters in the lord. **Tita answered**

Why have you chosen to disown them? **Mr. Oronde asked**

I am now a born again Christian, a chosen elect of God himself, and those you referred as my parents and sisters are pagans. They have not repented from their sinful ways. **Tita said**

You saw your parents and sisters in the Assemblies Mission? **Mr. Oronde asked**

Yes that is exactly where they are. **Tita answered**

My son that is not the way it works down here, if you have chosen to join a particular Christian denomination that should not blindfold you from distinguishing between your mere church members and your biological parents and sisters, and being a member of the Assemblies Mission 'must not deter you' from carrying out your family responsibilities as the only son. **Mr. Oronde said**

I no longer know them and all other similar relatives. **Tita replied**

What? What did you just said? **Mr. Oronde asked**

I don't know them anymore and it's been long since I told them that. **Tita answered**

If so, why are you here? **Mr. Oronde asked**

Visiting. **Tita answered**

Visiting who and who? **Mr. Oronde asked**

Visiting my house. **Tita replied**

Do you see that there must be something wrong with you? We all know you in this village and also know how much you have done. Listen my son, some of us also have children who have chosen to abandon our traditional beliefs and formed alliances with the so called western religion (what a mess-a religion that originated from the present day Middle East renamed), especially protestants who today operates from many make-shift houses. And frankly most of our sons do understand their family needs and never abandon their parents while fighting for the faith. **Mr. Oronde said**

I have done that, and I have decided to be where I want to be. **Tita replied**

Whatever wrongs you must have done concerns you the most. We are telling you that this "New Order" is a disastrous option. Following the ways of a particular religious design should not prevent you from taking good and adequate care of your parents. We know how rough the townships are and we understand that you could choose such an option to cover your skin and protect yourself from the risks of the township, but when that happens it should not consume you completely to the point of abandoning your parents for any reason, especially when they are not in any way at fault. **Mr. Oronde said**

I can't continue to take care of them unless they follow me in the same Faith. **Tita replied**

Mr. Cazembi did you hear what he said? **Mr. Oronde asked**

That is impossible. I cannot abandon my Traditional Beliefs for any rip-offs or passionate encounter, and in the name of any God that has chosen to elevate himself far higher than the real source(s) that produced him/her. I am a completely traditional person and all of you know that. Invention of any God or gods so as to enrich ones pocket is nothing but only and only exercises in futility, no front end and back end loads respectively. **Mr. Cazembi said**

Tita, you have heard. Your father cannot go back to lick his own vomit, he forbids that. So, if you have chosen to deviate from the family traditional beliefs, for any reason you can do that but not molesting your parents and sisters, abandoning your family responsibilities disowning all relevant relatives and making yourself a social outcast. So what final answer do you want to give us concerning taking care of your biological parents and sisters? **Mr. Oronde said**

I have told Mr. Cazembi and his family since years back that I have no parents etc in this home village, and for the past years now I have not given them any of my money because I do not desire them anymore. I cannot say more than I have already said. **Tita reiterated**

Mr. Cazembi have you heard what he said, we cannot force him any further but pity are those who out of gluttony, passion, quick wealth syndrome, and other forms of material acquisitions, fabricated and forged in the name of the Supernatural Being, for their journeys shall be endless, and they shall seek and shall never found and there days shall be mired with bloody conflicts and deaths endlessly. **Mr. Oronde said**

Yes. **Others responded**

Thank you my kinsmen for answering my emergency call, and may it be well with all of you. My first daughter Kalonji is married I can rely on her husband's assistance to continue with existence, but left for Tita, my only son, I am done with him unless he repents. You are my witness. **Mr. Cazembi said**

I want that, I have done that and I will never change. **Tita said**

His kinsmen left and asked him to take it easy and not to allow the thought of his son's blindness to destabilize family. **Mr. Oronde said,** and they departed

CHAPTER THIRTEEN

Tita Ordained a Deacon

As Tita continued to dedicate his time to preaching and other church activities he was nominated to be ordained a deacon as was approved by their pastor and the Ordination Council of the Assemblies Mission (OCAM) of his branch. He was perplexed by the news of his nomination and he accepted the offer with enthusiasm. OCAM selected Tita after seen that he had dedicated most part of his time to the services and growth of the church both financially, materially and religiously. They decided to retain Tita within their congregation since he still had something left in his shop no matter how small; they were also dependent on that. His connections were of immense help to most of the church members because through him they could have access to the other traders, especially within his market line. Besides, Tita always assisted them in making buck purchases from the outside market where he went for 'whole sale' purchases because in that case things were relatively cheaper.

With consultations with Tita a day for the ordination was confidentially selected by him and he was told about the necessary religious wears accustomed to his religious denominations-Assemblies Mission. He provided money for the purchase of the relevant wears and other accompanying attires, and also money to buy things like meat, soft drinks etc that will be used to attend to those that would be invited for such never held before ceremony by him, while he provided the needed quantity of rice, beans and other ingredients necessary for its cooking. After the provisions of all the things requested from him, Tita extended his invitation to his relevant friends, that is, fellow Born Again Christians from other religious denominations and those who continued to relate to him despite his religious ideology and absolute dedication ignoring all family ties. Some of the invitees accepted his invitations without questions while the rest refused and merely congratulated him.

Tita used a substantial part of the meager amount of money still invested in his shop for the celebration of his ordination as Deacon. Many of his invitees attended his ordinations and that day they church was filled to the brim, and his visitors also attended with gifts of different kinds. Pastor Lasana described Tita as a young man who was lost in an ocean of sin without hope in sight and had spent days, losing all his energies and was gradually sinking deeper and deeper, and suddenly a fisher man on his fishing canoe found him and brought him back ashore and revived him and rehabilitated, re-energized him and returned him back to life ones again, and that 'that is today his un-sinful ways'. The pastor said that Tita had been tasted under differ degrees of the scorching sunlight and under different inches of downpours but he Tita remained resolute, determined and dedicated to follow this course, a road leading to Heaven where there is only bliss and happiness. 'Tita's is a true fellow of this journey to salvation'. He said that Tita was like a helpless child when he was introduced to him, and like a father he accepted him whole heartedly, "Tita had no place to turn to, no friends, no relatives, and absolutely nobody to offer him the needed help, but the Assemblies Mission received him like an orphan and made him whole again" and more so, that Tita had become not only successful but prosperous both financially and spiritually, and that Tita had reached spiritual climax which put him above others that 'he is today a Deacon of the Assemblies Mission. And he praised Tita and asked him to continue with his good works which was sure to yield the desired fruits. The OCAM of his church eulogized him and asked him to draw from his immense biblical experience to continue to set good examples before the other church members and outsiders as well whom he may be in contact with. Pastor Lasana also stated he was amazed by the large number of people that 'today come to worship with them, a sign of Tita's impact in the Assemblies Mission".

Tita felt elated and in smiles. He thanked their pastor for believing in him, for been there for him when he needed help, especially in his most hours of need, for been his brother's keeper, and for aiding him become whole again, especially during periods of uncertainties when he had no other place to turn to. He described their pastor "who like a good father saw his child crying and curdled him and consoled him and gently put him on the bed and he slept off only to wake up in the morning of another good day". Tita also expressed his gratitude to the OCAM for selecting him by merit without recourse to favoritism and relativism. He urged them to continue to express the teachings of the bible in actions and in deeds. And he also expressed appreciation to his invitees for coming to be with him that day leaving all that they could have gained. He admonished all that were present to embrace the bible and draw from its teachings in every of their daily dealings because 'a closed bible does not read itself, when it is opened and scanned through shall you really understand its full contents'. Finally, Tita promised to continue to do whatever necessary according to the Assemblies Mission rules so as to ensure that their church continued to care for its members in the lord's ways.

After his ordination as a Deacon, Tita's shop became almost empty although sometimes he had sales and also went to the outside market to purchase merchandize. The sum of money still invested in his shop was too small to go farther than that was necessary unless there was an influx of money into Tita's shop, the only option available for him would be to close his shop and become fully employed by the Assemblies Missions because in that way he was sure to eat and perhaps allowed to stay in his rented room probably with other church members. Worst, before his deacon ordination, he sold some of his household properties so as to provide the needed money for making all the necessary purchases and that further reduced his financial stand because he could sold some of those things and used the money for 'whole sale' purchase that would be retailed in his shop thereby giving him the needed hedge to stay in business at least a little longer. And he could no longer go home to ask his father to pledge another portion of land on his behalf because the one that was already pledged although he had paid back the money to the pledgee, his father may not be willing again to bring out any land for pledge on his behalf, and having disgraced his own parents in the presence of their kinsmen, he would not be accepted by him anymore unless he called those kinsmen and pleaded to his father in their presence and that Tita was not ready to do. And he cannot use force against his father because although his father was also the only son, if he does; his people, the youths like him would stone him to death. While his fellow traders felt for him and contemplated on such options that could ameliorate his situation, Tita was unperturbed and busy biting more than he could chew. He continued to be at their church even when not necessary, praying, preaching etc, until a stage when he could no longer continue without the assistance of the church when if nothing was not done quickly, he could lose all, room and shop etc respectively. And during all these crises he never turned to any of his relatives for any form of assistance nor travel home to beg his parents for forgiveness, especially his father whom he nearly fought.

Not knowing exactly what next to do he approached their pastor and explained everything to him.

Pastor. **Tita called**

Yes, my brother in the lord. **Pastor Lasana responded**

I came to see you. **Tita said**

I am always here for you my dear brother in the lord. **Pastor replied**

Please, things are no more as they used to be before, so if something is not done fast it could be over for me soon. I am on the edge financially without an exit route, and I will not tell you that I have anybody to turn to except you otherwise things may get out of hand. **Tita said**

Are you contemplating suicide? **Pastor Lasana inquisitively asked**

That is not yet an option, pastor. **Tita answered**

Waive any idea of suicide off your mind because it has not yet reached to that stage. **Pastors Lasana said**

I will always abide by your advice, Pastor. **Tita replied**

What exactly do you need? **Pastor Lasana asked**

Pastor, please, I need money to invest in my shop so that I can look good again. **Tita answered**

I see your point; unfortunately, the Assemblies Mission does not offer such opportunities because this place is not large enough for more members that their monetary contributions could leave behind substantial amount of money at the end of the day. **Pastor Lasana said**

Pastor, please, please, everything in my shop may be gone by tomorrow and I have nothing else to do, and I cannot go back to the village. What next shall I do? It has never been this tough for me before. **Tita pleaded**

Tita Mr. you understand that you are one of the most important members of this church and as a Deacon your position really matters. I will not ask you to return back to the village, no that is not for the good and benefit of this congregation. You know my position as the pastor that all my financial transactions are approved by the Church Committee on Budgets and Expenses (CCBE), in that case, I want to promise you that I will get with them and present to them your situation and see what they will decide. So get with me later to know what they decided. **Pastor Lasana assured**

Thank you very much pastor. Thank you so much. **Tita grateful**

Don't mention, we are one in the lord. **Pastor Lasana said**

Tita left and was partially satisfied by the pastor's response but was also troubled by questions like: what if the committee decided not to approve any money for him? Should such a situation becomes the only answer, what else that could be his options was the only thing in his mind. He never concentrated on anything because he had no other option left than either to pack his things and go home to his village or he joined those at the rough side of town and become like them comes the finish date. On the promised day, he hurried to see his pastor;

Pastor Good Morning. **Tita greeted**

Welcome my brother in the lord. **Pastor Lasana replied**

I am afraid. **Tita said in low tone**

There is no need to worry my brother. **Pastor Lasana replied**

I have come to know the outcome of your meeting with the CCBE. **Tita said**

I am very much aware of that. **Pastor Lasana replied**

Any hopes? **Tita asked**

Yes, they have made a decision. **Pastor Lasana answered**

Oh! Praise the lord. **Tita replied**

The lord is good. **Pastor Lasana responded**

All the time. **Tita said**

I have explained everything to them and they said that there was no much money in the church treasury box so as to offer you the needed help at this time, but as I insisted they approved a certain amount of CFA Franc for you on the conditions that it will be interest bearing. You will pay the interest at the end of every month and the loan is a twelve month loan, no extension of repayment is possible. **Pastors Lasana said**

Amen! Amen!! **Tita shouted**

Any month that you failed to make the need interest payments, the loan could be recalled, and you can either pay in cash or with assets when the loan is recalled. Do you agree to the terms and conditions? **Pastor Lasana inquired**

Yes pastor. What else can I do? **Tita agreed**

Do you understand that when our money is loaned to you as a member of the Assemblies Mission, you will continue to perform your necessary church responsibilities like before or even more? **Pastor Lasana asked**

Yes, I understand, pastor. **Tita answered**

Pastor brought out the money from the middle of his bible and handed it to Tita to count. And Tita counted the money, and told the pastor how much it was.

Yes, exactly that amount. **Pastor Lasana said**

But pastor Lasana, considering the 20% monthly interest attached to it, I thought that the committee could have increased it a little beet. **Tita said**

You see my brother, you were even lucky they considered your plights. This church doesn't normally give money out for arms like this; the committee really did you a favor because I pressured and because they have seen your contributions to the church so far. **Pastor Lasana replied**

I thank God that they ever considered me although this money is like a maintenance ration. After paying the interest, I will be left with nothing of the profits to feed myself. I will try to see how far I can go with this money. **Tita said**

And do not forget that as a Deacon we expect you to lead by example financially and materially. **Pastor Lasana said**

Yes pastor, I understand that. **Tita replied**

Before you leave, I want to tell you that having gone through your credentials, I came to realize that you are an intelligent person more than most of those in this church, and in that case I appealed to the Ordination Council to see if there is any way you could be helped through our other branches outside of this state, I mean, our other branches overseas. And they promised me that they would look into my request and sooner they would write a letter to the Assemblies Mission Headquarters to include you among those that could be selected based on a type of lottery system for Pastoral Training overseas. They told me to disclose that to you so that I can give them the feedback based on your response. **Pastor Lasana said**

Pastor, I didn't attend secondary school. I only stopped at the primary level. **Tita replied**

Do you have FSLC? **Pastor Lasana asked**

Yes, pastor, and I made a 'Distinction". **Tita answered**

That's great, wonderful. That is enough, it can serve the purpose. **Pastor Lasana said**

In that case I hereby accept the ordination council offer. Is there any string attached? **Tita asked**

Not that I know for now, but should you be selected, we will inquire about that. **Pastor Lasana responded**

Thank you so much for your concern pastor. **Tita said**

That is alright my brother in the lord. I will go ahead and relay the message of your acceptance to the Ordination Council, and let us just hope that you will make it. They selection happens every four years, and the next one is sometime next year. **Pastor Lasana said**

Again, I am very grateful pastor. I just hope that I got elected and get away from this condition of living and get myself trained like you. **Tita cheerfully said**

That's nice, that is what everybody wants. Imagine becoming a pastor and controlling your own parish. **Pastor Lasana said**

I will be going pastor (got up and left).

Have a nice evening. **Pastor Lasana said**

I will pastor. **Tita replied**

CHAPTER FOURTEEN

Tita Selected for Pastoral Seminary

Tita went and combined his church loaned money with the little money already in his business and it was still a far cry from bringing his merchandise level to a state that could sustain him for a reasonable number of times unless he put in extra efforts. Having known that his borrowed money could be the last straw that broke the camel's back, he intensified his efforts so as to make sure that he was not laughed at. He started coming to his shop and opening earlier than any other person in his market line and staying a little late despite the odds, and he began to refuse credit to most of his church members, telling them that the money invested in his shop belonged to another person who would not take it easy with him should he ever ventured to disappoint him. He also stopped all kinds of gift 'grab it from the shelf', and 'empty your bag offers' and was running so fast without looking back like a person whose 'clock has run late'. He also reduced his presence at the Assemblies Mission but always been their when necessary and his church officials did understood his point and they never complained.

Despite all his efforts to re-stock his shop to a more sustainable level, the twenty percent (20%) interest barrier placed on the loan made it difficult for him to stay a little more comfortable with his meager profits, because after the 20% monthly interest virtually nothing was left for him, and after paying his rent and feeding, he was almost left with only few CFA Franc out of his profit. And besides, his all night pleasure attitude never stopped, he continued to knack women without retrospection and that eventually gulped the remaining CFA Franc he could have kept aside at the end of the week/month for emergencies. Tita continued to live from hand to mouth, and also continued to hope that miracle could happen and he becomes one of those selected for the pastoral training overseas. Some of his friends were happy that at least he was still in business having elongated his days of been forced out from his room by the landlord or been forced out of his shop by the shop renter because he paid the shop owner monthly rent too. Months went by and Tita continued to make the 20% interest payments on his loan without owing any CFA Franc, and that prevented the loan from been recalled by the Assemblies Mission his lender.

At the time when he had almost forgotten everything about the pastoral lottery, pastor Lasana invited him. On arriving at their church, Tita saw other church members sited. He thought that maybe they were about to recall the loan whereas he does not owe them any interest.

Praise the lord. **Tita shouted**

Halleluiah **Church members responded**

Praise the living lord. **Tita shouted again**

Halleluiah **Church members responded**

Halleluiah **Tita said**

Amen. **Church members responded**

Tita, welcome our brother in the lord. **Pastor Lasana said**

Thank you (sat down). **Tita replied**

I invited you to shear the good news with you. The lord has finally answered our prayers. You have been selected for a pastoral training overseas for this year. **Pastor Lasana said**

Praise the lord! Praise the lord!! Praise is to the leaving lord!!! **Tita shouted**

Amen! Amen!! Amen!!! **Church members responded**

The lord our God has finally listened to my cries, our plea to come for rescue. **Tita said**

Yes, the lord our God is good. He has done great things for us because he loves us and we are his elect, the lord lives. **Pastor Lasana replied**

Today, this day, I have known that. I have known that. He is there . . . watching us. **Tita said**

Yes, our brother in the lord. **Church members replied**

Thank you so much my brothers and sisters. **Tita said**

We are happy for you. **Church member said**

And more good news is that you have nothing to contribute, the Assemblies Mission will take care of your travel expenses until you arrival at our Headquarters overseas and our brothers and sisters over there take over. **Pastor Lasana said**

Praise . . . ! **Tita said**

Halleluiah **Church members responded**

Your journey commences in few months time, so, you have to get ready before the time. Take (handed him over an envelope), everything about it is written down, and therefore, you must be ready in at least two weeks before the departure date. Your plane tickets etc are all in there, keep them safe and do not throw them away. The Ordination Council members who are also here will later get with you before your departure and the CCBE will also see you within few days. **Pastor Lasana said**

I don't believe this. What am I seen? That's marvelous. Me. Tita, traveling overseas? I will never forget you people, no I will ever. **Tita surprised**

That is why I invited you. **Pastor Lasana said**

Thank you my brothers and sisters and my parents. Thank you all so much. You have really given me another opportunity in life. **Tita replied happily**

Continue with prayers, everything will be alright. **Pastor Lasana said**

I will . . . **Tita replied**

Tita, I will tell you when to meet with CCBE as soon as possible. **Pastor Lasana said**

I will be around. **Tita replied**

Tita was so happy that his dream of becoming pastor had come true because since he ever joined the Assemblies Mission, he had been contemplating on how to become a pastor, and that was why he had dedicated most of his time and even assets to the church. He began to work the streets and his market line with his head high. Tita circulated the message of his selection to all that appreciated and approved of his membership with his congregation and they were surprised to hear that Tita, the guy that they thought was at the brink of self imposed disaster had seen hope down the horizon. That Tita had been saved from 'walk out of my shop' mockery by fellow traders. Some of them joined him in praising the lord and also wish him safe journey to his next destination in another country-overseas. And others asked him to remember them while overseas.

The news of his selection to pastoral training overseas immediately reached Mpyama who without delay sent information to Tita's parents, and Mr. Cazembi warned Tita to stay away from entrusting all his hope in a distanced land in the name of the Assemblies Mission. He warned Tita not to venture anywhere overseas because what he saw was more dangerous than what Tita was promised. Mr. Cazembi made it clear to his son that they said 'next destination' could be a heaven of hell let loosed. "Tita you should please my only son stay back down here in the country and continue with your trade because I think that is the best thing for you. do not out of folly follow a prostitute overseas in the name of the Assemblies Mission, because I am afraid you will not come back yourself again. To play this type of game is much better at home than overseas because when overseas, you also could be taken for a really rough ride. I am your father, we are your parents, I am completely not part of your journey overseas, and I wonder what you will turn out to be as a pastor. You abandoned us long ago and we still consider you as our own. Consider the pains that you have inflicted on your mother in particular, and please my son, please, does have a rethink. We your parents may be gone before your return from overseas". Tita received the message sent by his father and simply said 'nothing on earth will ever make me to back away from this journey overseas. I must become a pastor'.

Tita met with the CCBE and they informed him that they needed their money at least two weeks before his departure and that more money was needed to finalize his travel and to cover other minor expenses. Tita promised to sell all his merchandise off and give them back their money. And since what could be left out of his 'close sale' may not be enough, he also assured them that he would sell the remainder of his properties so as to complete the other requested money. They accepted his decision and informed him that there would be no extension on the money collection date, otherwise that could affect his travel and completely stopped him from traveling overseas for the pastoral training which he had long waited for.

Tita also met with the OCAM and they disclosed to him everything concerning the pastoral training in the areas of education and learning. They told him that pastoral training involved enrolment into the Seminary School of the Assemblies Mission that educates seminarians and get them more equipped with their would be professions' which has to do with thorough study of the bible. They also made it known to him that there were other relevant aspects of the training which should be in line with the Order of the Assemblies Mission, and that all his feeding, basic needs and school fees would be taken care of by their international branch overseas which happened to be the Headquarters of the Assemblies Mission for the African Division. They urged him to be himself and never to disappoint their church, and Tita promised to make them proud.

Tita made good all his promises to CCBE, and a sendoff party was scheduled in honor of him. Meanwhile, Sanga who just got married scheduled to pass a night with him before the sendoff party in about two days time, and Tita accepted the offer and had another sexual pleasant night with her. Tita's sendoff party was a huge ceremony and many people were at present to celebrate with him in their church compound and other members of their church outside his branch were also present. And Tita spent his last card in contributing to the success of his sendoff party. Like before Tita was again described by pastor Lasana this time as somebody who had been called upon by the good Lord himself for pastoral ordination overseas so that tomorrow he would stand on the temple preaching the gospel of truth to the hearing of the people. In his words 'Tita has become like me in part as he is here today, his traveling overseas finalizes his journey to the plateau of truth where God reveals Himself to all his elects. He travels overseas to the Assemblies Mission Headquarters to learn, know and understand the bible and its teachings and will one day come back to be a living testimony of the Son of Truth'. He described Tita as a precious asset to the Assemblies Mission that could not easily be bought anywhere in the market. Tita expressed his gratitude to all that were at present and asked them to always remember him in prayers because as a new person the foreign land's shocks were expected, and to overcome such shocks their prayers were so vital.

On the scheduled departure date Tita was accompanied to their International Airport by select members of his church. After which he boarded an airline to his 'next destination' overseas where he would receive all the necessary trainings and education needed to become an ordained pastor. What happened next time will surely tell.

CHAPTER FIFTEEN

Tita Overseas

Tita's journey to his next destination overseas lasted for several hours on the air before their airplane finally touched down at the designated International Airport of his host country. He had not been in an airplane before and had his first liftoff experience, and as the airplane gradually ascended to a stable level and continued to cruise forward; he paid absolute attention to the flight attendants instructions of emergency measures. Before liftoff, the flight attendants instructed all passengers to put on their seat belts which were located right there on their seat belts, and that was necessary to reduce liftoff turbulence effects. Tita without wasting time carried out the flight attendants instructions, he found it a little difficult to fastened his seat belt but politely requested the help of one of the flight attendants who so willingly came to his side and showed him how to. Few hours after the aircraft liftoff, he was served either water or soft drinks depending on his choice and depending also on special orders as could be placed on his behalf by his sponsors if any. Tita chose to sip soft drinks. About half way to touch, he was served light food based on his selection which was mostly bread with either chicken or fish with other appetizers. In the morning about one hour prior to touch down, he was served with either coffee or tea with small slices of bread depending on his choice. And while the airplane lingered in the air, Tita fall asleep and had to dose most of the flight hours off, and that saved him from the fatigue due to long hours of flight. Before the airplane finally touched down, Tita again fastened his seatbelt and the airplane gradually descended and later touched ground. And the airplane spent a couple of minutes on the runway before it finally docked at one of the dockets, and the flight cabin crew said 'you can now exit the plane, thank you for flying with us'. And Tita unfastened his seatbelt and took his luggage and headed straight to the exit door and exited the airplane and walked through the corridor to the reception lounge.

Tita entered the lounge and there were a lot of people in that place; some of them were returning passengers, some of them tourist, some of them taxi/bus drivers looking for passengers while the rest were those like his host (members of the Assemblies Mission) who came to the airport to welcome relatives, friends and visitors. Some of those who came for reception carried kind of placards with names of those they were waiting for boldly written on them, and to enhance transparency, those placards had white background with black words. Inside the lounge Tita got confused and since he had not seen any of his host before, the best thing to do was to stay one place and enable them easily find him. As he stayed looking at some of the returning travelers, he noticed some of them carefully looking at the placards and talking to some of those placard holders after which those returning travelers followed them. So, Tita decided to approach the placard holding area and read them through as they were held to see if he could find his name in any of those signs. And he continued to read them;

he eventually saw his name on the placard held by one beautiful average age women, as he greeted the woman;

Good Day. **Tita greeted**

How are you? **Woman asked**

I am fine. **Tita answered**

Are you Tita? **Woman asked**

Yes, I am. **Tita answered**

What is your religious denomination? **Woman asked**

It is the Assemblies Mission. **Tita answered**

What is the name of your pastor? **Woman asked**

His name is Lasana. **Tita answered**

Come over this way (left the line). **Woman said**

Alright. **Tita replied**

The woman joined another group of church members.

Here is the young man. **Woman said**

How do you pronounce your name? **Man asked**

Tita. **Tita answered**

So, you are Tita. **Man said**

Yes, he is. **Woman replied**

Welcome to our country. **Man said**

Thank you, sir. **Tita replied**

A lot of hours on the air haah **Man said**

Yes sir. **Tita replied**

Welcome to our world. **Man said**

Thank you, sir. **Tita replied**

Welcome on board. **Woman said**

Thank you. **Tita replied**

Follow us. **Woman said**

Tita followed them to a vehicle park designated area for passengers' pickups, and they entered a bus with "The Assemblies

Mission" written on its side body, and the driver of the vehicle was inside there waiting for them. As they entered the bus, they limited their conversations until they finally arrived at the Headquarters of the Assemblies Mission that houses the Assemblies Mission Seminary and other administrative offices, and buildings of their church. They opened the vehicle door for Tita and he gradually came out of the bus and they ushered him into their reception room where there were other students of his type as well as other pastors/lecturers and church official members. They welcomed Tita and asked him few questions about his home country branch of the Assemblies Mission, he politely answered them and they told him that they had heard about his spiritual call to duty before he was ordained a Deacon and that facilitated his been entered for the Pastoral Lottery that eventually culminated to his coming overseas to their country. After series of cross examinations to make sure that the guy that entered their country through their church was exactly the guy that they sent for, his host further introduced him to some of the seminary students from Africa and other countries that were on training. Those students welcomed Tita and exchanged greetings with him. And Tita was later handed over to another beautiful young lady named Ronette whom he was told would show him his room within the community, and the young lady smiled to Tita and took him to his room.

Ronette took Tita to his room and showed him around on how everything worked as per the toiletries. She told Tita that the seminary cafeteria served meals three times a day and also told him that morning, afternoon and night bell ringing respectively signified time for those meals, and she advised him that he would have verities of foods to chose from and that as time goes on he would get used to all the types of food served on campus. She also showed Tita how to operate the electronics and made sure that he understood them all, which Tita acknowledged. She told Tita that it could be few months before their school officially started and that she would be visiting his room every day to make sure that everything was going fine. Tita thanked her and she left.

Tita took his time to put his cloths and few other things that he came with in place. He reasoned that for him to survive in such a foreign land that he knew no place to go to, he must not miss his meal times' otherwise he could emaciate and lose weight, energy and strength, and when that happened he could no longer get focused on his education and training. So, he inclined his ears to the ringing of the bell based on Ronette's instructions and by also focusing at time using the wall clock hung on a particular spot in his room. That night Tita heard the bell and went for his dinner, and as Ronette said there were verities of foods to chose from, so, he carefully made his selections and also drawing from the plate sizes of other students, he ate to his satisfaction. The following morning Tita again went for breakfast, beverages were served and Tita opted for creamed coffee and sipped that in with fried eggs. Tita who was not used to coffee got the first taste of it. In the afternoon shortly after launch of that day Ronette returned to ascertain how things were.

Hello. **Ronette greeted**

Good Morning. **Tita replied**

Tika, how are you today? **Ronette asked**

I am fine. **Tita answered**

Are you finding everything alright? **Ronette asked**

Yes I am fine. **Tita replied**

I came to know whether you have any concerns. **Ronette said**

Everything is fine. **Tita replied**

It's good to hear that. **Ronette said**

Ronette who was sitting on his room locker with her legs crossed and with her lapses flashing visible, stayed few hours in his room and finally told him "see you tomorrow, Tika", and left.

In the night of that day Tita stayed awake until the following morning because the coffee which he drank in the morning of it never allowed sleep to pass through his eyes. He stayed absolutely awake rolling from one side of the bed to the other. He thought that maybe Ronette had asked those white cooks to add poison for him in his food and that he was dying as fear gripped his entire being, but he did not realize that he was allergic to coffee. So, coffee drinks could cost him endless sleepless nights. When he later realized the impact of his newest introduced beverage (coffee) he called it quit with ever taken coffee and that restored his sleep hormone.

Ronette continued to visit Tita on daily basis and after about five consecutive days, one late afternoon she entered his room with three white men and two other ladies, and after series of questions and answers sessions with them, they bluntly told him that Ronette would be of assistance to him until his school started in few months time and maybe longer. They told him to always work with her to ensure his success as well as his retention in the Assemblies Mission Seminary, and that defiling Ronette's directives could leave them with no other options than to seek for his repatriation back to his home country. Tita agreed to comply with Ronette and follow all her directives. They following day Tita went with Ronette to the cafeteria and they had launch together and some of his fellow students looked at them with interest and concentrated on their lunch.

During one of the weekends on a Sunday early evening, Ronette arrived at his room and after exchanging conversations as usual she brought out a book full of naked beautiful women in their bikinis. She handed the book to him and told him to be reading the book as well as his bible. Tita was astonished because he had not set his eyes on such a number of nakedness before even when he was peeping at the ladies of the 'other side of town' in his home country. More so, Ronnette put a cassette in the stereo slut of his room TV and another bomb shell exploded, beautiful naked young women of all colors filled the screen. "Obviously, the entire room was full of their bodies, sweaty bottoms and chic, chic things". Tita managed to resist the urge but couldn't control the erection of his 'dig' as Ronette continued to watch the television and continued to call him "Tika do you like this, Tika do you like that". Ronette continued to canvass with him until dinner time when she told him "its dinner time, go grab your food, please make sure that you always eat well". And she also told him "continue to watch that on TV whenever you want" and left.

Tita glued his eyes to the television and continued to watch those films and also got focused on reading the text book she handed to him, and he committed little time to his bible. Having known the exact times that Ronette used to come to his room, so during such times he would turn off the television and concentrated on reading the bible so that it would appear that he never loved watching them nakedness too much. Tita was later introduced to some of the key officials of the Assemblies Mission and was taken to different locations within the Headquarters' compound by Ronette. She told him that he was not supposed to meet any of the officials in their various offices without her knowing of it and without her approval. And she warned Tita that as long as she continued to be his personal assistance, she remained the only girl friend he should allow to visit his room, no other female despite their intimacy should ever be seen at his hostel room, otherwise she would terminate her assignment with him and that would definitely result to him been flown back home. Tita promised her that he would not accept any other female in his hostel room even under duress except her.

As Ronette continued to visit Tita, she consistently made watching videos of such naked women her custom, and whiles the videos played she continued to look at Tita inquisitively waiting for him to throw the first shot, looking at him, releasing sparkles of passionate intimacy to his side. But Tita pretended to be a sacrosanct doing as if he does not understand the vibrating signals which had already got gripped of him. Whenever she noticed him fully erect, she would go closer to him and looked at him straight in the eyes as she spoke to him, yet he continued to hide his sexual feelings. After days of waiting for Tita to say something, and he instead preferred to die in the agony of passion, one day the lady noticed that 'it has protruded again and so warm", she approached Tita and began to caress him and pulse waves overtook him, and he became transfixed and was only mopping at her as she mover her finger nails across his chin.

As Tita nearly groaned, she gradually removed her hand and told him "not today Tika, not today, just get yourself together". And Tita never wanted her to remove her smooth fingers from him thereby stopping the flow of energy that had already built up. The lady stayed as usual and left.

Tita postponed his closer encounter with other female ladies who worked at the Assemblies Mission Headquarters because any unnecessary relationship with them could prove fatal. As a new person, an assumed minor mistake could send him parking because the eyes of her personal assistant could all be on him watching every of his moves. So, to the other ladies, he simply greeted them, and answers their ordinary questions when asked. He began to form closer ties with his fellow seminarians who some of them were in the same situation that he was in-new students with beautiful ladies as their assistants. After about one month of stay at the Seminary Hostel, one late morning Ronette came to his room as part of her daily duty, and it was almost three (3) hours before lunch, she exchanged conversations with him and in minutes she proceeded to slot another video cassette and the TV screen became filled with all kinds of 'man and woman' naked encounters—a real chocolate of a show. Ladies were busy given them all kinds of it; those men out there were attached to them ladies like very sticky glues, and never seemed to be tired for more. Immediately Tita looked at them he became attracted and lost himself and stood still.

Tika. **Ronette called**

Mm . . . mm . . . **Tita answered**

What is wrong? **Ronette asked**

Mm . . . mm . . . mm . . . **Tita answered**

The lady approached him and began to caress him once more, and took him by his hand and tossed him on the bed, and Tita never uttered a word because the passion stimulus had already sealed his lips. The lady lay on top of him and immediately removed her dress and bra and grabbed Tita's two hands and use his palm to feel her breast.

Tika feel me. **Ronette said**

Mm . . . mm . . . mm . . . **Tita replied**

Feel me with your hand Tika, feel me. **Ronette continued to request**

Mm . . . mm . . . mm . . . mm . . . **Tita replied**

Feel me, touch me as much as you like, Tika. Please . . . touch all of me. **Ronette demanded**

Mmmmmm . . . **Tita continued to reply**

The lady used Tita's hand to caress herself and continued to plead with Tita to act manly without further delay. Tita slowly grabbed her breast and gave it a little massage and gradually extended his touch to all over her body and began to take control.

Tika, I need you, please continue to touch me, take me, do me as much as you want. **Ronette requested**

Mm . . . mm . . . mm . . . I will, I will, I will . . . **Tita responded**

As the video continued to play, she continued to guide Tita through all the processes of love making and continued to partake, groaning in passionate pleasure for more. As the game continued and reached lunch time, and the bell ranged, she told Tita to stay back in the room and be ready for more playing while she went to collect his food for him. Tita immediately accepted and stayed back in the room pumping more blood to the necessary zones for more output. When she returned with his meal she open one small tube-like pill and sprayed the contents on Tita's meal. Tita consumed the meal fast without questions and minutes after eating the food, his 'dig' became so enlarge and stronger and all his body was hearing only "I want more, I want more". She grabbed him the second time and Tita followed without resistance and she gently tossed him on the bed and dominated him, and the love making continued with full participation by both parties until late in the evening when perspirations covered Tita's body and still he was ready for more. She congratulated him and told him that they had had enough for the day and Tita remained speechless and she departed.

CHAPTER SIXTEEN

Tita in the Seminary

The passionate encounters with Ronette continued and after about one month of the initial sexual triangle, Tita got enrolled in the Assemblies Mission Seminary as a freshman. Meanwhile, before his enrollment into the seminary, she never stayed with him without going through his bible; she also contributed to his knowing some of the vital things before his school officially started. Tita was welcomed in the classroom by his lecturers without reservations, and since it had been a long time since he was in the classroom last as a student, so he had to readjust himself so as to face the classroom challenges. He was lucky to have engaged himself into preaching and teaching of the bible while he was in the town because that helped him to master the act of speaking, reading and writing more efficiently. Since he did not attended secondary school it was initially difficult for him to understand some of the tones used coupled with his ability to easily comprehend and understand the courses. More so, his lecturers were also more than willing to explain to him any areas that he found difficult to comprehend. And some of his fellow course mates were always eager to work closely with him and assist him by answering whatever questions that he may have which they could answer, and also the areas of assisting with note taking-giving him their notes after classes to make his own notes. Initially he found it a little difficult to understand what was going on, to understand some of the languages spoken-as were used while delivering lectures, and to meet up with the sped of the lecturers in note taking, especially when notes were delivered via dictation. Furthermore, he always had to be in class minutes before the start of classes more than most of his course mates so as to sit in the front row in order to see the blackboard well and as well be able to copy efficiently.

Tita had no problems mingling with the rest of the students of the Assemblies Mission Seminary, and he associated politely with his lecturers which were mostly pastors, and also with other school officials, and these ensured that he received all his stipends for miscellaneous expenses which were giving to him as at when due by the Students Office of Foreign Affairs (SOFA). He complied with all the school rules and also studied hard combining unavoidable pleasure with his studies. While enrolled in the seminary, his love of twinkling with the beautiful lady continued and he was also introduced to other women whom he had sex with. As the semesters' progresses, the love making offers and love making affairs became messier and messier. Tita could have loved to reduce his involvement with those young ladies and women to a level that could allow him more time for his studies, but he had no other option than to obey the rules of the game as was been stipulated by Ronette who was fair to him anyway. Tita already knew that saying no to her could cost him all the efforts he had already put in his studies and sent him parking. So, he decided to play by the rules so as to finish his seminary successfully and as well become a pastor.

Combing the time for his studies with that of sexual gratification left him with little time for his studies which began to show in his test scores. So, to offset the effects of such intellectual downgrading, he decided to do his studies mostly in the night when there were fewer disturbances while waiting during the days for the next female visitor who may propose another sexual encounter which he would definitely complied with. As he spent his semesters and ads months and years as a student, Ronette gradually reduced her monthly visits to him to a minimum but he continued to meet with other ladies in his room as was approved by her. Tita flopped during his early semesters at the Assemblies Mission Seminary which nearly put him on probation, but gradually climbed the ladder to a better grade as the semester progressed. He manifested intelligent and continued to impress his lecturers.

In about one semester before his graduation Ronette came to his room one day during the hours when she used to come for prolonged sex. And that day Tita was somehow tired but full of under paint energy, and he couldn't even easily exchanged their usual greetings because in the previous night he spent hours reading his books and doing project writings. She followed her usual behavior of turning him on and putting him on the bed, Tita did not refuse the processes, but as soon as his back hit the bed and she began to caress him, he bitterly complained that he was so tied and never 'slept last night', and she refused to listen to him. Tita pleaded with her and tried to make her understand his condition, but Ronette insisted more on love making and continued to do that because she had already noticed that Tita's 'dig' was ready even though other parts of his body may be weak. On the lady's insistent, Tita forcefully got up and jumped down the bed and went and sat on the seat staring at Ronette and said: "what are you trying to do with me? Do you want me dead? Do you want me to die for you? Why can't you understand? Ronette smiled, and went and held the door for a couple of minutes while gazing at him, and she angrily left his room.

Ronette went and reported Tita's conduct to her superiors and Tita was immediately summoned to appear before the Office of Student Conduct (OSC). Tita appeared at the scheduled date, venue and time and Ronette was also present, and Tita was grilled by the officials of OSC through Mr. Integra its chairman. They consistently queried him on why he treated his personal assistant like a persona non grata-with absolute disdain.

Tita. **Mr. Integra called**

Yes. **Tita responded**

Do you know this lady (pointing at Ronette)? **Mr. Integra asked**

Yes. **Tita answered**

Who is she to you? **Mr. Integra asked**

She is my personal assistant. **Tita answered**

Do you know her name? **Mr. Integra asked**

Yes. **Tita answered**

What is her name? **Mr. Integra asked**

Her name is Ronette. **Tita answered**

What happened on the morning of August the 24th? **Mr. Integra asked**

Nothing happened. **Tita answered**

Are you sure? **Mr. Integra asked**

Yes. **Tita answered**

How much sure are you? **Mr. Integra asked**

Very mush sure, sir. **Tita answered**

Did you see Miss Ronette in the morning of August the 24th? **Mr. Integra asked**

Yes. **Tita answered**

Where did you saw her? **Mr. Integra asked**

I saw her in my room. **Tita answered**

Why was she in your room? **Mr. Integra asked**

She is my assistant, sir. **Tita answered**

Why was she in your room? **Mr. Integra asked again**

She was on duty sir. **Tita answered**

On duty doing what? **Mr. Integra asked**

Miss Ronette was in my room on the said morning carrying out her assignment as my personal assistant, and that was it. **Tita answered**

Did she offend you for any reason while carrying out her official duties in your room on the said morning? **Mr. Integra asked**

No sir, she never did. **Tita answered**

Did she ever approach you in a way that offended your traditional beliefs or in any way that offended you as a person that you never liked? **Mr. Integra asked**

No sir, she never did. **Tita answered**

Did she ever request any form of help from you while assisting you in the said morning of August the 24th? **Mr. Integra asked**

No sir, I have forgotten. **Tita answered**

Are you sure that Miss Ronette never requested for your help on that day? **Mr. Integra asked**

No, yes . . . **Tita answered**

Therefore, why did you shoved her by the exit door and used harsh words at her on the morning of August the 24th? **Mr. Integra asked**

I am sorry if I ever did, sir. I just cannot remember anymore. **Tita answered**

Did you ever jumped on something that frightened Miss Ronette on the morning of August the 24Th while she was on duty? **Mr. Integra asked**

I was not myself sir. I have certainly forgotten if something like that happened. **Tita answered**

Why weren't you yourself? **Mr. Integra inquired**

I do not know, sir. **Tita replied**

Do you understand that these premises forbade the use of hard drugs? **Mr. Integra asked**

Yes, I do. **Tita answered**

Were you on drugs on the morning of the day in question? **Mr. Integra asked**

No sir, certainly not. **Tita answered**

This office has evidence to believe that on the morning of August the 24th, Miss Ronette while on official duties in your hostel room, she requested for your assistance for a particular job assignment and you bluntly refused and instead jumped on something that scared and frightened her. And when she insistently demanded that 'you should please help make her work easier', you instead shoved her by the exit door and used harsh words on her. How do you want to plead; guilty or not guilty? **Mr. Integra said**

I plead guilty by mistake, sir. **Tita replied**

Do you understand the implications of been found guilty of such an offense as written in the Students Code of Conduct Handbook (SCCH)? **Mr. Integra asked**

Yes, I understand but I acted out of sense. **Tita answered**

. . . . Silence as OSC officials quietly communed to decide on Tita's faith. And after deliberations;

OSC has finally reached a verdict on your case, and based on its principles of equality, equity and fair play, we have decided your disenrollment from the Seminary School for the next semester which unfortunately is your graduation semester. Your offense could have earned you outright expulsion, but considering that this is your first offense of this nature and that you have always complied with the previous such requests by any of our employees. We thus reduce your punishments to the loss of only one semester. This implies that you will no longer graduate next semester as you ought to, your graduation will now be next two semesters if you are found to be of good conducts. You are hereby placed on probation to be monitored by you assistant Miss Ronette. Tita you were very lucky not to have received a higher sentencing otherwise the next aircraft to your country could have had you as one of its passengers. Do not do any other thing that will make you to face OSC again until you graduate else you will end up leaving the Assemblies Mission Seminary without certificate after 'years of efforts'. **Mr. Integra said**

Thank you so much sir. Thank you so much sir. How on earth could I have explained this to those that sent me to here? I will never try it again, I will never. **Tita at ease**

Tita became dumfounded and never had any other choice than to obey the rules and continue to read his book. He reduced his speed of reading and occasionally read in the nights because there was no need for the vigil anymore since his last days on campus had been postponed by the school officials-the mercenaries of Ronette. Having reiterated their decisions and having been again be betrothed to her, Tita wallows deeper into the dumpsters of love making and continued to satisfy her and all other women who wanted to have that with him through Ronette. In few of the occasions Tita saw himself in the mist of naked ladies who had complete raw sex with him and he always tried to nozzle as much as he could, releasing all his loaded bullets and leaving the empty cartridges to cool off. As the re-enrollment semester was approaching Ronette applied different types of tricks to maneuver so as to understand if he had ever learnt his lesson. Tita passed all the lady's examinations and he was later re-enrolled to the Assemblies Mission Seminary for his final semester in school. Meanwhile, during his probation, he used his spare time to go through all that was supposed to be covered during his final semester.

Tita was certified 'compliance complete'(probation passed), and he reentered the classroom to start from where he stopped. Although he had passed his probation, he was still under Ronette's apron string because should he refused to carry out his assignments as it pertained to 'pleasure duty' he would definitely lose out and this time he could not win again despite the importance he attached to himself or they attached to him. However, Tita followed her cautiously by been friendlier than never before and showed her more concern and appreciation since she never needed his money. Tita took his final Seminary Examination and comfortably passed. The time he spent doing extra reading during his probationary period never was a waste, it certainly paid off, giving Tita a leap more than some other students, although most of his former course mates had already graduated a semester ago, but those of them who failed their final graduation exams and those who were in the same boat with Tita either repeated or lost a whole semester. In the special graduation ceremonies held at the Assemblies Mission Headquarters, Tita and other grandaunts were ordained pastors, and he was hailed to have achieved his dream of becoming a pastor-the start of his spiritual call to duty.

Ronette's assignment ended shortly after Tita's final examination and during her last visit to his room she made the last love with Tita, again given him all herself and as well allowing him access to every of her. She truthfully congratulated Tita for reaching the epicenter of his seminary education which never came so easily.

She told him that many students of his type lost out during their final years in the seminary because of their unruly and headstrong attitudes, and that "you are lucky to have scaled the odds and that has crowned you with a graduation cap". She chipped in to him that he should not accept any offers from some of the Assemblies Mission officials to be retained either as a 'minor teacher or a support pastor' because there offers were like a 'tip of the iceberg'. She told him that "as soon as you are confirmed a pastor, do have no other option than to go back to your home country as soon as possible. They will not kill you; just tell them that you prefer it out there in your home country. Do not accept their offers of gold because all that glitters is not gold, because at a certain stage it results to 'bumper to bumper sexual encounter'. I need you home a cleaner man. Their offers come with bags of our currency, but you can equally make that type of money in your country. You are the only person I have advised like this before because I love you and I don't want to hurt you". As she left pastor Tita decided to adopt a wait and see attitude.

Two days after his graduation a messenger came and informed him that they needed to see him at a designated office in the afternoon after lunch. Pastor Tita went to see them and the office was full of expensive furniture and looked so well equipped. Inside the office there were about two men and two women.

Welcome pastor Tita, I am Ruttkay.

Thank you. **Pastor Tita replied**

Thank you for coming. **Ruttkay said**

Thank you. **Pastor Tita replied**

We invited you to let you know that you have been selected for employment to work for us as a Support Pastor (SP) here in the Assemblies Mission Headquarters. We have gone through your credentials and your qualifications matched our needs. **Ruttkay said**

That is good, sir. **Pastor Tita replied**

You will be paid thousands of our currency per month, so you will be looking at hundreds of thousands of CFA Franc per month and millions of CFA Franc annually. If you accept to work for us we will cover for your feeding while you can purchase the rest of your needs, you will also receive parts of the gifts and donations from members of the Assemblies Mission. **Ruttkay said**

It is nice, I mean . . . **Pastor Tita replied**

The employment goes with other conditions attached to it which must be necessary for any monthly payment of employee salaries. That is, for you to receive your monthly payments, you must comply with the terms and conditions of employment. **Ruttkay said.**

It is fine. I like that. **Pastor Tita replied**

To give you a hint of the other terms of your employment, look here, we have a Secret Code of Ethics (SCS) that we do follow which is based solely on employer-employee relationships. We do relate to each other in the areas of love making, and we do expect every of our employees to comply with us for full payment. We have homosexual sex and heterosexual sex relationships all for pleasurable gratification. This position we are offering you pays a huge sum of money as we have earlier told you, and do hope that you will not miss this opportunity to climb the ladder of success. Will you accept this employment position or not? **Ruttkay said**

Pastor Tita kept silence and contemplated for a while.

Pastor, take your time to reason it out; we are waiting for your response. **Ruttkay said**

How long will the employment last? **Pastor Tita asked**

The employment is sure to last for a very long time as long as you continued to comply with us. **Ruttkay said**

This is a very big amount of money. **Pastor Tita said**

Yes, the money involved in here is really big. Your one month salary couple with other benefits could last for a life time back there in your country. **Ruttkay agreed**

Yes, the money is really, really big. I'm going to bet on that. **Pastor Tita replied**

So, are you accepting the employment offer or not? **Ruttkay asked**

I will sure accept the offer. **Pastor Tita answered**

Have you or haven't you accepted the offer? **Ruttkay asked**

I have accepted the offer of your employment as a Support Pastor. **Pastor Tita answered**

Congratulations for making such a good decision. It is good to be rich. **Ruttkay said**

Thank you so much, that is what people are here for. That's what everybody is here for. **Pastor Tita replied**

We will make the needed arrangement to relocate you from your student hostel room immediately. As you reach your room wait there for us, we are coming to move your things to the place designated for our pastor retained. Make sure that you do not go about telling anybody about this agreement or your relationship of any type with us. After one month of work you will receive your first payment in our country hard currency-you know what that means. Meanwhile before your first pay we will cover all your expenses including feeding. How does that sound? **Ruttkay said**

It sounds so good. **Pastor Tita replied**

As soon as you are relocated, your employment becomes effective but it could take days before your initial assignments on the other aspect. When you are approached and asked why you have never gone back to your country yet, just tell them that you are retained as a SP. We expect to work longer with you as one of our employees. **Ruttkay said**

Pastor Tita loved money and accepted the offer to be retained as an SP at the Assemblies Mission Headquarters ignoring all advises given to him by Ronette an insider, and instead focused his mind on converting 'hard currency' to local currency (CFA Franc) that would yield him millions and made him instant millionaire-a billionaire maybe, and perhaps made him the richest person in town. Pastor Tita understood the moral implications of his employment offer as SP and he went ahead and accepted it. Pastor Tita knew so well that it was highly immoral and forbidden for same sex sexual relationships and he went ahead and accepted an employment offer that had such as its terms. Pastor Tita knew that it was traditionally forbidden in his home village by his tribe to even talk of same sex relationships and he went ahead, and without hesitation accepted the employment offer. Pastor Tita understood that having such an affair(s) implies only death by hanging in his village when discovered and he went ahead and accepted it. Pastor Tita knew that smuggling in such highly forbidden toxic immorality in his village could affect the pure and innocent of most of her inhabitants, and he went ahead and accepted it. Pastor Tita was very much away that engaging himself in such immoral sterns was unnatural and would make him an instant pariah thrown away to an evil forest and he went ahead and accepted such an offer. Pastor Tita understood that such same sex relationships could castrate him when discovered, and he went ahead and accepted the employment offer. And he also knew that he could equally make millions in his home country and he went ahead and betrayed his innocent villagers, community and tribe in particular and other relevant sections of his country in general. Pastor Tita had indeed loved money. Oh how dare you Tita for thee have loved money! You remember his boss days at the market as a business owner, but today Tita loves money.

CHAPTER SEVENTEEN

Pastor Tita as Support Pastor

Pastor Tita was relocated to a very comfortable room that had all the modern furnishing in it. Pastor Tita had everything he needed in his room for making life more enjoyable. He felt above the world for having accomplished such a good fit that he was been cherished, admired and accepted by his employer-a section of the Assemblies Mission. Within days of his relocation, he was explained to further on what his job really entailed. He was thereafter assigned with the responsibilities of preaching to a small number of people who were probably church members and others involved in the ball game. He does his preaching as an SP in sizeable like room patios but a little larger than his living room. He as an SP spent all the needed times based on his schedule as provided to him by his employers. As his days of work as an SP went by Tita's room was consistently visited by some of his employers who oftentimes brought church members with concerns to him for solutions. His employers always made sure that he had no problems continuing with his work and they were sometimes present during his preaching schedules as a Support Pastor.

After about two weeks of the start of his work, on a Sunday afternoon he was visited by a young lady in his room. The lady told him that she was sent by his employer based on their agreement as part of his conditions for continued employment.

Welcome to my room. **Pastor Tita greeted**

How are you? I'm Lucia.

I am very much fine. **Pastor Tita answered**

Get yourself sited. **Pastor Tita offered**

Appreciated. **Lucia replied**

Yes, what can I do for you? **Pastor Tita asked**

Your employer sent me based on your agreement with them as part of the conditions for continued employment. **Lucia replied**

Agreement! **Pastor Tita wondered**

Are you aware of the existence of such an agreement? **Lucia answered**

Please just give me a second while I take myself memory lane. **Pastor Tita excused himself**

You have all the time you need. **Lucia approved**

Pastor Tita kept silence for a while as he reflected, pretending to do as if he never remembered easily again.

I now remember. **Pastor Tita said**

That's fine. **Lucia replied**

I did make such an agreement with them, I just forgot. **Pastor Tita said**

Take this in and slot it in there (Lucia gave him a video cassette), and he collected it from her and slotted it and relaxed back on his seat. They cassette started playing and he and Lucia got their eyes focused on the television. On watching the TV, the film was raw sex involving all kinds of sexual adventures and some part of the sex were homosexual (gay) sexual relationships and while the rest were heterosexual relationships. The film instantly turned pastor Tita on who began to shift his legs uneasily from one location to the other, and Lucia been a well trained prostitute in that profession also got caught up by the wave of love making as was synonymous to many professional prostitutes. She got up from her seat and approached pastor Tita on his seat and held him closer and removed the chest section of her dress and exposed her breast and gently touched his face with her breasts, and she dipped one of her fingers into pastor Tita's mouth who instantly began to lick it like sucking. She removed her dress completely and began to make dancing moves with only her under pants on. Pastor Tita's 'dig' became stiff and he found himself in another sex passion mania, this time with a completely different lady sent to him by his employer. She licked his neck consistently and he became dazed. She took him by the hand and pushed him down on the bed and removed his wears and used her hands to direct his 'dig' to penetration and pastor Tita simply obeyed. They had all kinds of sex while the film played with sexual musical undertones, and the encounter lasted for hours and ended in the late evening. Pastor Tita nearly got exhausted because his newest sexual counterpart was so sexually rough that all parts of her were only ejaculation spots. And that made him to lose more energy as well as sexual continuation power. When the encounter was finally over for the day, she got up and smile and took her video cassette and told pastor Tita 'bye bye, see you around'.

Pastor Tita already knew that what he just completed was part of his agreement with his employer without which his employment with them would be terminated. He kept mute of the encounter as he promised and continued with his work as SP. Few days later, Lucia came to his room this time with another man when pastor Tita saw them he thought that maybe she had informed the authorities of the encounter with her and that they could be after him. So he got kind of frightened but Lucia told him to take it easy because they never came to hurt him but to share with him.

This young man with me came to witness our sexual escapades. He came to watch me and you perform the sex tricks. **Lucia said**

How? **Pastor Tita asked**

He will be watching us while we have sex and after sometime, he will join us in the sex games. That is also part of your agreement with your employer. I hope you are not offended? **Lucia answered**

I have no worries whatsoever. I am ready to get involved with you because I deserve. **Pastor Tita said**

She gave the young man with her the video cassette to slot in, and the young man did so. As the film got started and progressed, she undressed and approached pastor Tita again following her initial processes and he got overtaken by the spirals of passionate waves and she went to the other men and got him turned more on, after which she returned to pastor Tita. She took him to bed and as they began to go through the processes the man joined them and they shared the ladies genital and oral openings while she used her hands to rob mess out of their balls. As the sexual encounter intensified and her counterparts were approaching climax, she used pastor Tita's hand to grab the other man's 'dig' and as she robbed him, pastor Tita gradually followed suit until the other man ejaculated in pastor Tita's palm. And they continued with the cycle of sex play vice versa until when pastor Tita got tired of continuing to participate and the other young man had more with her until their sexual encounter came to an end for that day. The other young man shake pastor Tita's hand and gave him a pat on the back and also congratulated him and referred him as a great guy to work with.

When they left, pastor Tita nearly vomited because he had not had such a passionate encounter with a fellow man before. It was his first time of robbing a fellow man's 'dig' to ejaculation, and more so as he grabbed his 'dig' robbing him, the young man never cared and was busy touching the other side of her. Pastor Tita suspected that an encounter of such nature could eventually result to a male to male sexual relationship which they made mention of in his agreement with them. Pastor Tita thought of how he would feel if ever he penetrated a fellow man and asked himself 'where will I put my 'dig' in such an encounter since a man has no sexual reproductive openings other than the tiny aperture of the 'dig'. I will wait and see". And he reasoned that should they chose to have him like a woman how could that ever happened, 'perhaps facilitated by human invention of wield'. After his unusual encounter he continued to go about his normal duties without disclosing to anybody what he had encountered because it was forbidden for him to tell anybody about any of the sexual relationships with him otherwise he was good to go.

Before one month of the start of his work with them, one afternoon Lucia and another man called Jack entered his room for the same purpose. As the sex game started and they continued with their usual the lady asked pastor Tita to position himself like a lady.

Tita. **Lucia called**

Pose like a lady for sure. **Jack said**

How? **Pastor Tita questioned**

Bend in such a way that your 'roundish hole' will be exposed upwards. **Jack instructed**

How do I do that? **Pastor Tita asked**

Lucia showed pastor Tita exactly how to do that.

Why should I do that? **Pastor Tita asked**

I want to pump your ash. **Jack answered**

Have sex with me? **Pastor Tita bewildered**

So, you don't remember again. Position yourself otherwise you are not going to get paid. **Lucia said**

Pastor Tita hesitated for a while and contemplated that there was huge amount of money involved as his salary, and with that type of hard currency, in their local currency he was sure to be the richest coupled with other opportunities, and he realized that such an act was an instant passport to the world of outcast, a complete self alienation from his traditional village and family, but to him "I need money, I want to be rich, very rich. I can't go back; I need those bags of money, that money must be mine. After all, who will ever know that I did such things, it is only me here I must go for it, I don't even need that tradition anymore, it has been long when I walked my way and abandoned it". While refusing, Jack come closer to him and started touching his 'dig' and Lucia from the other side was caressing him. Pastor Tita assumed the position as was directed by the lady, and Jack had complete anal sex with him releasing his entire flood inside his 'roundish hole', and the process continued until when he felt like he had had enough of such encounters.

In their absence pastor Tita got confused on how on earth a man could have complete sex with a fellow man using the anal aperture as 'dig' entrance way, and that was never heard of in his home country. He also kept to himself, and never spoke on it and while he taught the bible as SP, he never made mention of such sexual encounters to anybody. At the end of that month, pastor Tita went to where he was directed for payments and got all his first month salary and other things from donations and gifts by those that attended his teachings. He felt above the world for getting such huge amount of money that was just for the initial pay. And without delay he wrote a letter to his home country township branch of the Assemblies Mission informing them that he had been employed overseas as a "Support Pastor", and that he was moving along with them fine. He made it known to them that he appreciated work with the Assemblies Mission Seminary and that he was looking forward for good number of years of work with them. Meanwhile, while in the seminary his home branch of his church always wrote to him inquiring about his condition and study.

Pastor Tita continued to work for his employer getting all the attentions that he needed and doing as they instructed him to do. They gay sex aspect of his sexual assignments continued to the point that he sometimes had gay gang sex with them which resulted to the point where he began to suck their 'dig' or oral sex. After his initial oral sex, he vomited all that he ate shortly after his male sex partners left his room but by that time it was too late for him to turn back. Pastor Tita later became very popular among some of the members of his division of service to the point that they always invited him as a special quest of honor, testifying about him as one of their best candidates and also asking him to 'stand in' for some of their key officials during important ceremonies.

Months of his employment with his employer made him a rich person in his home country standard as he hoped to continue to work for them for more hard currency-more CFA Franc o . . . o . . . o . . . o. As pastor Tita continued to obey the rules of the game, at the eleventh month of his employment, he was invited by his employer for a job review, and pastor Tita honored their invitation.

Welcome, pastor Tita I'm Fidler.

Thank you. **Pastor Tita replied**

Have a seat. **Fidler offered**

Appreciated. **Pastor Tita replied**

We invited you so as to take a look at your performances so far since you started working for us. You are aware that this is the eleventh month since you started with us as one of our employees. **Fidler said**

Yes. **Pastor Tita replied**

Having gone through your record, we regret to inform you that your employment with us as SP is hereby terminated with full pay. Henceforth, you are no longer one of our employees on the conditions that you have not been performing your assigned duties diligently. Having observed you for a couple of times, you always performed below our expectations, and some of those who benefit from your duties are no longer satisfied with your services, therefore, we can't continue to retain you. Here is your salary for this month and that of next month (handed him an envelope) and here is your airplane ticket back home (handed him his ticket). It was very hard for us to take such a decision but there was nothing we could do. You are advised to vacate these premises on the indicated date and catch your flight home, after that day, the security officers in charge of this place will come and lock your room. **Fidler said**

But sir, I want to work for you. I have been doing everything you asked me to do well and have also been doing my job to the best of my knowledge and the appreciation of our church members. **Pastor Tita replied**

Young man, this decision was not taken by us, and therefore, there is no way we can help you. The Assemblies Mission Seminary has decided to terminate your employment with them and there are no two ways about that. Please, be advised that you don't make any other extra effort(s) as to meet with other officials of this compound, I mean, the Assemblies Mission officials, because if you are caught doing so you will be sentenced to jail, and we hope that you will not want it that way. Do you have any other thing to tell us? **Fidler cautioned**

Since you have said, I do not have any other thing to say. **Pastor Tita replied**

Bye, bye and safe journey back home to your country. **Fidler said**

Pastor Tita got up and left.

Pastor Tita left with no other options than to return back to his home country. He immediately packed his bags and baggage ready for the departure date. He was afraid to negotiate his way because the guys could deal with him should he ever ventured, and more so, there was no need trying such a thing because his stay officially expired shortly after his graduation and was ordained a pastor. All those ladies and men that always came to him for all kinds of 'do me, I do you thing' disappeared and he saw only new faces that seemed unrecognizable. One thing was certain, pastor Tita had made money more than any people in his village and more than many people in his country, but 'despite the market value of shit, it is still really, really shit'. On his departure date he left his room and as he was leaving he saw a couple of ladies canvassing with their backs facing his room direction. He finally boarded an aircraft billed to his country and had a safe trip home to his country. Meanwhile his employer had already informed his home country Assemblies Mission branch that he was about to be home, and few of his fellow church members went to the airport to receive him. They were happy to see pastor Tita back home once again from a long trip and years of stay overseas.

CHAPTER EIGHTEEN

Pastor Tita Returns Home to His Parish

astor Tita back home stayed in his Assemblies Mission pastoral residency where he was comfortably accommodated in one room. He was received home by the official members of his church who expressed their satisfaction for his conduct oversea, as well as his successful completion of his seminary which eventually culminated to his ordination as a pastor. And he thanked them for giving him such an opportunity to serve, and promised to serve them with humility and dedication. After receiving news of pastor Tita's arrival, church members, friends and relatives came out in mass to welcome him and as well express their happiness for his successful return from overseas because 'some of the times, not all those who were sent stayed and completed their assignments'. Pastor Tita received all of them and thanked them for believing in him and also expressed his readiness to work with them.

Pastor Tita stayed in his Assemblies Mission pastoral house and declined to ask about his parents, sisters and other of his relatives at home. Meanwhile, his second sister got married to a wealthy farmer when he was overseas and news of her marriage reached him, and he never for one day wrote a letter to his parents through their church or through any of his friends. After days in the Pastoral House, he sent messages to his parents that he had returned home from overseas, and that his father should come and see him, and he gave money to one of his church members to go and bring his parents to come and see him. When his father received the message he vowed that 'I will never step out of this house to go and see that foolish boy, if he wants to see us, he should come to this place. How many years did he spend overseas? 'He now knows that we are important to him'.

Pastor Tita was told exactly what Mr. Cazembi said. And after weeks of his return, one day he travels home with the help of one of his church members, Mani (came from the mountain), who offered to give him a free ride home. On his arrival home, his parents and Jawanza were at home, and on seen his father;

Papa! Mama! **Pastor Tital called**

His father turned and looked at him and never responded.

Papa! Mama! **Pastor Tita continued to call**

Who are you? **Mr. Cazembi asked**

It is me, Tita your son. **Pastor Tita replied**

Why are you here? **Mr. Cazembi asked**

I'm home from my trip overseas. **Pastor Tita answered**

Did you travelled overseas? **Mr. Cazembi asked**

Yes, I travelled. **Pastor Tita answered**

Why have you chosen to come back to this place? **Mr. Cazembi asked**

I came to see you. **Pastor Tita answered**

Did you know that we were alive before you traveled? **Mr. Cazembi asked**

Yes, Papa. **Pastor Tita answered**

Did you inform us? **Mr. Cazembi asked**

Pastor Tita never spoke.

Who is that young man with you? **Mr. Cazembi asked**

He is one of our church members. **Pastor Tita answered**

Did he travel overseas with you? **Mr. Cazembi asked**

No Papa. He did not. **Pastor Tita replied**

I will let you into this house because of him. Come in. **Mr. Cazembi said**

They went into the house where his mother was sitting having rest and Jawanza was there too. On seen his mother;

Mama! Mama!! **Pastor Tita called**

Who is that my husband? **Mrs. Dunduza asked**

He said he is Tita. **Mr. Cazembi answered**

Which Tita? **Mrs. Dunduza asked**

Ask him. **Mr. Cazembi answered**

Mama is me Tita (advances to embrace her mother)

Do not ever touch me. I am ashamed of you, you made mockery of me, you spitted on my face. My only son Tita was dead long ago and it cannot be you. You please stay away from me. **Mrs. Dunduza said**

Mama! Mamaaaa! Is I your son Tita (tried to embrace her again)

Are you not hearing? Don't you have ears? I said stay away from me, you are not my son and your kinsmen can bear witnesses to that. You have long gone, and now what is left of you. Look at me, you have defiled yourself, what else do you need of us. Please stay absolutely away from me and do not try to embrace me again. My son is gone. **Mrs. Dunduza warned**

Mama. **Pastor Tita called**

I shall weep no more for your sake, for my womb's wound had been healed in your absence for years. I shall weep not again for a son that never was. Please call me no more. **Mrs. Dunduza pleaded**

Pastor Tita stood still and bowed down his head and when he sat down, he called her sister by her name.

Jawanza my little sister

Did you hear what my mother said? We have no person here by your name Tita. So, please, allow me to rest and take yourself back to town. I desire no other thing from such a callous person like you. You had already done that and they all know. Stay away from our lives and do not come here again. Is that clear? **Jawanza warned**

Little sister, I never meant to hurt you, I am now a pastor, which was all that I was fighting for. **Pastor Tita said**

I don't desire you, I have seen pastors before and I have heard of those that travelled overseas before, those that are even better than you. You have gotten there to do your wish and now you are wealthy. What else do you need from us, go away with your money bags and never call me again? You stumpy stink. **Jawanza refused him**

I'm sorry if I have . . .

As pastor Tita was trying to plead with his parents, his father left the room and walked away.

I attended the Assemblies Mission Seminary overseas and after my graduation I was ordained a pastor. And I just returned back few weeks ago and decided to come and see how you people are doing. I don't mean to offend any of you. **Pastor Tita said**

His mother and sister kept silence and never spoke to him.

I mean, I don't want to be rude anymore. **Pastor Tita pleaded**

Mrs. Dunduza and Jawanza continued to remain silence and his mother moved her face away from him and looked at another direction.

Is anything wrong my pastor? **Mani asked**

No not at all, only that they objected to my . . . nothing. **Pastor Tita answered**

So your parents never approved your going overseas, my pastor? **Mani inquired**

Not at all, but . . . yes, yes, just because I was . . . yes. **Pastor Tita answered**

Mr. Cazembi returned from the outside.

Papa! Mama! **Mani called**

We Papa and Mama no more, when you two are tired of staying in my house you are free to go. **Mr. Cazembi said**

Papa, Mama . . . I (as Mani was saying)

(Cuts in) I said don't Papa and Mama us again. Please keep your tongue, it was all over by your pastor's approval and disgrace long ago, it is all over and will remain all over. **Mr. Cazembi said**

I heard that Nyahuma is also married and I will like to know who married both of them and where they are married to respectively. **Pastor Tita requested**

Mr. Cazembi looked at him and said;

Let it be the last time you will ever made mention of my daughters. Did you just hear me? **Mr. Cazembi warned**

I am just trying . . . (As pastor Tita was saying)

(Cuts in) we don't know you, and you (pointing at Mani) tell him to stay absolutely away from our daughters for good. He had done his wish and he will live with its consequences the rest of his live and beyond. **Mr. Cazembi said**

Please we will be going, we will be going. **Pastor Tita hurriedly said**

His parents kept silence and never cared to talk to him.

Pastor Tita opened his briefcase and brought out bundles of CFA Franc and placed them on the table.

Please, Papa, you keep this money for the family needs. I'm so sorry for all my past behaviors. **Pastor Tita pleaded**

His parents remained unmoved and never touched the money.

I will be back some other time; right now I have a lot of assignments with me. **Pastor Tita said**

His parents still remained absolutely silent.

Let's go (pastor Tita told Mani). They got up and as they were about to leave, Mr. Cazembi grabbed the whole money and threw them away to the outside and said;

Go to hell with your money. Nonsense, did they tell you that we are begging for food? Rubbish, nonsense. Make sure that you do not venture to bring that bunch of useless papers of yours back into my house, else you will show me this afternoon. **Mr. Cazembi warned**

What is all these my pastor? **Mani asked**

I don't know. How can I . . . I need to be on my way. Gather the money; let us get out of here real quick. **Pastor Tita answered**

It is unusual (Mani said) as he picks the money.

Never ever tell anybody that something like this happened when we visited my home in the village otherwise I will be done with you. Understand? **Pastor Tita warned**

Yes my pastor, no need, is all our money, the church . . . we can handle this. **Mani replied**

Handle what? Let's get out of here. **Pastor Tita stammered**

After picking all the money they horridly left.

CHAPTER NINETEEN

Pastor Tita at AM

P astor Tita continued to receive well wishers at the Pastoral House in the Assemblies Mission (AM) compound, and he continued to admonish them to be good followers of the son of salvation through observing the teachings in the bible, and also he continued eavesdropping to ascertain whether Mani would make good his promise of not disclosing to anybody what happened in his village. Pastors Tita's call to the temple celebration was held in his Assemblies Mission compound and the ceremony attracted thousands of people, both church members and those from other works of life, especially his allies and representatives from other Assemblies Mission drawn from throughout his country's main branches. At the end of the celebration a good sum of money was realized and pastor Tita was given a sizable share of the money, their main pastor had his own share etc while the rest was used in running other church related activities.

Pastor Tita was retained as the Assistant Pastor (AP) of his branch of the Assemblies Mission this time as the second in command. His new assignment was a complete prestige to him and he was regarded, revered, honored and trusted by all those affected by his ministry, and also retained friends and well wishers.

Pastor Tita's preaching energized his church members more, and easily spread across the township which attracted more members to the Assemblies Mission and also lured some people to come closer and watch him deliver sermons. He gradually became the order of the day as one of the most eloquent and powerful preachers of a protestant church within the vicinity of his own side of township. Meanwhile shortly after his return from overseas, he began to give aids in the form of financial assistance to some of his church members in desperate need and some of his friends, relatives and community members who had dire needs for financial assistance and that branded him "he that gives", consequently, other non church members became convinced that by joining his congregation they could as well have the opportunities to draw from pastor Tita's wealthy pockets so as to be able to solve their personal problems, thus, increasing the number of both ordinary church attendants, the value of donations and the number of church members.

As his days increases as AP, he began contemplating on how best to reach out to his clansmen in particular and his community in general. He realized that he once made an open statement in the presence of his kinsmen whereby he disowned them and his parents and relatives, and vowed not to have anything to do with them again. So, he never knew how best to mingle with them and convince them to forgive him. He decided that the best method of approach was to attend one of their community gatherings during which he could speak to all the people present. And luckily such community gatherings took place once every month during which solutions were proffered on tackling community and certain family problems. He retrospect and understood that ordinary speaking to them could not convince them to believe in him because his kinsmen would tell them not to have anything to do with him haven disowned them. So, to buy the supports of some of them he needed to give them good financial donations, in that way, they could now give him the necessary supports-a system of divide and rule.

Prior to one of the Community Development Initiative (CDI) gatherings in his home village, he bought one new car and during the CDI gathering his car was used to convey him to the venue by his driver who was also a member of his church. On arriving at the CDI venue one early afternoon, his community people were perplexed to see pastor Tita with such expensive car, so all eyes were glued on him. His driver gradually opened the door and pastor Tita stepped out and was offered seat by few of the youths who stood up from their seats and asked him to sit down while his driver remained in the vehicle. Towards the end of the gathering, pastor Tita asked the relevant officials to permit him to speak to them because as they were aware he had not been around for some time. They approved pastor Tita's request without hesitation and as he step forward to speak, there were sporadic voices like; "who allowed that stupid man to talk to us? I cannot listen to whatsoever he wants to say; he is done with us, we are his kinsmen; we don't need him anymore; he is a surrogate doing his master bindings; he is an evil in a pretending flesh; he has betrayed our traditional ideals; pastor Tita is only immoral; he has castrated himself, therefore, he is no more one of us; we are done with this gathering etc". The officials appealed for calm and asked pastor Tita to say what he wanted to say.

Pastor Tita thanked them for allowing him such an opportunity to be in their mist and as well to speak to them. He expressed his appreciation of how they kept on keeping their community going in his absence although he was so small and therefore handicapped to contribute meaningfully at that time. He told them that he had finally returned home from overseas where he went for his pastoral training, where he attended Assemblies Mission Seminary and that as some of them were aware he had been ordained a pastor and was an assistant pastor of his parish. He made it known to them that he had the interest of the entire community at heart and wants to contribute financially and materially through CDI. He said that he had no much time to speak to them and he gave them tens of thousands of CFA Franc as a token of his readiness to work with them and as well continue to contribute whenever needed. Pastor Tita's speech was greeted with a round of applause and cheers and jeers. Officials of CDI accepted his money and asked him to continue to show his support to the community because by so doing they could achieve more.

At the end of the gathering some people went and exchanged greetings with pastor Tita as they thanked him for his understanding and show of supports, and some collected his township address. He departed back to town without a stoppage at his family to trouble his parents again. After one and half years as AP, pastor Tita who had already became cherished and accepted by most of his church members subsequently he was later promoted to the Assemblies Mission main pastor-pastor number one. His colleagues received his promotion with lots of admirations and there were celebrations everywhere to mark his ascension to the first position in their church. The former main pastor, pastor Lasana, was transferred to a different location, thus pastor Tita retained the revenue controlling seat. He became satisfied as a pastor and as a wealthy man whose wealth had been further fortified by his position. He continued to give aids to the needy, especially financially based on the amount requested. And he intensified his reaching out to his community members both in the township and at home in his village. Some of his community members in town relocated to his own side of town where it would be easier for them to be in closer contacts with him and as well attend church at the Assemblies Mission so as to impress him and make him help them out financially and materially.

Pastor Tita continued to employ all the available means to make his parents believe in him and they continued to reject all his gifts and pleas for acceptance. His parents warned him that he was free to mingle with the rest of the extended family if they chose and the community in general if they wanted, but for them all was sealed. Few of his extended family members started to collaborate and connive with him while he continued to assist them financially, materially and religiously. As time progressed he purchased a very large piece of land in his home village and built a mighty house that surpassed that of all other residents within his home community. His show of wealth attracted many friends who decamped to his side, especially the youths who did not know about him and his dealings overseas, those that needed help, and those who laughed at Mr. & Mrs. Cazembi decided to be parents and advisers to him. Pastor Tita bought a land because Mr. Cazembi refused to accord him the needed paternal rights, and built a house that could turn the entire community to his favor if they were to be ruled and masterminded for by material gain, wealth and monetary acquisition. They moralists and traditional believers in his community remained rigid and unmoved by his 'show of shame'. He continued to show his support to his community this time with more substantial CFA Franc through CDI, and he also used the same avenue to appeal to, especially the youths to come forward for his assistance.

CHAPTER TWENTY

Pastor Tita Banished

P astor Tita completed his house in less than no time and got his compound fenced, and as well constructed a pipe borne water that had an outlet pipe where the rest of the communities fetched water for free. To win more admirations of his people and get them give him more supports, he was always at his home village every month end on none busy church schedule days. During his stay at home his visitors ate as if they were partying and he also gave out monetary gifts. About one year after his occupation of his house, one young man in his early twenties called Mugabe (Intelligent) came to his house one late morning and after exchanging pleasantries, he ushered him in, and while with him, he went out and locked all the doors that led to the entrance where they were sited. Mugabe just finished his secondary school and needed assistance to continue with his education because he was an intelligent young man.

You are welcomed to my home my brother. **Pastor Tita said**

Thank you, pastor. **Mugabe replied**

What kind of drink do you like? **Pastor Tita asked**

Pastor, I do not want to drink anything today. **Mugabe replied**

Again, you are welcomed. **Pastor Tita said**

Pastor. **Mugabe called**

Yes, by brother. **Pastor Tita replied**

Please, I need your help. **Mugabe said**

What can I do for you? **Pastor Tita inquired**

I have finished my secondary school for the past one year and I cleared all my papers with better grades, and I do not have money to proceed to the higher institution. **Mugabe said**

Oh congratulations, it's happy to hear that. **Pastor Tita replied**

Thank you, pastor. **Mugabe said**

You know what, I made 'Distinction' in my FSLCE, and I found myself in the same position you are today. **Pastor Tita said**

That is good, pastor. **Mugabe replied**

So, what exactly do you want me to do? **Pastor Tita asked**

Pastor, I . . . Pastor I . . . I just do not know exactly how to say this. I . . . I came to know if you could be of help to me. **Mugabe answered**

You mean, if I can sponsor you to the higher institutions like the university. Is that correct? **Pastor Tita inquired**

Yes pastor, it is exactly what I mean. **Mugabe replied**

There is no problem; I can see what I will do. **Pastor Tita said**

Thank you very much, pastor. **Mugabe said happily**

This sponsorship will involve a real amount of CFA Franc; all the same, I will see how I can help you get there. **Pastor Tita assured**

Thank you, pastor. **Mugabe replied**

Have you gone to any other place to seek for assistance before coming to me? **Pastor Tita asked**

Yes, I have gone to all those I know, and my father has even tried his best but there was no fruition. **Mugabe answered**

Wait, a second I will be right back (pastor excuses himself and went inside a room).

Mugabe remained quiet, looking around the sitting room satisfying his eyes with impressive pictures and artifacts hung on every conspicuous corner/side of the sitting room. While inside pastor Tita changed his attire and put on shorts so loose without his cloths and he re-appeared to the sitting room.

You were lucky to see me here when you came. I could have gone out long ago and only one thing I was about to finish before you came kept be back. **Pastor Tita said**

That happens, pastor. **Mugabe replied**

Come over here to my seat, I need to show you something. **Pastor Tita said**

Mugabe got up from where he sat and approached him to his seat and pastor Tita held him by the hand and started touching his neck. Mugabe was curious to know what he pastor Tita exactly was trying to do.

I love you so much pretty young man, and I feel you, uh, uh, I need you, I want you to succeed, I really, really need you, uh, uh pretty young man, oh I need you. **Pastor Tita said growing in passion**

Pastor, I need your help to get me out of this mess, I certainly do. **Mugabe replied inquisitively**

Pastor Tita gradually used Mugabe's hand to touch his protruded 'dig' with his left hand while using his right hand to begin rub Mugabe's bottom. On feeling pastor Tita's 'dig' Mugabe looked at him inquisitively in aware as pastor Tita had already grabbed his buttocks.

What is that pastor Tita? **Mugabe said,** and jumped back

I don't mean to scare you, I need you, uh, uh, I want you by my side, I want you on bed, uh, uh, I want you pretty young man. **Pastor Tita pleaded in passionately**

What is that pastor? **Mugabe got scared**

Come closer, come, I want you. Come closer, I need you, come and do that with me my love, pretty young man. **Pastor Tita continued**

I said what is that? **Mugabe shouted**

Please, lower your voice; I don't want outsiders to hear your voice. Come closer, I want to have sex with you. I promise to sponsor you to any level of choice. Come, come closer, please come. **Pastor Tita pleaded**

Sex with me! Are you a woman pastor Tita? Sex with me! You pastor Tita having sex with me? Villagers' o . . . o . . . o . . . o! Villagers' . . . o . . . o . . . o . . . o!! Villagers' . . . o . . . o . . . o . . . o . . . o . . . o!!! **Mugabe shouted**

Unfortunate it was a work day when most people had gone to work and to school.

Will you shot up or I shoot you now. If I ever hear your voice again here I will kill you and your villagers will not save you. I said shot up your mouth or you will be dead. **Pastor Tita threatened**

Mugabe immediately closed his mouth as fear gripped him; he began to walk from one side of the sitting room to the other thinking of what next to do.

Listen if I ever hear you tell any person of what happened here today, you will be dead in this village. You know who I am, and you know that playing with my name will cause you your life in this community, try me and you will be dead. Should I even kill you immediately for goodness sake? **Pastor Tita said sternly**

Please don't kill me I won't tell anybody pastor, I won't tell anybody, I want to stay alive, please spare me, I won't tell. **Mugabe pleaded**

Are you sure you won't tell. Are you sure? I see you as a person who harbors no secrets. Where is my gun so that I can kill you? **Pastor Tita threatened**

Please sir, pastor, sir, pastor, please, I won't tell anybody, spare me please, sir, pastor, please I won't tell anybody, I won't (kneeled down before pastor Tita, and with his two hands, pleading). **Mugabe continued to plead**

Don't tell anybody and I will sponsor you through the higher institution in any university of your choice. Did you hear me? If you don't tell, I will make sure that you are a university graduate. I will not kill you here today because I am a pastor an elect of God Himself, a true follower of the son of salvation. **Pastor Tita said**

I will never tell anybody about this even my parents will never know it. I won't tell them. I promise I won't tell. **Mugabe assured**

Pastor Tita opened one of his drawers and brought out a bundle of CFA Franc and handed it to him.

Take this money as a startup for your higher education schooling and make sure that you never told anybody about what happened here today otherwise I will kill you. Did you hear me? **Pastor Tita cautioned**

I will never tell pastor. I will not. **Mugabe replied**

You can now go, when that money is finished, you can come back to take another one, either here or in my parish of the Assemblies Mission in town. **Pastor Tita said**

Thank you very much pastor Tita. **Mugabe expressed**

Pastor Tita opened the doors for Mugabe to go and as he was about to leave;

Bad ass boy. **Pastor Tita said**

Mugabe rushed out of his compound with his heart in his mouth.

Pastor Tita left the village very early morning of the next day to town. When Mugabe reached home he explained everything to his father Mr. Lumumba (Brilliant) and also showed him the bundle of CFA Franc as evidence. Mr. Lumumba immediately went to the house of their eldest kinsmen Mukuru (Elder) and told him everything that Mugabe told him. And Mukuru sent emergency messages to all their kinsmen who were at home. They all gathered at his house and he asked Mugabe to narrate his story to them. Mugabe truthfully narrated his ordeal to them. They immediately sent representatives to pastor Tita's father to inform him of what happened, how their son Mugabe was immorally approached (an abomination) by his son Tita. And that they needed pastor Tita's presence within two weeks so as to resolve the issue otherwise pastor Tita's house in the village must be burnt down and their young men would be after him.

On delivering the message to Mr. Cazembi of his son's immoral conduct and violation of the traditional norms, rules and values, Mr. Cazembi denied pastor Tita absolutely as his son and told the messengers that for years he had cut ties with the 'Son of Disgrace' called pastor Tita and that his own kinsmen were witnesses to that. Mr. Cazembi directed them to his own eldest kinsman called Diop (Ruler) to deliver their message. And the messengers angrily left his house and he accompanied them to Diop's house where the messengers finally delivered their message. Diop promised them to do whatever he could to make pastor Tita to be present at home within the given time period and to make him pay for his abominable behavior if found guilty. Diop consulted Mr. Cazembi and other of their kinsmen and an SOS (save our soul) was immediately sent to pastor Tita by dispatch of few young men. Pastor Tita received his message in person.

Pastor Tita arrived home and was present in person on the hearing day. He was interrogated by both Mugabe's and his kinsmen respectively through their leaders Diop for Mugabe and Mukuru for pastor Tita. That is, Mugabe's eldest kinsman questioned pastor Tita and vice versa.

Pastor Tita. **Mukuru called**

Yes my clansmen. **Pastor Tita responded**

Do you know why we asked you to come home and be present here today? **Mukuru asked**

No my clansmen. **Pastor Tita answered**

Tell pastor Tita the allegations leveled against him. **Mr. Nyongpua** (A new thing has come) **resolution moderator said**

This young man here (pointing at Mugabe) is our son. Have you seen him before? **Mukuru asked**

Excuse me pastor Tita, you understand the implications of this type of allegations, therefore, we ask you to say the truth and nothing but the truth. **Mr. Nyongpua said**

Yes, I have seen the young man before. **Pastor Tita answered**

Where did you see him? **Mukuru asked**

In my house my clansmen. **Pastor Tita answered**

Can you please tell us his name if you still remember? **Mukuru inquired**

I guess his name is Mugabe. **Pastor Tita replied**

Did Mugabe come to your house based on an invitation? **Mukuru asked**

No, it was not by my invitation, my clansmen. **Pastor Tita answered**

Did he come to deliver a message to you or to any of the occupants of your house? **Mukuru asked**

No my clansmen. **Pastor Tita answered**

Did you welcome him to your house when you perhaps opened the gate and saw him? **Mukuru asked**

Yes, I welcomed him. **Pastor Tita answered**

Did you ever asked him to leave your compound after seen him at the entrance of your house immediately after opening the gate and he refused? **Mukuru asked**

No, I never did ask him to leave. **Pastor Tita answered**

Did you ever allow him entrance in any of your maybe sitting room(s) by yourself? **Mukuru asked**

Yes I did take him to one of my parlors. **Pastor Tita answered**

So Mugabe never forced himself on you did he? **Mukuru asked**

No, he never did. **Pastor Tita answered**

When Mugabe was ushered into your parlor by you and was perhaps offered a seat which he humbly accepted: did he ever tried to still something maybe in your absence as you went inside to get him something like drinks as a visitor and you caught him? **Mukuru asked**

No, he behaved himself and never tried to still anything. **Pastor Tita replied**

When in your parlor as you said, did you ask him to leave that the conversation was over and he insisted on staying? **Mukuru asked**

No, I never asked him to leave. **Pastor Tita answered**

So, you made us to understand that Mugabe's visit to your house and his short stay with you were all accepted by you? **Mukuru asked**

Yes I welcomed his visit. **Pastor Tita answered**

While in your room pastor Tita; did Mugabe displayed an immoral behavior that forced you to repudiate him? **Mukuru asked**

No, not at all, he ever did. **Pastor Tita answered**

No further questions my clansmen. **Mukuru concluded**

It is now your turn to ask your questions Diop. Mugabe I hope you were briefed by your kinsmen before this resolution hearing that it is against our tradition to knowingly fabricate, forge or level false allegations against an innocent man or woman so as to tarnish his image or hang him/her on a stake without cause. Therefore, you must say nothing but the truth. **Mr. Nyongpua said**

Mugabe why were you in his house? **Diop asked**

I went to ask him for help? **Mugabe answered**

What type of help did you went there to ask him for? **Diop asked**

I went to pastor Tita house to ask him to help me with my higher institution education. **Mugabe humbly said**

You went to ask him for help with your education and what else? **Diop asked**

I told him that I needed financial assistance with my university education because I have finished my secondary school with all my exams cleared. **Mugabe replied**

Was that all? **Diop asked**

Yes, that was all I went there for. **Mugabe answered**

Pastor Tita is that true? **Mr. Nyongpua asked**

Yes my clansmen that were exactly what he came there for. **Pastor Tita answered**

Did you agree to sponsor him? **Mr. Nyongpua asked**

Yes, I did. **Pastor Tita answered**

Is that true Mugabe? **Diop asked**

He forced me to something that I still do not understand, and when I rejected that he threatened to kill me and later he gave me money. **Mugabe answered**

What did he ask you to do that you rejected? **Diop asked**

Pastor Tita drew me closer to him and touched my buttocks and grabbed my hand to touch his 'dig', and told me that he wanted to have sex with me. **Mugabe answered**

What was he trying to do? **Diop asked**

He knows I am not aware of that. **Mugabe answered**

Pastor Tita wanted to have sex with you like a man and woman, is that right? **Diop asked**

Is pastor Tita a woman? I am a man; I do not know whether he is a woman. **Mugabe answered**

You heard him pastor Tita. Are you a man or a woman? **Mr. Nyongpua asked**

I am a man and my 'dig' is right here with me inside my panties to prove that. **Pastor Tita answered**

If you are a man as you said, why did you touch Mugabe passionately and wanted to have sex with him? **Mr. Nyongpua questioned**

That was a mistake I made, I was under the influence of alcohol, and so, I lost myself and never knew what I was doing again. I took him to be one of my lady friends. **Pastor Tita replied**

What happened next after you refused his approach Mugabe? **Diop asked**

Pastor Tita threatened to kill me, to shoot me to death. **Mugabe answered**

Why did you threatened to kill Mugabe pastor Tita? **Mr. Nyongpua asked**

I have forgotten everything that I told him that day. I took him to be one of those ladies that had gulped me a lot of money and who always promise to marry me, and at the end they disappoint me. So, I wanted to use all kinds of fear inducing methods to have it with them and make them pay. **Pastor Tita answered**

When he threatened to kill you what happened next? **Diop asked**

I shouted and shouted and shouted. **Mugabe answered**

When you shouted what happened? **Diop asked**

That was when he threatened to kill me as he warned me to shut up my mouth. **Mugabe answered**

When you shut up your mouth, what happened? **Diop asked**

He pleaded with me that I should not tell anybody about that otherwise he would kill me, and I told him that I would not disclose it to anybody just to pacify him because he had already started looking for his gun to kill me with. **Mugabe answered**

What else happened? **Diop asked**

Pastor Tita gave me money. **Mugabe answered**

Where is the money? **Diop asked**

Here is the money (Mukuru brought out the bundle of CFA Franc) and placed it on the table. The money is still like that, nobody touched it. **Mukuru said**

After accepting the money what happened? **Diop asked**

He told me that he would sponsor me to any of my desired level in the university as long as I do not tell anybody. I agreed and he opened the doors and asked me to go home. **Mugabe answered**

No further questions. **Diop said**

Pastor Tita since you took Mugabe to be a woman, why did you plead with him not to tell anybody and why did you refer him as "pretty young man"? **Mr. Nyongpua asked**

I cannot remember referring him as a pretty young man, I thought him to be a woman. I pleaded with him because based on my status in these village/communities his disclosure of such an act would tantamount to tarnishing my image which I do not like. **Pastor Tita answered**

Should we accepted that you misidentified him to be a young woman. Why did you choose the option of rape so as to satisfy your sexual desire or as the best method of procreation that is immoral? **Mr. Nyongpua asked**

I never wished to do that with him, I thought he was one of my ladies. **Pastor Tita answered**

We understand that: why did you choose two traditional immoral options as the best method of achieving your goals in this case whatsoever? **Mr. Nyongpua queried**

I am sorry for trying to subvert the Traditional Beliefs and imposing my own method of sexual gratification, my clansmen. **Pastor Tita replied**

Why did you gave him money after he rejected your approach and you told him that he should use that as a startup money for his university, and that he should come back to collect more either at your house here in the village or at the Pastoral House? **Mr. Nyongpua asked**

I remember giving him money but I have certainly forgotten the exact amount or any other promise made. **Pastor Tita answered**

Pastor Tita, are you aware that our tradition abhors all forms of abominations despite the importance attached to it? And are you aware that such development of passionate interest in a fellow man is a complete violation of the moral law as evidenced in our tradition? **Mr. Nyongpua said**

Yes, I am aware of that. But I ask you to please do forgive me for I acted under the influence of alcohol. I lost myself while under the influence and misbehaved. **Pastor Tita replied**

Pastor Tita: do you understand that involvement in such an action-having sex with a fellow man attracts only the death penalty traditionally? **Mr. Nyongpua asked**

Yes, I understand my clansmen. I implore you to please spare me this time, I promise not to allow myself to be controlled by alcoholic drinks next time, henceforth, I shall always try to verify the real gender of my visitor before advancing to him/her for sexual relationships, and more so, I promise to have sex with my sexual female counterparts avoiding all forms of immoral behavior forbidden by our tradition. **Pastor Tita answered**

Pastor Tita, do you understand that threatening a fellow kinsman, clansman, tribesman or any innocent person at all with death without cause is forbidden by our tradition? **Mr. Nyongpua asked**

Yes, my clansmen. I understand that, but I never meant to harm him. I mistook him to be one of those ladies I mingle with. **Pastor Tita answered**

Do you understand that there are punishments associated with such an offence if found guilty? **Mr. Nyongpua asked**

Yes my clansmen, but I put myself under oath not to try that again. I vowed not to harm him having understood his true identity in whatever methods. **Pastor Tita answered**

No further questions. **Mr. Nyongpua concluded**

They involved kinsmen asked pastor Tita and Mugabe to leave them alone while they made their decisions on the allegations level against him. They clansmen bowed their heads together. Diop said that he had nothing to say in defense of pastor Tita, that pastor Tita was guilty of traditional moral violation, in this case an abomination, that pastor Tita's defense of mistaking Mugabe to be a woman was pure fallacy, and that in a situation of no complete sex with the complainant an appropriate punishments must be enforced. And pastor Tita's father asked for a stiffer sentencing and that had it been that pastor Tita had what 'he called sex' with

Mugabe he could have faced the death option inevitably. The two involved kinsmen weighed the death option by hanging and agreed that for such an option to be effective, pastor Tita must first release into the man either through his anal opening, through his mouth or at any part of his body with or without the man's consent, or force the victim to rub his 'dig' to ejaculation with or without the man's consent. And those conditions must take place and based on Mugabe's testimony none of the conditions happened. It was on the processes to any of the conditions for a death sentence that took place. They frowned at pastor Tita's invention of sexual immorality and vowed to take drastic measures against him.

Pastor Tita. **Mr. Nyongpua called**

Yes, I am here. **Pastor Tita replied**

Mugabe. **Mr. Nyongpua called**

Yes, my clansmen. **Mugabe answered**

You two are free to come back and join us. **Mr. Nyongpua said**

Pastor Tita and Mugabe came back and rejoined them once more, and Tita was looking at those of his kinsmen and the others he knew inquisitively as if to say; "considering my importance, please I deserved to be spared".

Pastor Tita. **Mr. Nyongpua called**

Yes, my clansmen. **Pastor Tita asked**

We have reached a verdict on the allegations leveled against you by Mugabe. **Mr. Nyongpua said**

Do you understand that we all here are your kinsmen and as well your clansmen? And do you know that you are also important to all of us? **Mr. Nyongpua asked**

Yes, my clansmen, I understand that. **Pastor Tita answered**

We have truthfully looked into these allegations against you and discovered that you committed an absolute traditional moral violation. Never in the history of this place had we heard of any man in this community who acted the way you did trying to have male to male sex with a fellow man. And you certainly have no defense to your gross misconduct. As your clansmen we are dismayed by your actions to Mugabe, on that day he paid you a visit. Mugabe has proved to you that despite all your education overseas you are worthless and of no importance to us. You only went overseas to get yourself trained and deeply involved in all kinds of immoral behavior and you returned back home so as to spread evil seeds of immorality among us thereby infesting our conducive homes with contagious immoral diseases. Although you never invited him into your house on that day, and having made a public statement-an appeal, of your readiness to assist the likes of him in the community during a CDI, therefore, Mugabe had every notion to believe that you could equally be of help to him, hence, he visited your house uninvited, so, this absolves him of any blame and as well vindicated him. Pastor Tita, one step further could have sent you to the glutton and maybe tied a rope round your neck, you were so lucky that you did not complete your immoral mission this time.

Our Traditional Law made it clear that any person found guilty of having sex with his sister, mother, brother, father or with a fellow man or woman through either anal openings, reproductive openings, or mouth or through the body should be hanged on a tree until he/she dies and lives no more, and his/her head must be cut off with a very sharpened knife. And his/her remains be buried without proper burial procedures and also be denied mourning. Having cross examined Mugabe and you, we found you pastor Tita not guilty of any of the above offences. And our Traditional Law further states that any man/woman who had lustful contacts with his parents, sisters, brothers, or a fellow man or woman, should be avoided for a reasonable number of time and distanced from being one of us until the duration of his/her banishment is ended. Having cross examined you, we found you guilty of this offence, and therefore you will be sentenced accordingly. In addition, our Traditional Law states that any person of an adult age found guilty of the death of an innocent kinsman, clansman, tribesman or any person at all without cause shall be sentenced to death by hanging; and that any person of an adult age who knowingly sent a minor to commit such an offense so as to save his/her skin shall also be sentenced to death by hanging while such a minor shall receive a reasonable number of strokes of whips in public until blood gushes from his body and he/she confesses not to do that again unless such a minor was induced, coerced or forced by the said adult to indulge into such an immoral act. Pastor Tita, having examined you, you were found not guilty of this type of offence. Finally our Traditional Law made it clear that any adult who threatens a fellow kinsman, clansman or tribesman with a threat of death using any material that could cause harm or death, or any substance that could cause harm or death without cause and/or provocation shall be made to be responsible for the life of the threatened until his/her or the death of the threatened through natural causes, otherwise he/she will be liable for the death of the threatened and will be executed to compensate for the lost live(s) by the threatened. Tita, having examined you, you were found guilty of this type of offence, and you will be sentenced accordingly.

We your clansmen never made this Traditional Laws, and we will never change them because of any person and/or group of persons despite his/her and /or their social status or importance in the community. We have reached an agreement on the appropriate punishment(s) to be pronounced against you so that next time you must act sane like a reasonable person. We have decided that you pastor Tita will be banished from this village and the entire communities as governed by CDI for a period of seven (7) complete years starting from tomorrow for your immoral and inappropriate behavior against Mugabe—for your homosexual venture. And we have also decided that you pastor Tita will be bared for additional two (2) years from this village and the entire communities as governed by CDI for your threat of death against Mugabe after he raised alarm against your immoral and obnoxious approach towards him. Summarily, you pastor Tita is hereby banished for a total of nine (9) complete years starting from tomorrow for been found guilty of the violation of the stated section of our Traditional Laws. Besides, Mugabe's life is hereby entrusted into your hands until your death, should anything happens to Mugabe, you will be treated accordingly as stipulated forth by our tradition. We allow you today to put your things together and vacate this village very early in the morning tomorrow, we will send those who will come and check on you to verify whether you have traveled back to town. You will not be seen in any section of CDI communities or send the affected communities any of your CFA Franc for a nine complete years, without which you have chosen the option of death as your only punishment. Besides, you must turnoff your tap water, and you must not supply water to any of the CDI communities for nine complete years. Please, after here today, do not venture to approach any of us for any reason whatsoever, if you choose you can go to any of this country's courts for redress but we have spoken. **Mr. Nyongpua delivered**

Nine good years! **Pastor Tita exclaimed**

. . . . Silence . . . .

I thought . . . I. Thank you for not killing me, I mistook him to be . . . I mean, I never couldn't . . . Away from home so long a period? **Pastor Tita murmured**

. . . . Silence . . . .

Where else will I . . . Tomorrow and nine years? **Pastor Tita continued to murmur**

Those clansmen continued to remain silence without uttering a word.

I will . . . I have heard you, my kinsmen, oh . . . clansmen. Tomorrow I will vacate this place for good. All my properties . . . my house, I mean, all my . . . **Pastor Tita confused**

You have heard us, you can now go? **Mr. Nyongpua said loudly**

See you all later. **Pastor Tita said and left.**

In the morning of the following day without delay pastor Tita obeyed the Last Order and packed some of his relevant needed things out of his compound and locked his gate so that nobody enters his house. And early that morning prior to his departure, those sent by his kinsmen to observe his exit were present steps away from his residency.

CHAPTER TWENTY ONE

Pastor Tita Completes his Exile

News of pastor Tita's Traditional Law violation circulated in his village and his entire home community. Some of his community members were so astonished that somebody who called himself a pastor could indulge in such a stinking immoral behavior. They said that "how could somebody that had nobody chasing him ran directly to a snare and entangled himself. What does he expect? He had already crucified himself and is tempting everybody to put him to rest. Does he thinks that we are some of those obnoxious beings overseas who have no Innermost Beings, who are moral outcast? Pastor Tita ought to have known that moral death is the worst form of death, such a death there is obviously no resurrection". Those decided to distance themselves from such an entity who had long ago abandoned his parents who eked out livelihood so as to see him through during his young hood. They hailed the decisions of the affected clansmen as the best solution to his share moral decadence and threatening of innocent life. And said that he was lucky he never got hung for his man on man passionate imbecility.

Still another group of people believed that they had set pastor Tita up and brought him out to be hanged just like the biblical only son of God, because he made promises and donations to the entire community through the CDI. Those held the view that the enemies of progress had dealt stingily hard with innocent pastor Tita just because he was determined to make things easy for his home people. and they criticized the decisions of the affected clansmen as too heartless and without cause, and even though pastor Tita may have erred traditionally, there was no obvious reason to send him on exile for such number of years, but some of them feared doing anything in defense of him because of the mean traditional decision implementation.

Another section of his community members, especially those who seem to be benefactors of his ruins debunked all the allegations against him as well as his conviction of the alleged offences. They believed that pastor Tita was setup and immediately convicted without giving him the needed opportunities to self defense as should be allowed under traditional law. They said that his parents as masterminded by his wicked father had withdrawn him from view and took him away so that he could not be of help to them. They vowed not to have anything to do with such a wicked father and as well to fight on pastor Tita's behalf. Some of them indicated that they would travel to town to see him and contemplate with him on the best ways out of this jungle of imposition of limbo. They refused the affected clansmen's decision as stupid and uncalled for. And wondered why such a wealthy philanthropist should be banished at such rate despite his importance in the entire communities of CDI. The indicated that their society would soon be embroiled in an endless conflict if the decision against pastor Tita was not reversed quickly.

The last section of the people were neutral, they reasoned that pastor Tita maybe innocent but they could not say for sure because sometimes those who play the gods are the real devils themselves. "Pastor Tita could be seen and viewed as the messiah for our communities whereas he is a pure and absolute devil in innocuous skin. He could have promised heaven for the people but in truth he represents hell and damnation. More so, pastor Tita could be branded to be guilty of an offence he never committed based on pure greed, the desire for hindrances and obstructions of the communities developments which he contributes to". On the decisions by those affected clansmen, they said that they must have taken their decisions based on pure verification of evidences presented and testimonies by the offended, which he pastor Tita must have been asked questions on and allowed to respond accordingly. So, based on the traditional notion of equity, equality and fair play, those clansmen never had taken wrong decisions against him based on pure fallacy and false allegations". They reasoned that having noticed how he contributes to CDI and coupled with his help to others that needed assistance, his kinsmen couldn't had been left out in the pool of the assisted individuals, so to level allegations against him and got him convicted would mean a 'fool's gold'. They also said that "some of his kinsmen who have not benefited from his wealth could plot against him after series of request for assistance and he declined. Or those that do not like his influence in the community could look for a veritable ground to get him out of their ways". Thus, they concluded that in either situation there should be calm while the truth is out. And they refused to blame either side for their actions but believed that their tradition had not been contaminated by cultural influences so as to punish her sons/daughters without cause, and that although most still believe in their traditional rules, the use of false allegations shouldn't be the best option to convincing community members to re-accept traditional values and ideologies.

Pastor Tita continued his pastoral duties at the Assemblies Mission, and shortly after the circulation of the news of his immoral conduct, some of his sympathizers started coming from his village to visit him. They asked him what happened and he explained everything to them that he had a visitor in his room during which he only exchanged mere greetings and conversations and the visitor left. They asked him who was the visitor and whether the visitor was a male or female, and he told them that he never knew again but that he mistook the visitor to be a female during the time of visit, and that the visitor turned out to be one of his clansmen. And they asked him if there was really a decision taken against him based on the allegations that they heard. He replied that he had been suspended for a period of nine (9) complete years on the condition that he must not either come home or visit his village, either send any money or material things to CDI communities within the said time period, and that he must not do anything to harm the complainant or his relatives otherwise he must be treated same. They asked him who and who made such heartless decisions, and he told them that it was an agreement between his kinsmen and those of the alleged offended kinsmen based on their Traditional Laws.

Some of his sympathizers as led by Mr. Leza (One who besets) expressed their dismay of such a decisive traditional decision against a man of his person. And that they came to know the next line of action because they had not been happy since they heard of the news of his banishment from the rest of their entire CDI communities. They expressed their readiness to align with him and get something done so that he could return home to the village so soon. Pastor Tita told them that he had nine complete years to be free to visiting village home again. So, for him to be on a safer side he needed time to reach such juncture on the next line of action. They tried to convince him that they were determined to deal ruthlessly with those clansmen and kinsmen in a way that he wouldn't believe if he only chose to work collaboratively with them because his cooperation was the only go ahead order needed from him. Pastor Tita insisted that he needed ample time for decision making concerning the issue so as to avoid stepping on sensitive toes. Mr. Leza twisted him more in order to convince him to accept their readiness to combat those clansmen and the young man involved in this type of scandalous offence considering his importance to the entire CDI communities, and he revealed to them that nine (9) years was too much for him to be absent from their communities because they needed him most more than any other member of their communities. Pastor Tita saw the merits of staging a war against his banishers but decided against it because he was guilty of such an offence and, more so, some of those who came to align with him could be one of those affected by his passionate immoral actions. And besides, those clansmen could not easily be underrated because they were not only on the right side of the law, they could also have all what it takes to put him down completely.

Pastor Tita paid absolute attention to his sympathizers and insisted that he be given ample time after which his decision would be made known to them, and as they came and gone, he gave them monetary gifts of substantial amounts of CFA Franc. After one year of his exile, he got married to a female member of his church named Bela (To perch). Pastor Tita took this measure so as to make it appear that he was really under the influence of alcohol that made him to mistake Mugabe to be a lady. His marriage could make his offended kinsmen and clansmen to believe that his violation of the traditional norms and values and laws was not intentional, and also helped to convince them to begin to accept him again, and also buttress his support in the CDI communities, and his sympathizers were happy that he had gotten married as they went in numbers to his Pastoral Residence to congratulate him.

Pastor Tita kept his cool and continued to enjoy life with his wife at the Assemblies Mission Pastoral House, and he agreed with Mrs. Bela to postpone the issue of having kids until after a given number of years by that time his banishment could either be ended or about to be ended. Shortly after his return from the village and as his villagers and certain CDI community members, and other concerned individuals continued to come to sympathizes with him, in one of his sermons he admonished his congregations to be God fearing more than never before and to debunk all rumors and innuendos fabricated by the enemies so as to disorganize the Assemblies Mission and force its members to join other congregations. Pastor Tita told his congregation that such hand works by the enemies should and must be rejected by them with their last pinch of strength. He told them that "Since I returned back from my trip overseas where I had my training at the Assemblies Mission Seminary, there have been secret moves against my person so as to tarnish my image and as well cast aspersions against my innocent person. Some people never approved of my joining this church in the first place, and when I became the pastor they were not happy and hence they vowed to put me to a stop using any means possible. My successful completion of my pastoral assignment overseas angered them and they did all they could while I was overseas to repatriate me back home but their efforts were scuttled because our members over there never wished to put me to a stop without credible reasons. As at today those who were after me during the initial instance are at it again, this time they are using every means to put me out of work, withdraw me from view and as well get rid of me. Since my life is on the line again, I implore you to work closely with me because through your assurance of reverence and obedience to God my weakness will turn to strength and my enemies will never get hold of me".

In about two years of his marriage to Mrs. Bela, she requested that they visit home to see his parents and other villages and as well get her introduced to them. This was necessary because it was customary for a newly married man to introduce his wife to his parents, brothers, sisters especially and his relatives etc if they lived differently from his place of residency. Since pastor Tita knew her parents, it was therefore left for him to introduce her same. But pastor Tita told her that there was something at stake in his village and that forcing himself on them must terminate his young life untimely and that he wouldn't want to risk. And that since they are already married as time progresses one day she must definitely see his people, and that since she had agreed to postpone the issue of child bearing, before their children begin to arrive he promised her that they would be home in the village without excuses, so consequently, Mrs. Bela abided by his decisions.

As things happened before the end of his banishment and barely two years left to the end of nine years exile period, he realigned and convinced his wife of the need to begin child bearing after which they were sure to hit his village line. Mrs. Bela conceived and had a son whom they called Din (Great), and shortly after the birth of Din pastor Tita's banishment period came to an end and he was again free to enter and leave his village and CDI communities without hindrances and obstructions. He returned home to his village one afternoon, and those that he told that he would be visiting home with his wife and first son came out in mass to see him and welcome him back once again in his residence. Pastor Tita and Mrs. Bela warmly received them and thanked them for their continued supports in his absence during the days when he was serving the imposed punishment of banishment (PoB) pronounced on, and implored them to continue to work with him and his family as they joined hands in developing their communities, especially through CDI. And those welcomed him and assured him of their readiness to collaborate with him and stressed the need for his supports to both individuals in particular and their communities in general. Some of his visitors came to see him with different types of gifts.

Meanwhile, as his sympathizers continued to align with him, in about five (5) months left off to the end of his banishment, he reached a clandestine agreement with some of those he trusted through Mr. Leza and they decided to embark in all efforts so as to wheel the table of ruler ship to their favors. Pastor Tita began to spend time again in his house as was before his exile, sometimes with his families and also continued to hold secret meetings with his newly formed gang of disgruntled persons. In his first public appearance to the CDI gathering Pastor Tita was once again given the opportunity to speak to the entire communities. He expressed his regrets for his absent for about nine (9) whole years from any of the CDI gatherings. He told them that his absence was necessary so as to avoid meeting his untimely death because having been cornered; there was nothing he could do. He begged them to forget everything they must have heard about him in the past and to continue to cooperate with him in their pursuits for community developments and assistance to one another. He said that he had been brandished as an immoral person by some wicked minds and dares anyone whoever said that he was guilty of a gay sexual relationship, and warned them that "anybody found guilty of circulating such false news or directly tells him that in person, will be severely death with" as pastor Tita was speaking Mrs. Makemba (goddess) rushed out from the middle of nowhere and spitted on his face and spit covered his face, and she shouted "Outcast! Outcast . . . o . . . o . . . o . . . o!! Outcast . . . o . . . o . . . o . . . o . . . o . . . !! And she disappeared from view.

Following the interruption by Mrs. Makemba who never speaks out in vain, there were temporary disruptions and people began to murmur and some of them instantly left the CDI gathering with Mrs. Makemba. And there was an appeal for calm from the CDI officials and later normalcy returned. CDI officials pleaded with pastor Tita to continue with his speech as he must be away of Mrs. Makemba's mission because she never comes into the open like that in vain. Pastor Tita used his handkerchief to wipe his face, and he appealed to them to forgo the temporary disruption caused by Mrs. Makemba's sudden appearance and continue to listen to what he was telling them. He made it clear to them that he was not the guy to play with and get away easily. To buttress his supports he gave them a donation of tens of thousands of CFA Franc more than he usually gave, and they accepted his usual supports and asked him to forget about the past and concentrate on the present because there was no way the decisions by those affected clansmen could be revisited, and they encouraged him to continue to contribute towards the development of their communities.

As the years added pastor Tita began to get himself involved with land disputes and also began to lay claim to pieces of lands that were neither inherited by his father nor bought by him, although he Mr. Cazembi was alive and healthy he started grabbing lands that never for once belonged to them. But his father consistently objected to his notion of ceasing innocent people's lands as theirs, because there had never been a time he, Mr. Cazembi, either inherited or purchased those lands from their owners which pastor Tita had his interests on. So, on pastor Tita's farmland 'use of force acquisition spree', he never defeated any of those that he seized their lands in the presence of their clansmen who were responsible for resolving such land disputes and they never backed him up in any court. Pastor Tita continues to grab farmlands and continue to ignore his father's advice and plea to back off innocent community members farmlands and he continues to lose.

Pastor Tita made solemn promises of free education, provision of employment, financial assistance and overseas sponsorship to any country of their choice etc to the youths of his village in particular and the CDI communities in general. Consequently, he again won the admirations and supports of some of the Youth Wing Association (YWA), especially those who never cared to take themselves memory lane of his conduct, and those who are family brigands, and those in dire need of assistance and those who assume that their successes lies in a foreign land. As time progressed, he opted for the position of the president of CDI and subsequently spent a lot of money to carry his campaigns across the entire CDI communities through using Mr. Leza as his campaign chief. He pleaded with eligible CDI voters to nominate him the President of CDI on the conditions that he was the most positioned candidate to ascend to the throne as could be evidence by his immense contributions to both CDI and the members of the entire communities in persons. He urged YWA to choose him because he was better positioned to understand their needs better and as well offer them unquestionable helping hands. He later dispatched gifts so as to win the support of the entire people and also gave huge amounts of money to his clandestine gang of distracters simply known as Community Development Union Alliance (CDUA) to distribute among key officials of CDI so as to convince them to vote for him. CDUA embarked on a community wide house to house campaign in order to convince the people on the merits of voting for pastor Tita, especially based on his status as a pastor, he was deemed to be in the best position to fill the positions of the president of CDI, and based on his philanthropic ideals, he was best positioned to be of most assistance to their people none discriminatorily and most responsive to their individual needs. They used his free tap water as an example because he had no restrictions placed on it and it ran free to the benefit of the CDI communities in general.

Elections were held and pastor Tita came fourth (4[Th]) among all those that were voted for. Furious on seen the results and determined to impose himself on CDI as its president whatsoever, he immediately rejected the outcome of the election on the grounds that it was not only unfair but rigged to favor the wrong candidate based on discrimination because he was once wrongly accused of immoral conduct which he had already completed the necessary punishments for. He met with CDUA and they appealed for the cancellation of the result of the election and the hosting of a new election. CDI election committee chairman Mr. Zola (Productive) rejected CDUA appeal and boldly told them that CDI forbids any form of riggings or manipulations of election results, and that contrary to the notion that the elections were rigged in disfavor of pastor Tita based on his past records, there was not a time his previous bad records were put under consideration otherwise he should not had been allowed to contest in the first place. Furthermore, "our people are still traditionally minded and therefore most of them may have chosen to prefer the traditional ways". And Mr. Zola made it clear to them that the outcome of the election was final and stays absolutely irreversible. CDUA still irate employed the use of all strategies to get CDI officials revisit the election, but to no fruition.

CHAPTER TWENTY TWO

Pastor Tita Secedes and Becomes a Maniac

Having completely lost hope of being the president of CDI, pastor Tita without delay called for the secession of his village from the rest of the CDI communities. In less than no time after his call for secession, pastor Tita declared the secession of his village from the rest of CDI control communities-the CDI communities are communities that made up one autonomous community. In his secession message delivered in his house flanked by CDUA members and also organized through its vice president Mr. Leza, during the swearing in of the newly elected CDI president, pastor Tita told them "I with the supports of CDUA, and my village/community and as the rightful president of CDI has decided to secede from the rest of the community villages comprising CDI. Our decision to secede became necessary after a careful review of the elections that produced Mr. Sebehive (Bearer of good fortune) the assumed current president of CDI who is currently being sworn in today. My village, our village has been deprived the opportunity of producing the next president of CDI based on pure discrimination, greed, hatred, and inequality as you all can see. Our village/community can't continue to mingle and intermingle with the other villages as CDI members while we are been deprived of our merited position as CDI president. Therefore, I hereby call upon all of you to give me the needed supports and also to buttress me as your leader while we marched on to independence as a free village from the rest of this obnoxious, heinous, and nefarious autonomous community and its CDI". CDUA promised to corporate with him in their quest for an independent village on the conditions that he pastor Tita deserved his victory as the next president of CDI, and it called on all his villagers/community members to alliance with him and CDUA and support all his decisions so as to reclaim the mantle of leadership which had wrongly be taken by Mr. Sebehive. Those that attended his Declaration for Secession (DS) speech were mostly youths some of them members of YWA, especially those that fall within the categories of; education continuation seekers, overseas lobbyists, employment seekers, or had other needs. The YWA member, Baranyanka (They hate me), who spoke on the behalf of their village, assured him and CDUA of their supports, and told him that they would do whatever that was necessary to make sure that success was achieved. They expressed their readiness to ensure that pastor Tita reclaimed his rightful position in the power echelon of CDI by doing everything within their reach to ensure that he was sworn in as the president of CDI through either an electoral college or a reversal of the election results. They encouraged him not to worry, that although Mr. Sebehive has become the president of CDI but with the mercenaries already in place they could still reach a compromise whereby he would be made a president of CDI before the end of the tenure that started as they speak. Baranyanka appealed to pastor Tita to weigh his promises, especially to YWA before making them because false promises and caricatures are what anger the youths most, and "If you do not play with our resolve as YWA, we will not play with your preferences and choices". Pastor Tita thanked them for their understanding and said that henceforth there village/community remained a free village that could now embark on her own activities uninterrupted. And he later told them that the promises which he initially made to the CDI communities were now theirs while they wait to see how CDI through its surrogate president Mr. Sebehive reacts to his decision.

Pastor Tita returned back to the Assemblies Mission to stay with his family and also to continue with his profession. CDUA continued with the operations of ensuring that everything went smoothly and that CDI's influence was barred from his village. And CDUA loyalists continued to intensify their supports to him and to pressure for the independence of his/their village. Pastor Tita provided money for the building of their Village Hall but his village heads led by their leader Mr. Tugiramahoro (Lets have peace) declined to accept his money and as well provided a place where the proposed hall would be built. So, he bought a place with CDUA's connections and built the hall for CDUA and its supporters. During their independence agitation, the CDI never cared to recall him and his CDUA. Most of the adult members of his village made it known to CDI that their village remained intact and a strong member of CDI, that there was never a time it had separated from CDI and had never for once had the notion of been independent from CDI member villages, and that they will continue to contribute and donate to CDI without hindrances, and that they still abide by the rules of their autonomous community with absolute reverence to the autonomous community king. CDI continued to show its supports to pastor Tita's village and urge CDUA and its supporters to shun any act that could result to destructive violence despite the merit attached to it, and to address their concerns appropriately. CDI urged CDUA to avoid confrontation with CDI communities' autonomous leader because any act to jeopardize the stability, continuity, existence and coexistence of their autonomous communities would have disastrous consequences whose outcome may not be favorable to any person or group of persons found guilty of such infractions. And Mr. Sebehive reiterated Mr. Zola's decisions that the results of the elections that brought him into power was final and had no chances of been revisited despite they calls and clamors by those 'who out of their selfish aggrandizements to represent all sexes lost out in the leadership battle, after all what position did they occupied, a far cry from real victory itself'.

CDUA continued to hold meetings with or without the presence of pastor Tita its president but been presided over by its vice president Mr. Leza, urging their supporters to continue to buttress CDUA activities and they sometimes shared gifts among member supporters. CDUA later began its development programs drawn from the formats of CDI but with minor modifications. Those of pastor Tita's village members who refused to identify themselves with his self declared independence from the rest of the CDI villages for no obvious reasons continued to distance themselves from CDUA and having anything to do with him. Those reasoned that pastor Tita had been bedeviled overseas and was no more worthy of their trust and collaborations, and that he had once been convicted of abominable encounters and therefore he deserved not to speak for them. Pastor Tita continued to express his usual readiness to assist his villagers, especially those who believe in their independent in whatever ways financially, materially and religiously possible.

CDUA continued to attract supporters both within and outside his village mostly among the youths and the needy. In one of CDUA's meetings, pastor Tita gave money to students who wanted to continue with their education for their one semester/ term payments and promised to give money to those involved in, with different kinds of businesses like trade, crafts and handiwork the next time that CDUA' meeting holds. Unfortunately, before the next CDUA meeting when he would make good his promise to the second recipients, pastor Tita was transferred out from his branch of the Assemblies Mission to another branch located in one of the far distanced states within his country. He was posted to his new location so as to assist with the developments of that branch of the Assemblies Mission. His relocation was with immediate effect and it posed a problem of promise fulfillment for him because the Assemblies Mission of his new location had few members and was located at the village side of township. The place of his new location was religiously pluralistic (that is, it had missed religious beliefs with less than the majority as protestants of different denominations, and their financial strengths of its members as well as their donation values were far less than half of that of his old location).

Pastor Tita made it clear to CDUA that he had been suddenly posted to a new location far distanced from his old parish which summarily implied a complete one and half (11/2) days of travel on the road unless he took flights which was not possible because of his home village location. He told them that as a result, he could only be around for the meeting few times a year, especially during crucial decisions periods, and that his transfer affected his savings which meant that if he does not make extra efforts to be on the expected level financially, he could not be able to meet all the necessary financial obligations as would be required of him, but assured them and the rest of his followers that he would do whatever good that was necessary to make good his promises to them, especially the youths. CDUA acknowledged his predicaments and its effects on their resolve for permanent separation from the rest of CDI villages, and assured him that they would continue to do their best and that although CDUA could have the ability to raise money when needed but wondered what could come out of it if there was not enough money available so as to continue to pacify frayed nerves. Pastor Tita attended one of the meetings from his new location, and while coming home to attend the meeting, he spent nearly two days on the road with his wife. He never mad good his promise to the other sections of the youths, but he implored them to bear with him because relocation was unanticipated, in his words "when such a thing happens, I hope I deserve no blames. I still remember what I promised you and I will make good my promises in due time, please do not give up". They gave him all the needed supports that he deserved and he spent few more days at home before going back.

As YWA adopted a wait and hope attitude, the distance barrier created an unanticipated shortfalls in his revenue generation casted aspersion on his ability to make good his promises but he continued to draw from his existing financial pockets to attend to the needs of his followers in terms of hosting of meetings. And pastor Tita with time added more kids to his family which increased his family monetary consumption. Pastor Tita then stayed months, years without making good his promises, instead he kept on promising them that there was hope on the horizon, that he would multiply his promised monetary gifts to them by a reasonable number. "I will surprise you in my next visit home with the money; you are just not going to know. I am still pastor Tita, and you all know that. Trust me

I will never ever disappoint you, especially my youths, my own guys".
CDUA always helped to plead with YWA supporters to reason with
him because he was not a type of guy who brags without fulfillment,
and that they all saw his contributions to CDI which he committed
part of his assets more than any other wealthy member CDI villager.

YWA CDUA supporters continued to believe in pastor Tita and
continued to trust in him while growing older and older until at a
certain stage when most of them lost hope of relying on his help
to achieve their very future dreams. Not knowing what next to do
YWA through its village branch leader Baranyanka confronted
CDUA vice president Mr. Leza and he absolved himself and CDUA
of any wrong doing and asked them to wait for pastor Tita's next
visit home. YWA accepted his directives and continued to give
supports to CDUA. In pastor Tita's next meeting attendance, YWA
demanded that they must be compensated as he promised or they
part ways with him and CDUA. Pastor Tita pleaded with them and
openly told them that 'his boat has jammed sea rock, and that
things were no longer as they used to be, and that they should
have to understand that. "We formed this CDUA with the vision of
reclaiming our fatherland, our lost village and making it look better
than before and ascend to the glory that it deserves. I have spent a
lot of money to ensure that we achieved that, unfortunately, after
my relocation, my pocket has become drained below an expected
level. So, as a result, I no longer have that kind of money to make
good all my promises to YWA especially, therefore, I implore you to
bear with me. I ask you to go and look for where to lay your hands
on so as to earn a living if you have not done so and can't have
hope and continue to work with us while things improve".

After pastor Tita's statements most of the YWA members in
particular and other youths in general started shouting against

him calling him all kinds of names, saying things like: "foolish man who deserves you; that was why you wanted a man for that; who never knew that it was you who had it over there and came back to introduce that to us; so, you don't want us anymore, now what else are we going to do? You have deceived us out of your wickedness and immorality; come closer pretty boy was your tone; we need our village back; I am back to CDI; CDI I apologize". Some of them advanced towards him shouting 'Rukorikibi" (he does bad things) and nearly fought him, while the rest of the youths, especially the 'I have already lost hope ones' and the cowards still believed in him.

Pastor Tita sudden change of mind confused his youth supporters who were mostly (YWA) members of his village, those who had already began to count the value of their 'hard currencies' to be earned when overseas began to calm down and work with their heads low. Those who had already counted it all complete as per higher institutions graduates became dropouts, and those who contemplated of owning one of the most expensive businesses in town began to reflect for places to fix themselves in, and those who relied on his given stipends for occasional feeding and miscellaneous expenses began to look for places of jobs to at least kept things going. And some of those who cannot tolerate disappointments resorted to minor village theft while the rest cruised out to the townships to form criminal gangs, and the lazy ones began to roam the streets eating only when given and begging to make ends meet. But pastor Tita remained defiant and continued to contribute only to the sustenance of CDUA although it's a child destined to natural death at birth.

Pastor Tita's empire supporters began to crumble block by block after he lost the full supports of his village YWA in particular and other youths in general. Having understood the implications of the departure of some of his key supporters, and having lost his financial stronghold and with no hope in sight of been transferred to a basket of offertory place where he could rebounds back to his financial might, he connived and conspired with CDUA and introduced another method of furthering his desire for independence. CDUA met and one of its members Mr. Yero (Born a solder) suggested that the best way to suppress the increasing anti CDUA perception for an independent village was to move secretly against the lives of those deemed to be in strong disfavor of CDUA. But Nzeobatniya (I will be very careful around them) objected to that and reasoned that outright killing of such would make their village members to point accusing fingers at CDUA and as well compel them to stage a counter attack, and since it was mostly a traditional society, the village could abide by the traditional laws and get them executed before their times. The other members agreed that the best thing would be to deal with the selected sections of them clandestinely using not easily verifiable means to get rid of the marked ones if possible. So, they agreed to lay traps for any person in his village in particular who knowingly or unknowingly ventured to criticize CDUA despite his/her social standings, and they also agreed that such most be accomplished through administration of poisonous concoctions whenever the opportunities presented itself. And they accepted the option of 'lure and capture' as the best method to use against such suspects. And Pastor Tita promised to also deal with those who may venture to visit his end in the township either uninvited or for whatever reasons as long as they stand on CDUA's way. CDUA decided to avoid facial confrontations with dissidents because they were fewer in number and could not combat the whole village that had chosen the traditional way of lives as their best method of existence and coexistence.

CDUA's president fallout with the youths drained most of his village and communities supports and redirected most of his former followers to CDI who expressed their regrets for joining an immorally confused mission that had no merits and no end in sight. Despite all the troubles and problems caused by pastor Tita and his CDUA, he remains a maniac in his village, a real crisis to himself, and nearly a snag in CDI shoes, and a threat to his autonomous community, trailing all human lives with evil intents. But how long will his maniac last—maybe another open secret.

Pastor Tita mingled with only ruin, disaster, destruction, decadence, immorality and rottenness during his visit to the 'Next Destination' only because of the love of bags of CFA Franc.

THE END